SWEET HOME ALASKA

CAROLE ESTBY DAGG

Nancy Paulsen Books

Nancy Paulsen Books
an imprint of Penguin Random House LLC
375 Hudson Street
New York, NY 10014

Copyright © 2016 by Carole Estby Dagg.
Penguin supports copyright. Copyright fuels creativity, encourages diverse voices,
promotes free speech, and creates a vibrant culture. Thank you for buying an authorized edition
of this book and for complying with copyright laws by not reproducing, scanning,
or distributing any part of it in any form without permission. You are supporting writers
and allowing Penguin to continue to publish books for every reader.

Nancy Paulsen Books is a registered trademark of Penguin Random House LLC.

Library of Congress Cataloging-in-Publication Data
Dagg, Carole Estby.
Sweet home Alaska / Carole Estby Dagg.
pages cm
Summary: In 1934, eleven-year-old Terpsichore's father signs up for President Roosevelt's
Palmer Colony project, uprooting the family from Wisconsin to become pioneers in Alaska, where
Terpsichore refuses to let rough conditions and first impressions get in the way of her grand adventure.
[1. Depressions—1929—Fiction. 2. Frontier and pioneer life—Alaska—Fiction. 3. Family life—
Alaska—Fiction. 4. Moving, Household—Fiction. 5. Alaska—History—1867–1959—Fiction.] I. Title.
PZ7.D138Swe 2016   [Fic]—dc23   2015016755

Printed in the United States of America.
ISBN 978-0-399-17203-8
1 3 5 7 9 10 8 6 4 2

Design by Marikka Tamura.
Text set in Adobe Caslon Pro.

To Helen and Randi,
my sisters and best friends forever

CONTENTS

CHAPTER 1

Terpsichore Johnson Cooks Dinner

November, 1934—Little Bear Lake, Wisconsin

IT WAS BECAUSE TERPSICHORE WAS THE ONLY UNMUSICAL Johnson that she dragged a hatchet across the yard toward a pumpkin as big as a pickle barrel. She stumbled over an icy hillock of mud where her mother's roses had been uprooted to make way for potatoes. The wind howled and whipped her skirt around her knees. It snatched notes from her sisters' piano duet, which escaped through the crack in the parlor window and swirled up to meet the chimney smoke. If Terpsichore had not made that foolish bargain with her mother, she could have been inside with her sisters, warm. She would not have to attack that monster pumpkin like a lumberjack.

She raised the hatchet over her head and heaved it down with the full weight of her seventy-three pounds behind it. The strike vibrated up her arms and clear through her shoulders to her jaws. After several more blows, she finally hacked off a section light enough to carry into the kitchen.

Terpsichore's father said she was a wizard with pumpkins. After all, she could turn a hunk of pumpkin into pumpkin pie, pumpkin soup, pumpkin muffins, pumpkin pancakes, pumpkin custard, pumpkin cookies, pumpkin bread, and pumpkin fritters. A good thing, too, because pumpkin was about all that was left to eat.

By the time she'd boiled the pumpkin long enough to make it edible, though, everyone was too hungry that night to wait for her to turn it into muffins or fritters. Instead, she just mashed it and decorated it with a sprinkle of parsley from her mother's window garden.

"Yuck, Trip! Pumpkin mash?" Polly poked her fork at the mound of pumpkin on her plate. Cally poked her mound, too.

Terpsichore's ears cringed at hearing the twins' nickname for her that announced to the world "This girl's a stumblebum!"

"You're not a baby anymore, Polly. You can say my whole name: *Terp-sick-oh-ree!* And if you don't like pumpkin mash, don't eat it, fancy fingers." She shot the twins what her father called her piercing basilisk glare, a glare so intense that it usually bent them to her will, at least for a little while. "Let's see how good you are with a hatchet."

"What's a hatchet got to do with dinner?" Cally poked her mash again.

"I'm sure Terpsichore worked very hard to make us this nourishing dinner," Mother said. She spooned a bite of pumpkin into baby Matthew's mouth. With a flick of his tongue, the pumpkin oozed back out of his mouth, dribbled down his chin, and sat in a blob on his bib.

Terpsichore poked her own mound of pumpkin mash. She had bargained herself into the role of family cook to get out of piano lessons. Mother had always made time for Terpsichore's lessons, even when baby Matthew kept her up most of the night. One day last summer, after fumbling through the first few bars of "Für Elise," Terpsichore had slammed her palms down on the piano keys and said she would rather cook dinner for the rest of her life than practice one more hour at the piano.

Before one more *ticktock* of the metronome, Mother said, "Deal!" And that was the day her mother gave up trying to make a musician out of Terpsichore.

"I'll make pumpkin pancakes tomorrow," Terpsichore said. "It's just that everyone was so hungry . . ."

Pop reached over to squeeze Terpsichore's shoulder. "It's not your fault we're reduced to eating pumpkin for dinner."

Even though her father had dug up nearly every square inch of their yard and replaced her mother's flowers with plants you could eat, there was never enough food. The rhubarb leaves had grown big as elephant ears, but they were poisonous. The stalks were red as strawberries, but without sugar, they were more lip-puckery than a pickle. The pole beans were long gone—since Mother was not up to canning after birthing Matthew, they ate those beans fresh until their eyeballs turned green. They ate the zucchini last month before it went moldy. Her father had made sauerkraut out of the last of the cabbage just before frost.

This month they were eating their way through pumpkin

before it went soft. Then they'd have to face the sauerkraut.

Pop rolled up his sleeves, exposing new muscle earned by gardening instead of working as a bookkeeper at the mill. He balanced his knife on his forefinger and gently seesawed it up and down. Terpsichore watched the knife tip one way, then the other, as if her father were weighing choices.

Pop cleared his throat. "The Olsons got the paperwork about President Roosevelt's new Matanuska Colony project. They're going to apply." He was talking to her mother, but he was staring at his knife.

Mother laid her knife and fork slantwise on her plate.

"What Matanuska Colony project is that, Mr. Johnson?"

"It's where the government has set aside land in Palmer, Alaska—forty acres for a family." Her father finally looked up and let the knife topple so he could throw out both arms to show them how big forty acres was. "And you get a loan of about three thousand dollars to get started on your own farm."

"Alaska?" Terpsichore let out a horrified squeak as she thought about icebergs and endless winter.

Cally and Polly echoed "Alaska" one beat behind her. They exchanged goggle-eyed glances.

Mother clutched Matthew tighter on her lap.

Pop filled the silence. "With forty acres we could grow crops and still have room for your roses." He reached for Mother's arm, but she shifted on her chair, just out of reach.

"We could have pigs, a couple horses, a milk cow, and a few sheep." He forced a grin and looked around the table for answering grins, but there weren't any.

"You can't take a baby to the frozen wilderness!" Mother nuzzled Matthew's head.

Terpsichore edged forward on her chair. "Can we take pets with us? I won't go without Tigger!"

"How could we afford to get back home if we don't like it?" Mother asked.

"I'm not living in an igloo!" That was Cally, shaking her head in horror, which made her ringlets bob.

"I'm not eating whale blubber!" That was Polly. Her ringlets bobbed too.

"The piano would go out of tune!" Mother looked through the archway between the dining room and parlor toward her prized Chickering upright grand. Her voice cracked. "Would we even get to take the piano?"

Of course Terpsichore wouldn't miss the piano. What made her heart flutter anxiously was the thought of the stack of library books she kept beside her bed. She couldn't sleep whenever the stack of unread books became too low. Would there be a library in Alaska? And this house, how could they leave the house that her father had built for them—the plate rail with her mother's wedding china ringing the room, the built-in cupboards and buffet along one wall, the solid brass electrified chandelier overhead?

Pop heard them out, but when their reasons for not going to Alaska petered out, he took up his rebuttal. "First of all, I'm not saying we're going. After all, they're only choosing a few families in this county to go. But I do think Alaska would be a good chance for us. This is the Matanuska Valley, not the Arctic Circle. It won't be any colder there than here in northern Wisconsin. In the summer the sun hardly sets and it gets up to eighty degrees. I hear they grow pumpkins so big it takes four men to lift them." Her father winked at Terpsichore.

Judging from the worry lines in Mother's forehead, she wasn't sold. "You already have your answers, don't you? You're not just going for information tomorrow, are you?"

"Competition will be tough. If I have to move fast to get us one of those slots, I will."

"Even if I refuse to go?"

"Jiminy," he said, as he threw his napkin down on the table. "We have to face facts. We're one step from starving and I won't go on government relief and have church ladies coming around with charity baskets." He rose from the table and looked out the window, his back to the rest of the family.

Was their situation really as desperate as her father was saying? He had always told Terpsichore this was the land of opportunity. That if a person was willing to work, he'd never starve. But hard work wasn't always enough when there were hard times all over the country. They had worked hard and they still faced a winter with almost nothing left to eat but sauerkraut. Maybe Pop was right now. They would have to go to Alaska.

CHAPTER 2

Let Them Eat Worms

TERPSICHORE WATCHED HER FATHER AS HE STOOD IN front of the mirror by the front door to straighten the part in his hair.

Her mother watched too, her face grim.

Pop took his fedora from the hook by the door and adjusted it on his head.

"Don't I get a say in this?" Mother asked. "Why don't we just admit we're not making it on our own and apply for relief like most of the other mill families? Or we could move in with my mother in Madison. We don't have to do something as drastic as moving to Alaska."

He held up one hand against anything else she might say. "It's my job to provide for this family, not the government's," he said. "And I'm not saying we're going to do it."

"But you're sure acting like it," Mother said. "We belong here, where we have friends—and doctors and schools and libraries."

"This may be a ghost town soon," Pop said.

"Maybe the mill will reopen," Terpsichore said. "Maybe you'll get your job back and we won't have to move."

"Look out the window, Terpsichore. How many trees do you see on the hills?"

The hills were once covered with oak and maple trees that turned red, orange, and gold in the fall. Now all that was left was stumps and scrub. There weren't any trees left to feed to the mill.

Mother darted back and forth between the table and the sink as if the fate of the world rested on her having a tidy kitchen. Pop caught up with her to plant a kiss on the top of her head before he left the house.

At recess, instead of making snow forts in the fresh snow, everyone huddled to hear who might be applying to move to Alaska. It turned out that lots of fathers were going to the county building that morning.

Terpsichore and her best friend, Eileen, were a huddle of two. "Does your dad want to move to Alaska?" Terpsichore asked.

"Da thinks that we have to go if we can," Eileen said. "If we don't, we'll probably have to move in with Uncle Patrick in his apartment in Chicago."

"And if we don't go to Alaska," Terpsichore said, "we'll probably have to move in with Grandmother VanHagen in Madison." Terpsichore thought of Grandmother's house, where everything was so proper and quiet you were afraid to laugh out loud. Maybe Alaska wouldn't be so bad compared to that. "How will they choose the families who get to go?"

"You have to have farming experience, so my da thinks we'll have a good chance of getting picked," Eileen said. "I bet some people applying have never grown a radish or milked a cow."

"I don't know if a henhouse and vegetable patch would count as a farm," Terpsichore said. "So maybe we won't get picked." She shrugged. "And I don't even know if I'd want to go. One minute I think it would be a crackerjack adventure and the next minute I think of all I'd miss, especially you—if you're still here, that is."

"We won't be able to stay here long—and I don't want to live in my uncle's apartment, so I hope we go to Alaska," Eileen said.

"Then the only way we can stay together is to both go. We have to make it happen." Terpsichore took off the mitten on her right hand. "Pinky promise?"

Eileen took off her right mitten too. "Pinky promise!"

They interlocked little fingers.

"I do solemnly promise," Terpsichore said, "I will do everything in my power to help my family go to Alaska."

Eileen repeated the pledge, and with fingers still interlocked, they shook hands three times.

That evening, Pop told the family about his visit to the county building. "I got some crazy news today." He looked at all of them: Mother, his little Muses—Terpsichore, Calliope, and Polyhymnia—and baby Matthew in his cradle.

"In order to qualify for the Alaska program you have to be on relief. So because we've skimped and made do instead of going on relief we're not eligible. We're the kind of self-reliant people needed up north, but we were rejected before they even read my application. It makes no sense at all."

Pop's forehead wrinkled in frustration. Terpsichore had to agree with her father. It wasn't fair that they were disqualified because they hadn't gone on relief. When Pop lost his job last year, he had sold his car to Mr. Nostrand—the owner of the general store—and Mother sold some jewelry, so they'd have money to live on till they figured out how to make it without the income from the mill.

Terpsichore locked her pinky fingers under the table. She couldn't let Eileen's family go to Alaska without the Johnsons. What could she do?

Pop picked up the stack of forms he'd filled out and threw them in the air. "That's what I think of their requirements. I'd like to go to Alaska, but I would rather eat worms than go on relief." He stomped outside.

Cally started to cry. "I don't want to eat worms."

"Me neither," said Polly.

Terpsichore knew her father didn't really mean for them to eat worms, so she tried to make a joke of it. "Maybe if you dipped them in flour and fried them? Or chopped them up and mixed them with bread crumbs and baked them like a meat loaf?"

"That's disgusting, Trip." Cally gagged into her napkin.

Polly pushed back her chair and dashed to the bathroom. It sounded like she made it there before upchucking.

"Terpsichore Johnson! Now look what you've done," her mother said. "You'd think at your age you'd have more sense than to say things that send your sisters into gastric spasms."

"It's not my fault," Terpsichore said. "Pop talked about eating worms first."

Terpsichore crawled under the table to pick up the forms her father had tossed. There were forms for applying for relief and forms to apply for the Alaska program. She'd promised Eileen she would do everything she could to make sure her family went to Alaska. She'd think of something, or her name wasn't Terpsichore Johnson!

CHAPTER 3

Making Do and Doing Without

ALL WINTER, THEY STILL TRIED TO KEEP UP APPEARANCES. Pop and Mother drank their foraged chicory coffee out of the fancy blue-and-white Royal Copenhagen teapot and cups Mother had brought with her to the marriage along with her piano and sterling silver place settings. There was no point trying to sell the silver; no one in Little Bear Lake had enough money to buy it. One by one, the mothers of every one of Terpsichore's mother's piano students called to cancel their children's lessons, so the last bit of income was gone.

The school was about the only thing still operating on a normal schedule, but it seemed like every week another family left Little Bear Lake to move in with relatives in other parts of the country or look for work as far away as California. Maybe they'd even have to close the school if most kids left town.

The library was still open—but just on Tuesdays and Saturdays. On the way home from school one Tuesday, Terpsichore stopped by to see if Miss Thompson had any books saved for her under the desk.

She should have suspected something was wrong when she saw that the snow on the steps had not been cleared. She pulled on the brass door handle, but the door didn't budge. Then she read the hand-lettered notice taped to the inside of the glass:

Change of Hours

*Due to budget cutbacks, the library
will now be open only on
Saturdays, from 10–4*

Miss Hanna Thompson, Librarian

Cutting library hours again? Whose crazy idea was that? The library was one of the most popular places in town, especially after the mill closed. People couldn't afford the movies or the roller-skating barn, but they could come to story hour and check out books for free. Even folks who didn't read much huddled around the heat registers at the library. Terpsichore returned her books through the slot. The hollow clunk they made as they hit the bin inside was as hollow as her heart.

She started back down the steps slowly, but then her cheeks grew hot and she started running and huffing like a mad bull. Cutting library hours to six hours a week was the last straw. Now Miss Thompson would probably have to move. Terpsichore flung open the kitchen door and shouted, "The library's closed today!"

The house was silent. Polly and Cally's books had been dumped on the kitchen table, but Terpsichore didn't hear anyone practicing.

Then, from the parlor came their mournful voices. "Noooooo!"

Terpsichore dropped her books beside her sisters' and dashed to the parlor.

With one trembling finger, Cally outlined the large rectangle on the wallpaper where the colors of the pink cabbage roses hadn't faded. The large rectangle that marked the space where the piano used to be.

Mother came out from the bedroom. Her eyelids were red and the tip of her nose was pink. "It was the sensible thing to do, girls," she said. "After all, I don't have pupils anymore."

Terpsichore tried again to tell them about the library, but they had no room in their hearts for any sadness but their own.

When Pop came home from chopping stumps for firewood, Cally and Polly each grabbed a hand and dragged him to the parlor.

"I didn't think anyone had money to buy a piano," he said.

"I didn't actually sell it," Mother said. "I traded it to Mr. Nostrand for a hundred twenty-five dollar credit at the general store. I had to do it soon. Mrs. Nostrand already has the Smiths' Queen Anne dining table and the Nybergs' secretary desk, and pretty soon their house will be so overflowing with bartered goods they won't be willing to trade anymore."

Pop wrapped Mother in his arms. "I never would have asked you to give it up."

"I saved the music books," she said, pulling away and trying to smile. "When times are better we can always get a new piano."

CHAPTER 4

Fireside Chat

FOR THE REST OF WINTER, AND ON INTO SPRING, THE Johnsons ate food made from the flour and oats they bought with the piano credit at the store, eggs from their three remaining hens, an occasional rabbit, and sprigs of greens from Mother's windowsill garden. Two of the teachers at Terpsichore's school left town, so all the remaining fourth-, fifth-, and sixth-grade children met together in one classroom. On April 28, they all had the same assignment: listen to President Roosevelt on the radio.

Terpsichore was stretched out on her stomach in front of the radio console. Outside the front room window, the sky was black. Inside, the only light came from the fireplace, the pool of lamplight by her mother's mending chair, and the faint glow of the radio dial.

The volume had been low because the twins were already in bed, but at 8:59 P.M., Pop rose from his chair and leaned

16

over Terpsichore to turn it up just in time for the words, "And next, the President of the United States, Franklin Delano Roosevelt, with his seventh Fireside Chat."

Terpsichore yawned. If it hadn't been a school assignment to listen to the speech, she'd be in bed by now. Pop dragged his chair closer to the radio and sat leaning forward, elbows on his knees.

As soon as Roosevelt opened with *My friends,* Terpsichore pressed the right side of her face against the nubby cloth over the speakers. Feeling the vibration of the President's voice against her ear, she could imagine that she really was his friend, and that he was talking directly to her.

"Americans as a whole are feeling a lot better—a lot more cheerful than for many, many years," President Roosevelt said.

Pop snorted. "He obviously hasn't visited Little Bear Lake."

". . . the great work program just enacted by the Congress. Its first objective is to put men and women now on the relief rolls to work . . ."

Terpsichore glanced up at her father. His mouth and eyes were scrunched up small, probably in anger over programs that only helped people on relief. Terpsichore scrunched her mouth up small too, because Pop's prideful refusal to go on relief had made her miss her chance to join Eileen in Alaska. Just as Eileen had predicted, her family had been chosen to go to Alaska. Now they were boxing up everything they owned.

When the President started talking about banks and utilities, her attention wandered. Her feet began swinging back and forth, thunking the floor rhythmically like the slow beat of a metronome. She thought about Mrs. Eleanor Roosevelt. Everyone loved Mrs. Roosevelt because she seemed to care about ordinary people. Maybe Terpsichore should write a letter to her and ask her to explain to her husband that even people who were too proud to go on relief needed jobs too.

"Terp-sick-oh-ree, stop!" Her mother's scolding whisper cut through Terpsichore's thoughts.

Terpsichore froze her feet in mid-arc, sighed, and sat up to lean against the radio speakers. She looked at the clock. With only five minutes to the end of the speech he would be getting to the most important parts. She needed to pay close attention and take notes for school tomorrow.

"I, therefore, hope you will watch the work in every corner of this Nation. Feel free to criticize. Tell me of instances where work can be done better . . ."

Now that President Roosevelt was talking again about things she understood, she wrote as fast as she could.

"We have in the darkest moment of our national trials retained our faith in our own ability to master our destiny. Fear is vanishing and confidence is growing on every side . . ."

The radio speaker warmed her back and filled her with faith and confidence. She would do her best to be cheerful. She would have confidence that President Roosevelt's plans would work, but she would also have faith in herself, that she could master her own destiny.

She stretched her eyelids open, trying to make them sparkle with faith, optimism, and cheer. If President Roosevelt could see her now he might say, "Now, there's a fine example of the confidence I'm looking for!"

Pop stood and leaned over Terpsichore to switch off the radio. Turning toward Mother, he said, "I don't want a make-work job. I heard about a program started last year for homesteads—some right next door in Minnesota. We'll have to move somewhere when they close the school, so why not Minnesota? It's closer than Alaska."

Mother threw the sock she was darning into her mending basket. "Well," she said, "as long as we have to move somewhere, how about New York City? Surely they won't close the schools there. Cally and Polly's plan to go on Major Bowes Amateur Hour makes as much sense as homesteading in Minnesota. You should hear how they talk about all the money they'd make as the twin piano prodigies and vocalists." Mother forced a laugh to show she didn't take the twins' plan seriously.

Pop shook his head. "Good thing you're not encouraging that suggestion. Have you read about the hundreds of people who apply for every show? And some of the ones who get that far are gonged right off the stage." He shook his head at the folly.

Terpsichore imagined Major Bowes swinging a padded hammer and hitting a gong as big as the top of a bass drum. But of course, no one could be so hard-hearted toward the twins. Their curls bobbed in time to the music as they played their piano duets. Their dimples were so cute as they sang.

"You're right, of course, Harald," Mother said. She stood so she could look Pop in the eye. She lifted her chin. "We don't have to homestead in Minnesota or move to New York." She pulled one of Pop's hands from his pocket and held it in both of her own. "All we have to do is write to my mother. She'll sell something for our train fare down to Madison." Her coaxing voice was gentle, musical. She never took her eyes from Pop's.

The skin around Pop's mouth tightened. "Clio, you know how I feel about taking charity from your mother."

Terpsichore's own throat ached in sympathy with the misery in Pop's voice. Grandmother VanHagen would make them wear their Sunday clothes all day. Her neighbors were the kind of people who would not welcome children running and shouting outdoors. Grandmother was allergic to cats, so Tigger would have to sleep outside. Terpsichore liked Grandmother, but she didn't like the way she'd have to live if they moved in with her.

Mother seemed to remember she had an audience besides Pop. She sat on the floor and gathered Terpsichore into a hug. "I don't know what we're going to do if your father refuses the only reasonable option, moving back with your grandmother." She turned back to Pop. "Besides, it wouldn't be charity. You could replace her gardener and her chauffeur. And I could find piano students in a big city and contribute that way."

Mother squeezed Terpsichore's shoulder, stood with a sigh, and crossed from darkness back into the light by her mending chair.

· · ·

Terpsichore was in bed, but she could not sleep. She didn't want to move to Grandmother's house, or New York City, or Minnesota. She wanted to move to Alaska with Eileen. President Roosevelt wanted her to be optimistic. If Eileen was going to Alaska, she would find a way to go too.

Pop didn't want charity, but if the people in the Alaska project had to pay back the money they were loaned for a new start, that wasn't charity, was it? And if they were on relief only long enough to get into the Alaska project, that wouldn't count as charity either, would it?

She slipped out of bed and wiggled her fingers under the mattress to pull out the forms for going on relief and applying for the Alaska project that Pop had tossed away. She had heard Pop saying that out of over two hundred families who had been chosen to go north, at least one would back out and another family would be chosen at the last minute. Maybe that last-minute family would be the Johnsons if she turned in all the paperwork. If Eileen's family went to Alaska, her family would go too.

CHAPTER 5

Alaska Bound

THE NEXT MORNING, TERPSICHORE KNOCKED ON EILEEN'S front door and when nobody answered, she cracked open the door. "Hello," she called.

Eileen's mother looked up from scrubbing the floor around the woodstove. "Eileen's up there," she said, nodding toward the back of the house.

"Up there" was up a ladder to the attic. Eileen was the only one who had her own cot. Her seven brothers all piled into the two other cots or blankets on the floor. They were in the barn helping their father, so for once Terpsichore and Eileen had some space to themselves.

Terpsichore sat on the floor as she watched Eileen sort through her belongings. There wasn't much to pack. Eileen hugged Dolly, the rag doll her grandmother had made for her when she was four. Her Gran had embroidered bright green eyes on the face, and captured Eileen's lopsided smile in red thread. She'd dotted her face with rust-colored freckles and plaited its red yarn hair, just like Eileen.

"My mother said I can only take what fits in this apple crate," Eileen said as she held her doll out to Terpsichore.

"But your Gran made her for you—she looks like you."

Eileen grinned her lopsided grin. "That's the point," she said. "She'll remind you of me."

"But if my family goes too, I won't need the doll to remind me of you—I'll have the real you! I haven't given up yet on our pledge." She handed Dolly back to Eileen and leaned in to whisper. "And guess what? I turned in the forms to go to Alaska that Pop threw away."

"You didn't!" Eileen dropped her doll to hug Terpsichore. Then her smile faded. "It was clever of you to try, but isn't it too late?" Eileen asked.

"It's not too late until the boat sails," Terpsichore said. "If some family backs out, our application will be at the top of the pile. We'll be together yet!" Terpsichore held out a crooked little finger for another pinky swear.

A few days before Eileen's family was going to leave, Cally and Polly burst through the gate and nearly knocked Terpsichore and her father into the pile of mucky henhouse scrapings they were raking into the soil. "Pop! Trip! Mrs. Reilly is expecting!"

"Expecting?" Pop said as he regained his balance.

"You know," Cally said, as she outlined a rounded tummy, "expecting!"

"Frankie and Jimmy Reilly said they're not going to Alaska," Polly added. "Their mother told them she would never have baby number nine living in a tent in the wilderness!"

Pop shook his head. "I knew Mrs. Reilly didn't want to go." He tapped the loose dirt from his hoe and leaned it up against the wall by the kitchen door.

"I suppose that is good news," Terpsichore said as they all entered the kitchen. "That means Eileen doesn't have to go! We can still be together here in Little Bear Lake."

Mother looked up from a bowlful of batter she was dishing into a muffin tin. "I don't blame Mrs. Reilly for not wanting to go."

Pop said, "I wonder if another family will get to take their place."

No one noticed the panic on Terpsichore's face. What if they got picked now! This was not working out the way she had planned. She had put in their application so they could go to Alaska with Eileen's family, not take their place.

Mother jumped in. "Don't talk nonsense, Mr. Johnson. No family could get ready to go in two days. It takes weeks to decide what to take, and to visit relatives they might never see again . . ."

"Mother's right," Terpsichore said. "No one could be ready so soon."

But Pop wasn't listening. He left the door open, swinging in his wake as he strode—almost running—toward the courthouse.

Mother slammed the door.

At four o'clock, her father had not returned. Her mother paced the floor, clutching Matthew to her chest. Terpsichore paced the floor too.

At four-thirty, Pop burst through the door, catching his breath. "We have to move fast, or the caseworker will find another family to go! Everybody scrub up; we're going to the social service office so the doctor can certify our health."

Mother's eyes were wide and glazed, like the eyes of a deer in the oncoming headlights of a two-ton truck. "What?"

"I've signed the paperwork," Pop said. "We have just a few minutes before the office closes." He shooed Terpsichore and her sisters toward the bathroom.

As Terpsichore elbowed her way between Cally and Polly to brush her teeth at the sink, she heard her mother's voice. "What did you sign?"

"Our application for the Alaska program, of course! We're going to Palmer, Alaska!"

"Oh, no, we're not," said Mother. "Besides, I thought we didn't qualify."

"I guess someone agreed with me that we're just the kind of people Alaska needs." Pop turned to Terpsichore, who was hovering by the bathroom door. He winked. Did he guess what she had done?

Terpsichore's face felt feverish and her heart fluttered like the wings of a trapped bird. Yes, she had turned in the forms, but she hadn't done it just for Pop, she had done it for Eileen,

25

and now Eileen wasn't going to Alaska. She wanted a giant eraser that could wipe out her trip to the welfare office with Pop's paperwork.

Mother shook her head. "This is impossible," she said. "I thought we were going to talk about our choices . . ."

"We were, but I had to move fast, before another family was picked to take the Reillys' place. Clio, honey, there's nothing left for us here. How else will we get our way paid to a place where there is a new life waiting for us?" He brushed the back of one finger along her cheek to wipe away a tear.

Mother tightened her jaw and blinked back more tears. "One year," she said. "I'll give it one year. If we haven't made a go of it by then, we'll come home and move in with my mother in Madison."

"One year is not enough time for the land to prove itself," he said. "The first summer will probably be stump pulling. Give it until the first full harvest, at least. That's just four months past the first year. Give it a fair test. That'll still get the girls back to Madison in time to start school in the city if that's the way it goes."

Mother looked up at the ceiling as if looking there for advice, or patience from heaven to live another year with such a fool-headed, stubborn man as Mr. Johnson.

"All right," she said. "Until September after next."

In six and a half minutes, they were lined up with teeth and hair brushed and in clean underwear. Matthew wailed from all the to-do. Tigger the cat rubbed around Terpsichore's legs with a worried meow.

Terpsichore grabbed the cat. "Does Tigger have to be inspected too? She is going, isn't she?"

Her father looked at the clock. "We'll worry about that later. Come on now, line up like ducklings."

The exam was over in five minutes. Terpsichore still had the taste of the wooden tongue depressor in her mouth. The doctor had listened to her lungs right through her spring dress. Her heart was beating so fast and hard she didn't think he'd need a stethoscope to hear it.

On the way back home, Terpsichore stumbled along behind the rest of the family like a chicken that kept moving even when its head was cut off. The day after tomorrow they would leave for Alaska. If they froze to death in Alaska it would be her fault.

CHAPTER 6

Packing Up

As Terpsichore entered the living room to tell her parents good-night, they were still arguing over what to take. Her father said it was crazy to take records when they wouldn't have the electricity for a record player. Her mother said it was crazy to move anywhere that was so uncivilized it didn't have electricity.

Whenever Terpsichore woke up that night, she heard drawers sliding open and thunking shut as her parents sorted through everything in the house. When she woke up for breakfast, she halted at the kitchen door, agog at the mess. The table was stacked with dishes and silverware and Great-grandmother's pitcher and Aunt Katrin's flowered vase and all the things that had history enough to want to keep.

Mother was on her knees, wrapping teacups in old newspapers and fitting them into boxes.

"Teacups are hardly what we need most," Pop said.

Mother looked up. "They *hardly* weigh a thing, and I'm not giving up every vestige of civilization, Mr. Johnson."

Terpsichore cleared a path through the piles of pots and dishes that her mother had pulled out of the cupboards and piled on the floor so she could see everything she had to make choices about.

To their mother's piles, the twins added their Shirley Temple bowls and mugs. They had eaten box after box of Wheaties to get them and they weren't going to leave them behind.

Using some of the last of the flour, Terpsichore whisked in eggs, milk, and a dash of salt, poured the mixture into a greased cast-iron frying pan, and slid it into the electric oven for a puff pancake.

While it baked, Terpsichore surveyed the mess again. How could they be ready to leave by tomorrow? They could take a ton of stuff—literally a ton, two thousand pounds—to Alaska. But her father's tools and the furniture he had built were heavy. Their books and records were heavy.

After eating, Pop whistled as he built crates out of scrap lumber for everything they were taking to the railroad station the next morning. Terpsichore hovered over her father as he worked on Tigger's cage. He screwed hinges and a metal hook and eye latch to the front, and lined the bottom with wood shavings.

Once she was sure that Tigger would have a sturdy crate for the trip, she headed to Eileen's house. Her feet moved slowly. If she had done nothing, she would be staying in Little Bear Lake with Eileen, at least until one of their families had to move. Why had she meddled in grown-up business?

The Reillys' front door was open, so she climbed up the ladder to the attic. Eileen was sitting on the edge of her cot.

"Hi," Eileen said. Her voice was flat.

"I'm sorry," Terpsichore said. "I was trying to keep our pinky promise . . . I didn't mean . . ." Her throat was too tight to let out any more words.

Eileen shrugged. "We wouldn't have been together here for very long anyway, even if you were staying. We're moving tomorrow morning to Uncle Patrick's place in Chicago. Da says as long as we are packed we might as well go right away."

"So I guess this is good-bye, then," Terpsichore said. Her voice was raspy.

Eileen nodded. Then she looked up, and like a true friend, tried to cheer up Terpsichore, even though she was sad herself.

"Remember when we played Little House in the Big Woods last summer? Now you won't have to pretend to be a pioneer. You can be a real pioneer in Alaska and you can write and tell me all about it."

"Of course I'll write. I'll tell you everything." Terpsichore sidled up to Eileen for a super hug, one that would last. "And you write and tell me everything about life in the big city!"

Still feeling the pressure of Eileen's arms around her shoulders, Terpsichore ran home to fill her crate with her personal treasures, mostly books: the Anne of Green Gables series, *Black Beauty*, *The Little Lame Prince*, *The Princess and Curdie*, *The Secret of the Old Clock*, and, of course, *Little House in the Big Woods* and *Farmer Boy*. When she had read and reread the Laura Ingalls Wilder books, she'd daydreamed about what it would have been like to live sixty-five years ago in pioneer times. Just like Eileen said, she was about to find out.

As she opened the kitchen door, her mother slapped her forehead with a howl. "My mother! I haven't called her. She doesn't even know we're going!" She held out her hand toward Pop. "I need all your change—quickly!"

Pop emptied his pockets of quarters, nickels, and dimes, and Mother darted out the door.

"Where's Mom going?" Cally asked.

Pop closed the door Terpsichore's mother had left open. "The phone booth by the post office, I expect."

When her mother returned, Terpsichore greeted her with a cup of mint tea from the mint-patch-that-would-not-die. Before she went to bed that night, she dug up mint roots, wrapped them in damp newspaper, and put them in a tin can. If mint tea had calming powers, they'd better have a ready supply. They'd all need it up north.

By eleven o'clock that night, everything they were taking but didn't need until Palmer was crated and boxed up, ready to deliver to the train station in the morning. Tigger had hardly left Terpsichore for an instant all day, rubbing her shins and meowing questions about her future. That night, Tigger curled on Terpsichore's chest to make sure she went nowhere without her. Terpsichore slept—or tried to sleep—on a bare mattress on the floor. May 12, 1935, would be her last night in Little Bear Lake.

CHAPTER 7

By Land

Terpsichore's footsteps echoed as she wandered through the empty house one last time. As she closed the screen door, she tried to remember the exact sound of the squeaky hinge. She fingered the pumpkin seeds in her pocket, the seeds of the biggest pumpkin she'd grown last fall. She'd kept those seeds separate from the other seeds she and Pop had packed so she could keep them close to her.

Half the town—or what was left of it—showed up at the railway station to say good-bye to the Johnsons.

Terpsichore kept Tigger's crate next to her on the bench on the station platform and periodically slipped her fingers through the slats to rub Tigger behind her ears. "You'll have to be cooped up by yourself on the trip, but I promise I'll never abandon you. It's an adventure, Tigger. Pretend you're like one of your ancestors, sailing off on a Viking ship."

Tigger licked Terpsichore's hand, as if she were comforting Terpsichore instead of the other way around.

Mother clutched Matthew, the twins clutched their mother's coat, and Pop tapped his foot, held his watch to his ear, and leaned toward the southbound track to be among the first to see the train when it arrived.

Everyone on the platform turned from the tracks to the road at the sound of a bold car horn. Terpsichore stood on the bench and squinted toward the noise. It was a 1928 Pierce Arrow. Only movie stars, business moguls—none of whom lived in Little Bear Lake—and Grandmother Van-Hagen had a Pierce Arrow.

The car careened into a signpost and jolted to a stop. Grandmother VanHagen herself was at the wheel! She flung open the door, stepped from the car, and ran toward the tracks. Grandmother—running—instead of her normal stately glide. She wasn't a movie star, but with her elegant silk dress, she looked more like a movie star than anyone else's grandmother.

People parted for her as she made a beeline to Mother.

"Mercy sakes!" Grandmother said. "Thank goodness I made it in time."

Mother, stunned, said, "You drove all this way yourself?"

"Yes, the chauffeur taught me before I had to let him go. And good thing too, since you wouldn't listen on the phone last night," Grandmother said.

"I ran out of nickels; I didn't hang up on you," Mother said.

"But I knew if I could talk to you in person I could save you from a disastrous mistake. It was bad enough that your

Mr. Johnson dragged you here—two hundred miles from me and civilization—but Alaska is the back of beyond . . ."

Mother raised her eyebrows at Pop.

Grandmother continued, "Please, Clio, do us all a favor and move in with me."

Pop approached now. "We've decided—"

Mother interrupted. "Actually, it was you who decided, Mr. Johnson. But I did agree that we'd give Alaska a try through the first big harvest." Mother and Pop locked eyes and Pop nodded his head.

Mother turned back to Grandmother. "If it doesn't work out by next September, we'll take you up on your offer to live with you in Madison."

"Then I imagine I will have to go up there to get you when you admit you've failed," Grandmother said.

When the conductor shouted the all aboard, Grandmother's face crumpled and she hugged Mother so tightly that Matthew, squished in between them, squeaked. "I'll miss you, you know." She pulled back and touched each Johnson with her eyes, even Pop. "All of you."

Mother sat by the window so she could wave good-bye to Grandmother. Pop sat next to her on the aisle, turning his hat over and over in hands he could not keep still. On the seat facing Mom and Pop, Cally and Polly squabbled for the spot next to the window and Terpsichore clutched the side of her seat to keep from falling into the aisle as the train started rumbling down the tracks toward Seattle. Baby Matthew was lucky. He got his own padded box on the floor between their seats, and seemed so stunned by all the changes in the last few days that he didn't even cry.

After everyone got used to the swaying of the train car, some folks played checkers or cards to pass the time. The twins left their seat to chum with a girl who had a genuine Shirley Temple doll. Older girls huddled over movie magazines, mooning over Clark Gable and Errol Flynn. Boys passed around ragged copies of *Amazing Stories* and the Sunday funnies.

She overheard one young child complain about being cooped up on the train.

"Hush, now," said her father. "Only happy girls get to go to Alaska."

"Tell me a story," the girl said. "Tell me a story and I'll be a happy girl."

Terpsichore strained to hear the story, but she couldn't make out the words, only a low, comforting murmur as the father told his tale. Only happy children get to go to Alaska? He must have heard President Roosevelt's speech too, about being cheerful and optimistic. No matter what happened, she would try to be happy too.

She alternated between looking out the window and, despite the jostling of the train, rereading *Farmer Boy* and *Little House in the Big Woods*.

At the one long stop that first day, the train picked up more

Alaska-bound passengers and Terpsichore jostled for room at sinks in the ladies' lounge to get fresh water for Tigger, who was in the car reserved for pets.

As she entered the animal car, a dozen dogs barked, ducks quacked, and a bird cooed from a sheet-draped cage. Tigger cowered at the back of her cage, but crept forward when she saw Terpsichore. "There, there, kitty, I haven't forgotten you."

She nudged bits of sausage, left over from the free lunch in the diner car, through the slats and unlatched the door to slide in fresh water. "You'll like Alaska. Just dream of all the mice you'll catch once we get you out of this cage."

A boy about Terpsichore's age popped up from behind a crate at the other end of the car. "Actually," he said, "your cat is more likely to catch a red-backed vole, *Myodes rutilus*. Besides eating your plants, they sometimes even eat each other. They're cannibals, you know."

Yuck! Who wanted to know about cannibal voles?

The dog at the end of the boy's leash lunged toward Tigger, tail wagging.

Tigger leaped to Terpsichore's shoulders and dug in her claws.

"Don't be scared," the boy said. "She's just a puppy and wants to play."

"Well, Tigger doesn't want to play. Can you please control your dog?" As she stood, she looked more carefully at the boy's mouth instead of his dog. "What's that on your teeth?"

He wrangled his dog back into its crate, then turned and

smiled to show off his mouth hardware. "Orthodontia. My father's a dentist, and he's practicing on me to learn about teeth straightening."

The boy acted like metal brackets on his teeth were a privilege. Terpsichore thought they looked like torture.

The boy reached in his dog's cage for a parting pat. "In Alaska, I'm going to train her to be a sled dog."

"Ow, Tigger!" Terpsichore reached to her back to untangle her cat's claws from her sweater.

"Her name is Togo."

"That's nice," Terpsichore said.

"You know, like the dog who raced the longest part of the relay with the diphtheria antitoxin from Anchorage to Nome. Balto gets all the credit, but it was Togo who ran the longest." He reached through the slats to pat his dog as if she had made the heroic run herself.

"Did you know that seventeen of the twenty highest peaks in the United States are in Alaska?" the boy continued.

"Yes, I . . ." Terpsichore started. After all, she had studied Pop's atlas and the *World Book* article about Alaska at the library.

"And did you know that the Yukon River is nearly two thousand miles long, and is the third longest river in the United States, and Alaska has more than seventy volcanoes and has three million lakes and is twice as big as Texas?"

"Yes, I—" Terpsichore tried to answer again.

". . . And in 1915 the highest recorded temperature in Alaska was one hundred degrees at Fort Yukon, so it's not true that Alaska is all glaciers, although there are at least one hundred thousand glaciers in Alaska."

That was one fact Terpsichore had not known, but Tigger was squirming in her arms and couldn't wait another minute to get outside to do her business.

As she left, she heard the boy prattle on, something about the number of species of spiders in Alaska. She hoped Alaska was big enough that she wouldn't have to listen to that boy again.

CHAPTER 8

By Sea

As soon as they crossed the Cascade Range, Mother took the still-damp diapers down from where she had hung them on the overhead luggage rack and started repacking. Everyone wanted to be the first ones off the train to see Seattle, but a nurse boarded the car and made everyone line up so she could check for signs of measles. Anyone with fever or spots would have to stay in Seattle and wait two weeks to come up on the next boat.

Luckily, none of the Johnsons had spots.

Terpsichore was awestruck at the hubbub on the train platform. Young women dressed in yards of fluffy tulle, like princesses, held up a banner: **Welcome to Seattle!** Boy Scouts lined up to help carry the Alaska pioneers' luggage to the Frye Hotel for the evening before their ship would set sail.

Mother sighed when Pop closed the door of their hotel room. "What a relief to see real beds again!" she said.

Cally and Polly bounced on the other bed until they

noticed Terpsichore unloading an enormous basket of fruit and candy on top of the dresser. They raced to the dresser. "Trip, is all this for us?"

Terpsichore batted away their grasping hands. "Terpsichore! It's Terpsichore! And there's enough for one apple, orange, and banana for each of us."

"And Snickers bars!" That was Cally.

"And Tootsie Roll Pops!" That was Polly.

"Clio, they've thought of all of us," Pop said. "One of these drawers has a whole stack of clean diapers for Matthew, and in this drawer . . . a flannel nightgown! There's even something for me." He picked up a can of Hills Bros. Coffee and pretended to smell the coffee right through the tin.

Mother stood and held out her hands for the nightgown and rubbed it against her cheek. "Is there anything softer than new flannel? I hate to get into it after five days on the train without a proper wash, though."

Pop opened a side door and peeked in. "I think this will make you happy then," he said. "Ta-da! Your own private bathtub, my lady." He bowed.

Mother tiptoed toward the opened door, as if afraid she might make the bathroom disappear if she made a sound. "Yes," she said. "I'm going to soak for an hour in hot water and put on a clean nightgown and sleep for twelve hours in a clean bed."

Meanwhile, the twins had already eaten all the candy. Except for what Terpsichore ate, of course.

• • •

The next day at least two thousand people crowded the dock to see them off at the Bell Street terminal. Seattle had prepared a royal send-off.

The twins bounced like they were on pogo sticks. "We're famous, aren't we, Mom? Everyone wants to see us!"

High school girls handed out picture books, toys, and apples. Men in band uniforms milled around at the edge of the crowd, testing their instruments.

"Excuse me, excuse me," Pop said again and again as he elbowed his way closer to the ship where the Alaska-bound passengers waited to load.

Photographers motioned for families to move closer together for photographs, and everywhere she looked, Terpsichore saw microphones labeled NBC and CBS. The whole country would be hearing about the Johnsons and the other families going to Alaska!

On the other edge of the crowd, Terpsichore saw the boy from the railway car. He was watching the crane load piles of lumber and huge crates with **POTATOES** stenciled on the side. High above their heads, a crane plucked up one crate at a time and swung it over to the gaping loading door of the *St. Mihiel*. Somewhere in those hundreds of crates piled high on the dock, Tigger was probably howling for Terpsichore to rescue her. Poor kitty didn't care about being a part of a historic event. She just wanted her own place on Terpsichore's bed again.

As pioneers started to board, a man standing next to a

newsreel camera narrated in his official, deep, announcer voice. "And there they go, folks, brave families walking up the gangplank to their new lives, courtesy of one of President Roosevelt's programs to take families off public relief and start anew as Alaska pioneers!" After a moment, he motioned for the cameraman to stop cranking the camera, but gave the signal to roll again when he spotted Cally and Polly.

The twins had found a clear spot near the edge of the crowd, fluffed out their skirts, and set their mouths in little-girl pouts. Terpsichore knew that warm-up routine. Cally and Polly were about to break into their performance of "On the Good Ship Lollipop."

For Christmas, Grandmother had sent train tickets so they could visit her in Madison. She also treated the family to the movies. The twins sat through three showings of Shirley Temple in *Bright Eyes* and memorized every gesture. Now, all fifty-six ringlets on each head bobbed just like Shirley Temple's, and their hands moved in exactly the same patterns Shirley Temple had used in the movie. Their voices were pure and sweet. Who could resist watching them? Two photographers with large box cameras moved in for still pictures. Then several moving picture cameras rolled forward on tripods. Cally and Polly might be in all the newsreels!

As one of the cameramen swept his camera over the rest of the crowd, Terpsichore stood on her tiptoes behind everyone else crowding in to be included in the newsreel and waved. Her hand in a newsreel. That was probably as close as she would ever come to being famous.

If Eileen saw the newsreel, she'd see the twins for sure, but she'd have no way of knowing that somewhere in the crowd, Terpsichore was waving good-bye to her.

Their moment of fame over, the Johnsons walked up the gangplank.

The twins weren't the only ones trying to get in the newsreel—a man with a harmonica and another one with a guitar took up positions at the top of the gangplank. Terpsichore recognized the tune. It was Gene Autry's version of "Springtime in the Rockies," but they had changed the words. Terpsichore laughed along with the crowd at the new words: "When it's springtime in Alaska and it's ninety-nine below . . . Where the berries grow like pumpkins and a cabbage fills a truck . . . We want to make a new start somewhere without delay. So, here we are, Alaska, AND WE HAVE COME TO STAY!"

Just before sail-away, Terpsichore took two rolled-up streamers from a basket on deck. She held onto one end of each, then threw the rest of the rolls down to be caught by someone on the pier. The air was quickly filled with spools of yellow, blue, and pink streamers. The deck of the *St. Mihiel* began to vibrate with the engines and the ship gave out three long, deep bellows. The loose streamers grew taut as tugboats nudged the ship out of its slot. Terpsichore stretched her arms over the rail, trying to delay the moment when her streamers would snap, but she couldn't prevent the inevitable. First one, then the other snapped and the broken ends fell limply into the water. The Seattle docks and the pyramid-topped Smith Tower grew smaller and smaller as the ship edged out of the harbor.

In newsreels and movies, ship passengers had private staterooms and dressed for dinner as if they were going to a ball. Terpsichore quickly realized that the *St. Mihiel* was not that kind of ship. Pop and all the fathers and older boys were herded off to a dormitory in the bow. Terpsichore, her mother, sisters, and baby Matthew were herded to a vast open area that would house nearly all the women and children. Matthew added his distressed howls to those of all the other babies.

Terpsichore looked at the rows and rows of triple bunk beds. Only one of those triple bunks was for the Johnsons. Mother collapsed on the bottom bunk with Matthew, patting his back to settle him down.

Cally and Polly were still bouncy after being photographed by real moving picture cameras. "We call dibs on the middle bunk!" they singsonged. They slid into their slot to try it out.

Terpsichore clambered from her mother's bunk to the twins' bunk to reach the third tier. She closed her eyes to shut out the chaos around her, but she couldn't close her ears. Nearly seventy mothers and over one hundred children, including fifty-nine babies, would be crammed for the whole trip like sardines in a can. Mother slid cautiously out of bed and handed Matthew up to Terpsichore so she could tuck the long edge of a blanket under the edge of Terpsichore's top mattress to tent in the two bunks below. "A little better," she said.

Terpsichore bounced gently, testing the thin mattress.

Two sets of fingers poked into her back from below. "Stop it! You'll squish us!"

Terpsichore leaned over her bunk to see for herself. The springs supporting her mattress were particularly stretchy. She wasn't squishing her sisters, at least as long as they stayed perfectly flat on their own mattresses, but if she bounced and Cally or Polly chose that moment to roll over, they would collide.

Terpsichore leaned over and shook the blanket divider to get her mother's attention. "Where are our pillows?"

"I heard we're supposed to use our life preservers as pillows," Mother said.

Terpsichore heard a high-pitched toddler's voice. "Is this to pee in?" Terpsichore leaned over to see what he was referring to. It was a five-gallon lard bucket.

Another voice answered. "It's to throw up in. Each family has its very own." Apparently having your own upchuck bucket was the *St. Mihiel*'s definition of luxury.

Although the first night out was fairly calm, Terpsichore couldn't sleep. Somewhere toward one of the mess halls, she could hear someone strumming a guitar. More folks had learned the new words to "Springtime in Alaska," as they now called it, and Terpsichore mouthed the words along with them.

The next night was worse. The sea heaved, the ship pitched, buckets and suitcases slid, and unlatched doors slammed. The twins were suggestible—if one upchucked, the other followed soon after in sympathy. "It's their sensitive, artistic tempera-ment," Mother whispered.

For once Terpsichore was glad she didn't have a sensitive, artistic temperament. Her mother, Cally, and Polly were still moaning in their beds in the morning, but you wouldn't catch Terpsichore getting seasick. She was going to be strong and optimistic, just like President Roosevelt wanted her to be. Al-though the deck was wet with spray, she spent the morning breathing fresh air and watching for whales.

At noon, the captain reported over the loudspeaker that they'd be heading into "a little chop," and he ordered all pas-sengers to leave the open deck and stay inside. From a win-dow one deck up from their sleeping quarters, Terpsichore watched the storm. The ship hit twelve-foot-high swells, and the front end of the boat rose at the angle of a flight of stairs and everything not nailed down went sliding. And then, like jumping off a cliff, the front end smacked down with a jolt.

As she watched, the boy with the sled dog sidled up. "Sea-sick people are usually described as green," he said, "but I'd say you are more pale yellow than green. You'll find that you can minimize the effects of seasickness if you face forward or back and look at the horizon, which stays relatively in place, rather than to the side, where motion is more apparent."

Since she was not being climbed by a cat with claws out at this meeting, she had a better look at him. He was short, with sandy hair and features too big for his face: a nose he would have to grow into; a big mouth, literally and figuratively. Even his eyes were too big, or maybe it was just the magnifying effect of his glasses. And those braces! Terpsichore winced to think what it must feel like to wear them.

"I see you're admiring my brilliant dental appliances."

"Don't they hurt?" Terpsichore asked.

"They do when Dad tightens the arch wire."

For the first time, she felt sorry for this strange kid instead of annoyed.

"Mendel Theodore Peterson," he said, holding out a hand.

Terpsichore didn't let go of the windowsill to shake his hand. "Terpsichore Elizabeth Johnson." That would be one advantage of the move. In Alaska she could reinvent herself and finally escape her horrible nickname. "Terpsichore," she said. "As in—"

"I know, I know, the Muse of Dance," he said.

Terpsichore narrowed her eyes. "How did you know that?"

Mendel smirked. "You're not the only kid on this ship who knows Greek mythology. And my name, Mendel, is for—"

"The composer Mendelssohn?" Terpsichore wanted to show he wasn't the only one who knew his composers.

"No," he said. "Gregor Mendel, the guy with the twenty-nine thousand pea plants. The guy who figured out how two parents with brown eyes could have a blue-eyed baby."

"I knew that," Terpsichore said. "The reason I guessed Mendelssohn first is that my mother used to teach piano."

"And my mother used to teach botany, so I got stuck with 'Mendel.' Anyway, since I read up on sea travel in the library before I left, I've been able to minimize seasickness. At least I didn't toss my cookies."

"Toss your cookies?"

"Puke, vomit, upchuck, retch, heave, spit up, spew up, disgorge, be sick to one's stomach, be nauseated, return your breakfast, or blow your lunch."

"Stop!" Terpsichore said. "Just the words . . ." Who ever knew there were so many ways to say *throwing up*? All the same, she couldn't quite control the grin that quivered at the corners of her mouth.

"I should check up on my mother and sisters," she said. "They've been too busy tossing their cookies to leave their bunks."

"You catch on to the lingo fast," Mendel said. "See you."

Terpsichore gagged as she climbed down the stairs into the dormitory. Not everyone had made it to the slop buckets, and they were too sick to clean it up. Trying to hold her breath, she mopped up the area around their bunks.

"Thanks," Mother whispered. She tried to roll out of her bunk to help, but groaned and leaned back on the bed.

"Still pukey?"

Mother moaned. "I'm nauseous, not 'pukey,'" she corrected. No one as refined as Terpsichore's mother would do anything as crude as "puke." She paused to spit into the bucket again. "A touch of *mal de mer*." She rolled back on the bunk.

Matthew was restless in his own crate beside the bunk beds. Terpsichore changed his diaper, since doing it might make her mother throw up again. She felt better staying busy, so she played nurse, fetching small cups of ginger ale and soda crackers from the cook.

By the fourth day, everything Terpsichore owned had been upchucked on. The captain called their journey the worst crossing of the Gulf of Alaska he had ever seen.

Terpsichore was on the deck with most of the other passengers when the *St. Mihiel* pulled into the harbor at Seward. After a bone-rattling crunch and ear-splitting squeal of the ship against the wood of the dock supports, the engines went silent and the vibration under Terpsichore's feet halted.

Careening into the dock—what a way to announce their arrival in Alaska.

CHAPTER 9

Landing in Alaska

TERPSICHORE WATCHED HER FATHER WALK DOWN THE gangplank to the dock. He would travel ahead on the first trains to Palmer with the other men. Tomorrow they would each draw a number from a box that would decide where in Palmer they would make their home.

The next morning, the train returned for the women and children. After a stop in Anchorage, they were finally on the last leg of the journey to their new home. Terpsichore jostled with her sisters for window space. After miles and miles of unpromising land with stunted evergreens, they entered a gradually widening, more promising valley with dense bushes and birch, spruce, and poplar trees.

It was midnight when the train arrived in Palmer. Terpsichore was surprised there was still enough light to see that beyond the rows of tents, jumbled stacks of cut-down trees lay like abandoned games of pick-up sticks played by giants.

Somewhere in the throng of men hunkered down along the tracks in the rain and mud, Pop was waiting for them. Terpsichore's breath fogged up the window, so she pushed the latches on either side and tugged it down to see better. Mother nudged her aside and leaned out the window, disregarding the rain. She waved. "Mr. Johnson! Harald!"

A nurse tapped Mother on the shoulder. "Ma'am, I'm sorry, but you'll have to close the window. We've discovered another case of measles aboard, so we're going to keep everyone in the train tonight until we've had a chance to check everyone again."

"Not again," Cally and Polly whined.

Terpsichore felt like whining too. Measles was plaguing them to death.

The nurse slid the window back up. "You're just as well off here anyway. The CCC—that's Civilian Conservation Corps—crews are a little behind schedule and the tents for this group aren't finished yet. At least here you'll be warm and dry."

Mother snapped the window shut. "They don't even have tents for us yet?"

She continued to mutter through clenched teeth until Terpsichore pounded on the window. "There's Pop!"

He elbowed his way through the crowd and they shouted to each other through the glass, their faces inches from each other. Pop blew everyone kisses and Mother cried.

Soon after that, a nurse came through the train car with

blankets. Terpsichore leaned against her mother on the bench seat opposite the twins.

Outside, campfires still burned in the eerie twilight that passed for a late spring night up north. Row upon row of white tents reflected the light of moon and stars and the top sliver of sun that still hovered behind the mountains. Snuggled up against her mother, Terpsichore finally slept to the hum of a harmonica and a few stalwarts determined not to sleep, singing "When it's springtime in Alaska . . ." She was beginning to get sick of the song.

Later the next morning the nurse was back again, checking for fevers and spots. They passed inspection and were free!

"Yay! I can get Tigger," Terpsichore said.

Mother looked out the window at hundreds of fathers and families trying to find each other. "I don't see your father yet, so you might as well get Tigger now. Meet us right back here at this passenger car."

Terpsichore darted out the door to the baggage car to fetch Tigger. The only other animals left were a family of ducks she'd heard someone's family was saving for Christmas dinner if they didn't get too attached to them.

With Tigger's cage banging her shins, Terpsichore stepped down from the car and inhaled. Besides new tent canvas and spring cottonwoods, she smelled mud. Acres of mud, with rough planks serving as make-do sidewalks through the muck. But above the mud, mountains tipped in snow bordered the valley on two sides. So this was Alaska!

Over the noise of the sawmill and diesel Caterpillar tractors growling their way over the tracts to pull stumps, a thousand people were still calling out names, trying to get families back together. "Lars?" "Henry—over here!" "Rachel!" "Margaret!" "Agnes!" Tigger added her own calls, which Terpsichore took to mean "Where are we? When can I get out?"

"Soon," she said. "We have to get back to Mom and Pop."

Terpsichore was relieved to see both her parents by their railroad car. Pop held Mother's hand, pointing out the freight yard stretched out alongside the tracks with piles of lumber, stacks of steel pipe, and heaps of kitchen sinks.

"We're going to take this wilderness right into the twenti-eth century in a matter of months, and we'll all be part of it!" he said. Mother looked less enthusiastic as she tried to avoid ruining her shoes in the mud on the way to the huge map of the colony.

Pop slid off the rubber band coiled around the slip of pa-per he'd drawn out of a box in yesterday's lottery. Terpsichore bumped her father's hand with her head as she leaned over to read the tract number and legal description that was their future. Seventy-seven. Did that sound like a lucky number?

She had trouble finding their plot on the map because the numbers were often assigned haphazardly, with lot eighty-three next to lot one hundred and sixty-seven in one cluster, and lot forty-seven next to one hundred and seventy-nine in another cluster. Pop knew where they would live, though. He pointed to a little square on the map near a bend in the Mata-nuska River. "Here's our piece," he said. "It should be a good location, not too far from town. After the month the government allows for exchanges, we'll move our tent out close to our building site so we can watch our house going up."

Terpsichore stood on tiptoes to get a closer look at their plot on the map. What would their plot in the big woods look like?

Pop avoided Mother's face as he rerolled his lottery paper and carefully centered the rubber band around it. "They're a little behind on the building so everyone is in tents now. But as soon as the shipment of hammers arrives . . ."

Mother squawked in a most unladylike way. "They don't even have enough hammers to go around?"

"It'll be like a camping vacation," he said. "Summers are beautiful here, I've heard. In the meantime, we can clear land for the house and barn and kitchen garden."

"And where are the school, the stores, the church?" Mother looked around, as if hoping to catch sight of a steeple or school bell tower.

"The railroad's donated a passenger car for the primary children and I heard that older kids'll go to the school in Matanuska, between here and Wasilla, until there's a school in Palmer."

Mother's shoulders stiffened.

"Let's get settled in, then, shall we?" said Pop. "We'll be rooming temporarily with the Wilcox family . . ." Pop started to guide his family to the tent they'd share with a Minnesota family who'd arrived two weeks ago.

Mother jerked away from him. "What kind of disorganized mess is this? I can't believe they don't even have our tents ready."

Pop gently turned Mother toward him. "Now, Clio, we'll only be sharing for a few days, until our own tent is set up. The Wilcoxes probably aren't any happier than we are having to share their tent, so let's meet them with a smile and make the best of it."

Mother leaned her head for a moment against Pop's chest, then pulled back with an almost-smile. "At least we're on solid ground sharing a tent with just one other family instead of the hold of a ship with seventy other families," she said.

"That's my trouper," Pop said, and took her elbow to guide her through the mud toward the Wilcox tent.

CHAPTER 10

Rude Facts of Life in Tent City

POP KNOCKED ON THE POST SUPPORTING THE CANVAS ON the entryway of the Wilcox tent, and a man's voice called out from inside. "Please don't let the mosquitoes in!"

As the Johnsons quickly sidled in and secured the tent flap, Mr. Wilcox greeted them. "Well done. First rule of Alaska etiquette," he said. "Get through the door as fast as you can and close it behind you."

Terpsichore clapped her hands to smack the mosquito that had followed her inside and wrinkled her nose at the spot of blood on her hands. Mendel would probably know the species and the Latin name for whatever kind of mosquito it was.

While the grown-ups talked, Terpsichore examined the tent, which wasn't as bad as it could have been. The floor was a raised wooden platform. A wood and coal-burning stove to the right of the door took off the morning chill, and someone had brought in two more cots. Two, for all six Johnsons? At least the Wilcox family had only one child. What if they had had to share a tent with a big family like Eileen's?

A clothesline crisscrossed the room. One of the lines was already strung with diapers and a sheet, doing double duty as a partition for the Johnsons' section of tent.

When Mrs. Wilcox pointed out the screened window at the outhouse, shared by who knew how many families, Mother sniffed and shot a glare toward Pop that could have cut inch-thick steel. That look reminded Terpsichore which parent had passed on the gene for the basilisk stare.

Mrs. Wilcox touched Mother's arm and pointed to a corner of the tent that had been cordoned off with another sheet. "There's a chamber pot; you won't have to find your way to the outhouse during the night."

Was that supposed to be reassuring? One chamber pot? In a tent shared by nine people. Terpsichore's pioneer spirit was already flagging. In reading books about the pioneer days, she had never thought about things like outhouses and chamber pots.

"Thank you for all the trouble you've gone to for us." Mother smiled weakly.

Terpsichore didn't know how many times she'd heard her mother say "Good manners don't cost a cent and are the cornerstone of civilized life." Good manners seemed to be the only element of civilization left here.

"The line at the outhouse isn't too bad if you want to go right now," Mrs. Wilcox said. "It's a two-holer, so that makes the line go faster."

Mother, who was still patting Matthew's back into a burp, paused in mid-pat. "We're expected to go in two at a time?" She turned to Pop. "Really, Mr. Johnson, this is quite beyond the pale."

"The smaller hole is for the little ones, going in with a mom or dad," Mrs. Wilcox said, nodding toward the twins. "So they don't fall in the pit."

"We could fall in?" Cally and Polly clutched each other in horror.

Mrs. Wilcox smiled. "Don't worry," she said. "We haven't lost a little one yet." She went on to explain outhouse etiquette. "There's a checklist posted on the wall with a pencil attached with a string. If it's been a couple hours since the last person used lime, take a scoop from the bucket in the corner and sprinkle it in. It'll help keep down the smell and flies. Don't get any on your hands—it'll burn."

Mother wrinkled her nose. "Let's get it over with." She handed Matthew to Pop. "Ladies first," she said, and trooped valiantly toward the outhouse, followed by Terpsichore, Cally, and Polly.

Cally poked Terpsichore's arm. "Trip, do you know that boy? I think he's trying to get your attention."

Mendel waved his newsboy cap and called out from the boys' line. "Don't worry about spiders," he said. "There have been no confirmed sightings of deadly spiders in Alaska. There are a few that bite, but they won't kill you."

Cally and Polly clung to their mother's coat. "Spiders! There might be spiders!"

Even though Terpsichore turned her head away from Mendel so people would think he was talking to someone else, he persisted. "You might see some of the *Araneidae,* though, if the calcium hydrochloride whitewash doesn't keep them away." He drew a circle in the air. "*Araneidae* are the orb-weaver spiders that weave the great webs with spokes coming out from the center. The stink brings the flies and the flies bring the spiders hunting for a good meal."

Terpsichore swatted another mosquito. The stink—or maybe just the lines of people in front of the outhouses—also attracted mosquitoes. She glanced in Mendel's direction. Mosquitoes were attacking him, too. "*Aedes implicatus,* I think," he said. "Or maybe *Aedes intrudens.* It's hard to identify mosquitoes without a magnifying glass."

Terpsichore scratched another bite. As far as she was concerned, there was only one kind of mosquito: BAD.

That night, Pop draped mosquito netting over the clotheslines near the tent ceiling and down to the floor, enclosing each cot and Matthew's basket. Mother put a pillow at each end of the girls' cot so Cally and Polly could sleep one direction and Terpsichore the other. The tent was too cramped to unpack suitcases, so they slept in their clothes. If Cally, Polly, and Terpsichore all lay on their sides like sardines in a can, they just fit.

Outside, older children still played. "It can't be bedtime," one of them said. "It's still daylight."

"It'll still be daylight at midnight," a grown-up answered. "But my watch says it's bedtime!"

Daylight or not, Terpsichore was too tired to think of playing outside. She snuggled under her share of the blanket. The twins' toes were within inches of her nose. "Your feet smell," she whispered.

"Yours do too," the twins whispered. They hadn't had a bath since Seattle, so what could they expect? And they probably wouldn't get a proper bath now until they had their own tent and could fill a washtub with hot water. A few minutes later, when the twins had stopped fidgeting and started snoring, Tigger slipped under the mosquito net and jumped up on the cot. She paced up and down, trying to find a place to wedge herself into the narrow valleys between Terpsichore and her sisters.

Terpsichore's fingers sought the place on Tigger's jaw that she liked rubbed. "It's going to be all right," she whispered. "No matter where we are, as long as we're all together, we're home, and we're still your people." She felt the vibrations of a near-silent purr, then each paw-step as Tigger crept up to lick Terpsichore's jaw. Satisfied that all was well in this new world, Tigger slipped to the floor and found her own spot on the plank floor underneath the cot.

To the distant whine and screech from the sawmill and the closer whine of mosquitoes attempting to access fresh flesh, Terpsichore fell asleep at last.

The next morning, she woke to the sound of hammering and sawing, and the tickle of cold, wiggling toes in her face.

"That pounding is the sound of our tent going up," Pop said.

"I hope," Mother said. She was huddled under the blankets feeding Matthew.

"It doesn't take long to build a tent frame," Mr. Wilcox said. "They'll have everyone in their own tent in a couple days. Meanwhile, let's give the ladies some privacy. I'll take the rest of you on a tour."

Since they had slept in their clothes, Terpsichore, Cally, and Polly were ready as soon as they put on their shoes and visited the outhouse.

"Breakfast at the community hall first, I guess," Mr. Wilcox said. "You can always find it easy; it's the only frame building here. Even the bigwigs are living in tents for now."

Long plank tables and benches were set up in the mess hall. Another long table supported vats of scrambled eggs and bacon, piles of toast, urns of coffee, and pitchers of milk.

"This mess hall setup is just until everyone is in their own tent and unpacked," Mr. Wilcox said. "You'll get a welcome packet of bacon, eggs, and coffee when you get your tent, but from then on you'll have to buy food on credit at the general store."

After breakfast, Pop asked, "Can we see the lot where we'll be living?"

"Have to build the road to it first," Mr. Wilcox said. "You'll be assigned to a crew to help clear a path to your plot. Where will you be?"

"Seventy-seven," Pop said. "It's just south of town."

"The big map is deceiving," Mr. Wilcox said. "I expect that cluster south of town is going to be a couple miles away."

Mr. Wilcox turned to Terpsichore and the twins and shook his finger at them. "You girls stay away from the garbage bins behind the community center. They attract bears. And stay out of the way of the CCC workers the government brought up from California to clear land and build houses and barns. We want those houses built as soon as possible, don't we?"

The twins clutched Pop's coat. "There really are bears here!"

"Garbage is easier pickings than kids," Mr. Wilcox said. "Just stay out of their way and make noise as you go so they can stay out of yours."

Apparently all the children in camp had heard the advice to make lots of noise. Almost louder than the sawmill and tractors, groups of children whooped and yelled, reveling at having running room after being cooped up on trains and ships.

Mr. Wilcox was right. The tents did go up fast, and two days later, Terpsichore and her family were unpacking in their own tent in the sixth row back from the train tracks. The construction crews were still waiting for more hammers, but Pop had packed his own. He scrounged wood scraps and installed shelves in several of the packing crates so each of the girls had a make-do cupboard. Terpsichore had her own cot and the twins had stacked cots like bunk beds. Pop made Matthew a make-do crib out of pieces of packing crates sanded smooth.

Once her mother had covered the rough picnic table with a good cloth from home and Polly and Cally had set the table with silverware and their Shirley Temple dishes, they could try to ignore the whine of buzz saws and the roar of tractors and pretend they were back in civilized territory.

Until more land was cleared and folks could move their tents closer to their own plots of land, all two hundred and two families were together in one camp. For now, this was home sweet home.

CHAPTER 11

Terpsichore, Not Trip

TERPSICHORE HAD NEVER SEEN HER MOTHER DO ANYTHING as undignified as skipping, so she was surprised when Mother skipped into the tent after the mothers' meeting in the community tent. "Good news! The camp superintendent arranged with the Matanuska District to have a bus come and round up the fourth- to eighth-graders to take them into Matanuska for the last two weeks of school!" She beamed at Terpsichore expectantly.

"School?" Terpsichore's question came out as a whispery squeak. "I thought—that is, I heard some of the kids say— that since the school year was almost over, summer vacation might start early."

Mother humphed. "Just because we're in Alaska doesn't mean you can become hoydens. Besides, school will keep you safely out of the way of falling trees and bulldozers and excavators."

"But what about us?" Cally scooped up her jacks and stood.

"Yes, what about third-graders?" Polly stood too, clutching the red jacks ball.

Mother handed Matthew to Terpsichore so she could hug the twins.

"Tip," he said. "Tip carry!"

"Terp-sick-oh-ree," Terpsichore whispered, bumping noses gently with her brother. Maybe she could at least teach him to say her real name.

"The primaries will have school right here in camp in a railroad car," Mother said. "Won't that be exciting? You won't have desks, but the Matanuska school has loaned Palmer a teacher and a few primary textbooks to share. At least someone's trying to provide the basics of civilized society."

Cally and Polly looked at each other, trying to decide how they should respond. With twin telepathy they spoke in unison. "Fun!" they said.

"And, Terpsichore, you'll have to get up early because the Matanuska bus leaves the community center at seven forty-five tomorrow."

"Tomorrow?" Terpsichore said.

"Tomorrow!" The twins headed to their packing crate cupboards to decide what to wear on the first day of school in Alaska Territory.

Terpsichore scrubbed the muck off her Buster Brown oxfords and used her father's shoeshine kit to rub out the scuffs. Even if the only dress that covered her knees was made from a flour sack printed with roses, her shoes would be presentable. She found a pencil and what was left of a rough-paper tablet and arranged it under her cot next to her shoes. She'd never ridden a school bus before, and she was not looking forward to a room of classmates she had not grown up with, but she had done all she could to get ready.

The next morning, Terpsichore put a coat over her pajamas to beat the line to the outhouse. She ate her oatmeal and drank her reconstituted powdered milk, then brushed her teeth.

She had five minutes to dress. She knelt at the side of her cot, and then straightened with a howl that would have startled a wolf.

"What happened to my shoes?"

Cally and Polly rolled sleepily on their bunk-cots. Cally leaned over the top bunk. "Did you lose one?"

Terpsichore held up her shoe, pointing indignantly to the ragged end of a shoelace. "Somebody ate my shoelace!"

"It wasn't me," Cally said.

"Me neither," Polly said.

Mother took the shoe and wrinkled her nose at the shoelace. "More likely a rodent." She quickly thrust the shoe back to Terpsichore as if she were afraid of catching bubonic plague.

"But what am I going to do about my shoelace? There's not enough left to tie."

Mother cut a yard of waxed twine that had been wrapped around the packing boxes.

"String on my shoes?"

"You'll have to make do."

A loud honk announced the arrival of the school bus from Matanuska.

"You'll have time to fix it on the bus," Mother said. "Now scoot!"

Terpsichore slipped on her coat, picked up her lunch pail, tablet, and pencil, stuffed the string into her pocket, and slipped on her shoe, curling her toes to grip the inside sole to keep the shoe from falling off.

"Love you, honey." Mother kissed the top of her head and nudged her out the tent door.

"Don't let the mosquitoes in!" chorused the twins.

Terpsichore stumbled toward the bus by the community center just as the door started closing.

"Wait!" As Terpsichore ran to reach the bus before it pulled out, her toes lost their grip on her shoe and it tumbled off.

When she straightened from picking it up, she saw the row of windows on the bus, each one filled with kids laughing and pointing. She slogged through the mud in one shoe and one muddy sock.

With a pneumatic hiss, the door opened again and she puffed up the steps. She stood in the space by the driver's seat, holding her dripping shoe as she looked for an empty seat. The only one left was on the boys' side. And it was next to Mendel.

CHAPTER 12

A Mouse Ate My Shoelaces

MENDEL WAS SITTING IN THE FRONT SEAT, PROBABLY SO he could tell the driver what gear he should be using. He patted the seat next to him. Terpsichore pretended not to see him.

As she scanned the girls' side of the bus, a boy with a waxed crew cut in the seat behind Mendel hooted, "Who's the clodhopper?"

The boy poked Mendel in the shoulder. "I said, who's the clodhopper? She your girlfriend?"

Mendel turned in his seat to answer the shoulder-poker. "She's Trip," Mendel said, in the kind of shouting-whisper the whole bus could hear. "And she's not my girlfriend."

Terpsichore winced. Mendel must have heard the twins call her Trip.

"You can see why people call her 'Trip.'" The shoulder-poker jabbed a finger at Terpsichore as she stood at the front of the bus, still holding her muddy shoe. He sniggered and looked over his shoulder to see if all the boys agreed with him.

They did. But at least Mendel had clarified that he was not her boyfriend. She felt like bopping the obnoxious boy with her shoe. Instead she glared her basilisk glare. Once she had it perfected it would be so lethal that, like the legendary basilisk snake, one glance would still a man's heart forever. So far she hadn't killed anyone with a look, but even at half power, she could usually halt any noisome behavior from her sisters. Apparently she hadn't developed enough power in her eye beam for it to work on boys. They kept on sniggering and pointing.

"Everyone to a seat," the bus driver called. He meant Terpsichore.

"Psst, squeeze in with me." A girl with an orange sweater scooted next to her seatmate to provide six inches of room for Terpsichore. The older girl sitting next to the window begrudgingly slid over too.

"Thanks!" Terpsichore said. She plopped down but almost slid off the seat when the bus lurched forward.

"We girls have to stick together," the orange sweater girl said. "What happened to your shoe?"

"A mouse ate my shoelace last night." Terpsichore held up her shoe to show where the lace had been nibbled off.

The older girl, probably an eighth-grader, glanced briefly at the shoe and wrinkled her nose in disgust as Terpsichore peeled off her muddy sock and balled it and put it in one of her jacket pockets. She took a crochet-trimmed handkerchief from her other pocket and wiped her hands.

"Here, let me hold your tablet and lunch pail while you fix your shoe," the orange sweater girl said.

Terpsichore gave a shuddering sigh, forbidding her eyes to tear up. What a start to her first day of school in Alaska! With another sigh and trying to smile, she handed over her tablet and lunch pail.

Terpsichore started to pluck out the gnawed-on shoelace. At the next rut in the road she had to clutch the rail on the back of the seat in front of her to keep from sliding off the edge of her own seat, and the shoe slipped off her lap. As she reached under the seat in front of her to reclaim it, the bus bounced over a fallen tree limb and she hit her head.

"Fiddlesticks!" Terpsichore straightened, rubbing the back of her head. "I guess I'll have to fix my shoe later." She leaned over to slide her flopping shoe back on. "Thanks for holding my stuff." She knew her cheeks must be as bright as her seatmate's sweater.

The orange sweater girl acted as if it was perfectly normal to walk onto the bus wearing one shoe. "My name is Gloria." Her grin was, well, glorious and Terpsichore began to feel that maybe the day would start to go better.

"My mother named me Gloria after Gloria Swanson." She touched her crescent-shaped spit curls plastered against her forehead and one cheek. "I was in drama club at school."

Her collar was jauntily turned up in the back, and Terpsichore's eyes widened as she took a closer look at Gloria's mouth. "Is that Tangee lipstick?" she whispered.

"My mother won't let me wear even Tangee until I'm

thirteen." She leaned toward Terpsichore. "It's just a little Vaseline."

Spit curls, tilted-up collar, pretend lipstick, and drama club. Terpsichore wasn't sure this was a girl her mother would approve of, but Terpsichore already liked her.

"I'm Terpsichore," Terpsichore said. "My mother named me after the Greek Muse of Dance."

"Did your mother want you to be a dancer?"

"If she did, I'm sure she's given up that idea by now," Terpsichore said. She sighed again, and not just because of her shoe. Her mother had such grand ambitions for all her daughters. At least Cally and Polly were everything her mother had hoped for.

When they reached Matanuska and filed off the bus, the seventh- and eighth-graders peeled off to the line of older children, and the fourth-, fifth-, and sixth-graders were herded into a crowded classroom. There were only ten desks, and those were already filled by the old-timer kids whose families had settled the valley before the Palmer Colony. Folding chairs had been moved in and crammed every which way into the classroom for the new kids.

Gloria found a chair, but there wasn't another vacant spot next to her. As Terpsichore picked her way through the maze to find a seat near the back of the room, her lunch box clanged against a metal chair and she looked guiltily toward the teacher. Maybe the clang had only sounded loud in her own ears, because the teacher continued to stand with a patient smile until all the students had stowed away their lunches and wiggled out of their coats.

"Welcome to the Territory of Alaska! I'm Miss Burgess, and I'll be teaching the combined fourth, fifth, and sixth grades for your last two weeks of school."

She looked nice, with a soft ruff of auburn hair around her face, the kind of hairstyle you had to set in pin curls every night. But trousers? Terpsichore half stood so she could double-check. Yes, Miss Burgess was wearing trousers, and they were tucked into tall, laced boots. Mother would faint!

"We know that all of your families need your help to help get crops planted, so there won't be any homework"—she paused for cheers—"for the rest of the year. What we'll do in the two weeks left is focus on helping the newcomers learn about Alaska and make new friends. Let's introduce ourselves, shall we?"

She wrote her name in perfect cursive on the blackboard. "As I said, I'm Miss Burgess, and I've lived in Matanuska for two years, since I finished my education degree at the University of Washington. I came up for a year for the adventure of it, and decided to stay."

She smiled again. "Let's start in the front, and when it's your turn, come on up and tell us your name, where you're from, where your family will be living, and one thing you'd like everyone to know about you."

As old-timers from the front row trooped up, Terpsichore kept her eyes straight ahead so it would look like she was paying attention as she finished pulling the mouse-nibbled lace from each eyelet. After putting the old shoelace in her pocket, she started threading the twine through the eyelets.

She paid more attention when the Palmer Colony children started coming to the front. Somewhere among the Palmer kids she hoped to find a new best friend. Maybe it would be Gloria. The only one she recognized from the trip up was Mendel. Nearly everyone on the ship had been too busy up-chucking to do much socializing.

If she were back in Little Bear Lake, Eileen would already be coming up with ideas for fun things they could do that summer. They had planned to help Miss Thompson with the summer reading club at the library, but Palmer didn't even have a library. They had planned to learn to do the backstroke in Little Bear Lake, but Alaska would be too cold for swimming. Would she ever have a friend like Eileen again?

Most of the boys were automatic rejects for a new best friend. Teddy, the crew-cut boy, had been the best batter on his baseball team at home, so he claimed. Another had a stamp collection. Several girls had won ribbons in 4-H. Gloria had played the title role in their school production of *Heidi*. Then it was Mendel's turn.

"My name is Mendel Theodore Peterson. I'm from Wisconsin, and my family will be moving to lot one-eighty-five out at the Butte, about twelve miles southeast of Palmer, across the Matanuska River. I'm going into sixth grade, and the first thing you probably noticed about me is my handsome set of dental appliances." Instead of trying to hide the mess of metal in his mouth, he grinned to show it off and pointed to his wires to explain how they worked.

"See this arch wire? The arch wires sustain pressure on the tooth to activate a biochemical process called bone remodeling, during which the periodontal membrane is gradually stretched on one side of the tooth and compressed on the other."

Nobody seemed too interested in a lesson on torture by tooth, not even Miss Burgess, who interrupted him and asked him to tell about one of his interests.

"I'm an amateur entomologist, and I look forward to collecting specimens of all thirty-five species of Alaska mosquitoes," he said. He scanned the room to see if there was any interest in entomology, but as far as Terpsichore could see, there were no other bug boys in the class. Just the word *mosquitoes* made her bites itch.

The girl next to her went up and explained how she had organized a girls' basketball team back in Minnesota. "It's your turn," she whispered when she returned to her seat.

Listening for a new friend, Terpsichore had forgotten to finish threading the string in her shoe. Should she carry it, leave it behind, or try to wear it? She dropped the shoe to the ground, slipped her foot into it, and shuffled toward the front of the room.

Crew Cut, the boy who'd been sitting behind Mendel on the bus, stomped on her dangling shoelace.

Terpsichore tugged her shoe free with a stumbling lurch. "Trip, her name is Trip," Crew Cut said in a mock whisper as he jabbed his chubby finger in her direction.

"Terpsichore, my name is Terp*sich*ore," she hissed. But the damage was done. She ignored the giggles and whispers of "Trip," and tried to walk on to the front of the room as if she had not almost nose-dived to the floor.

"What's wrong with your shoe?" Miss Burgess asked, kneeling to take a closer look.

Terpsichore's stomach felt almost as sloshy as it had on the ship, and her cheeks felt feverish. She was probably coming down with measles. "A mouse ate my shoelace," she mumbled. What a miserable start to the day!

Mendel waved his hand, but didn't wait to be called on. "I bet it was a vole, a *Myodes rutilus*, a northern red-backed vole."

Miss Burgess ignored him and smiled at Terpsichore. "A mouse ate my shoelace . . . That's funny! I bet a lot of you have great stories to tell about coming to Alaska too." She put a hand on Terpsichore's shoulder, and then stood. "This afternoon at writing time, you can each write a real or pretend letter to a friend back home about the funniest thing that has happened to you so far in Alaska. Thanks for that, Terpsichore."

Miss Burgess laughed again and called up the next student, forgetting that Terpsichore had not had her turn in front of the class. Just as well; Terpsichore couldn't think of any interesting thing she wanted everyone to know about herself.

That afternoon, Teddy announced Terpsichore's arrival as she climbed the steps to the bus behind Gloria. "Here comes Trip the Clodhopper!"

Terpsichore pointed at Teddy. "And there sits an uncouth person from the back of beyond."

He thrust his foot into the aisle, but Terpsichore was onto his tricks and daintily stepped over it.

"Uncouth person from the back of beyond," Gloria repeated. "That's a good one. I'll have to remember that line."

This time Terpsichore and Gloria got a seat to themselves. "You didn't get a chance in class to tell about yourself," Gloria said. "So what were you known for back home?"

"Pop says I'm a wizard with pumpkin. I can turn it into cookies and soup and at least a dozen other dishes. Not as exciting as starring in a play, is it?"

"If you like cookies it is! And I sure do. I think there are lots of ways of being creative. Maybe you'll write a famous cookbook someday," Gloria said. "Hey, where's your tent site? I hope we're close together!"

"We're in row F, the back row, number twelve."

"Yes!" Gloria grabbed Terpsichore's arm. "My family is in row C, number fifteen, a couple rows ahead of you and a couple tents over. We're almost neighbors!"

CHAPTER 13

Letter Home

General Delivery, Palmer, Alaska Territory

May 27, 1935

Dear Eileen,
For today's writing assignment we all have to write
a letter home, and try to include the funniest thing
that has happened to us in Alaska. My teacher thinks a
mouse eating your shoelace is funny but I don't. Instead
I will write about what I like and don't like about the
Palmer Colony. I don't have much paper so I'll write
small.

Things I Don't Like:
- *Two-holer outhouses—the smaller hole is for little kids*
  so they don't fall in the pit. Yuck!

- *Mosquitoes and horseflies—we are all covered in itchy welts. Matthew's eye got swollen shut with one bite, and I have twelve welts on just one shin!*
- *Crowded-together tents instead of houses.*
- *No library—I will go crazy if I don't get something new to read!*
- *No radio! Jumping grasshoppers and leaping lizards! If you have a radio in Chicago please tell me how Orphan Annie got a message to Daddy Warbucks to rescue her from the pirates.*
- *No Eileen!!!*

So that's some of the bad stuff. But President Roosevelt wants everyone to be cheerful and confident, so I will try to think of things I do like about the Palmer Colony.

Things I Like:

- *My teacher is nice, even though she has an odd sense of humor.*
- *Mountains everywhere help you forget about the mud at your feet.*
- *No homework for our last two weeks of school.*
- *More room to grow pumpkins (Ha!).*
- *The sun doesn't set until eleven and with twilight another hour after that, I have plenty of light to read by at night, even without electricity.*

- *Mendel—the first kid I met, who happens to be the most talkative, nuisancy know-it-all in all of Alaska—will be moving to a lot twelve miles away, so I won't have to see him much all summer.*

As you can probably guess, I had to think hard to come up with an equal number of things to like about living here. We are plagued with measles. Because of them, two families had to stay in Seattle and wait for the next boat, and another family had to stay on the ship when we finally got to Seward. Between measles, mud, and mosquitoes, some family is sure to give up and go home. Maybe there'll be an empty tent just waiting for you if you don't like Chicago.

I wish I could TALK to you instead of writing, because my talking muscles last much longer than my writing finger muscles, and I would love to see your expression when I tell you about everybody throwing up on the St. Mihiel *and how we have to carry our chamber pots to the outhouse and how we have to make a lot of noise to keep the bears away.*

What are you going to do this summer? I got empty nail kegs from behind the general store and have planted seeds for pole beans, cabbage, carrots, mint, parsley, and pumpkins. Once we move the tent out of the main camp to our plot number seventy-seven, I will probably spend the rest of the summer digging up roots and rocks and hauling water so we can get a few vegetables planted and harvested before it starts to snow.

Please, please write and tell me how you like the big city of Chicago. Everyone here picks up their mail at the main camp, so your letters will get to me if you just send it General Delivery, Palmer, Territory of Alaska.

XOXO,
Terpsichore J. (as if you knew more than one Terpsichore!)

P.S. The X on the map shows where we'll be building our house.

P.P.S. WRITE SOON!!!

CHAPTER 14

Fire!

ONE AFTERNOON, AS SOON AS TERPSICHORE AND GLORIA stepped off the school bus, they smelled smoke.

Gloria sniffed. "Must be burning stumps again."

"It doesn't smell like stumps to me," Terpsichore said as they passed the first few rows of tents. By the time they reached the fifth row, the smell of smoke had gotten stronger.

The girls ducked under sheets hanging from a neighbor's laundry line and broke into a run. The column of smoke led straight to Mother.

Mother stood outside the Johnsons' tent, holding Matthew, who was howling like a fire engine. Cally and Polly jumped up and down like agitated tree frogs. "A fire! A fire in the oven."

Terpsichore skidded to a stop and gripped her mother's arm. "Mom, are you okay? What happened?"

"I'm not sure. When I restarted the woodstove myself for the first time, it spewed out smoke. The cake I'd planned is ruined, but at least we all got out in time."

When Terpsichore started toward the tent, Mother grabbed her by the collar.

"Don't go in yet!"

"If it's just smoke, not flames, we have to air out the tent," Terpsichore said, securing the tent flap in the open position.

Holding her nose as the smoke billowed out, Terpsichore found a pot holder and opened the oven door. She darted back, waving her pot holder to diffuse the smoke.

Gloria dove toward the stove and shoved the door shut with a clang. "I bet it's the damper. Your father must have closed it when the morning fire went out, to keep the heat in the tent, and when your mother lit another fire to bake something, the smoke couldn't get up the stovepipe." She dragged a chair to a spot in front of the stove and climbed up. She held out a hand. "Pot holder," she said.

Terpsichore handed up a pot holder and Gloria leaned over the stove to turn the damper handle on the stovepipe so it was vertical, to the open position.

Gloria stepped down from the chair. "Fixed that—easy peasy when you know what you're doing." She turned to look at the rest of the Johnsons' tent and ran a finger over the linen tablecloth on the rough-hewn table that the CCC made for every tent. "Pretty snazzy!" she said. "No way my mother would wash and iron a tablecloth. We use a wipe-down oil-cloth on our table." She picked up a fork and squinted at the back. "Sterling silver! You guys must have been rich. How did you get into the program?"

Before Terpsichore could answer, Pop burst into the tent,

followed by Cally and Polly, Mother and Matthew. "Is every-one all right?"

"Mom was baking a cake!" Cally said.

"The tent almost burned down!" Polly said.

"We almost died of smoke inhalation with that infernal woodstove," Mother said. "I wish we could have brought my Hotpoint electric range. Oh, but I forgot." She blew her bangs out of her eyes. "Here in the Alaska wilderness there's no elec-tricity." She stomped out of the tent.

Pop followed and stood outside beside Mother to address the crowd that had just gathered, all poised to fight a fire. "Just smoke," he said. "And the only casualty was a cake."

Terpsichore heard laughter from the crowd.

"Anyway, we don't need your water, but it makes me proud to know I have so many neighbors who are ready to help."

Terpsichore peeked outside to see Pop wave to the Wilcox family, who had shared their tent the first two nights. She saw Mendel and his folks too. They had all brought buckets of water.

Terpsichore heard someone say, "Hey, are those the twins who sang in church last week?"

As Terpsichore scraped the charred remains of the cake into the trash can, she could imagine how tickled the twins were at being recognized.

Gloria stepped away from the tent opening, where she had been listening to the gossip too. "I see Mom and Dad in the crowd, but before I go I'll get you started on using a woodstove so you can make something that bakes fast, like biscuits, to make up for the lost cake."

"Good idea," Terpsichore said. "It would be great to learn from an expert!"

Together the girls measured flour into a bowl, sprinkled in a dash of salt, cut in shortening, mixed dry milk powder with water, and lightly kneaded the dough. They rolled out the dough on the breadboard, and cut out the biscuits.

Gloria peeked in the firebox and the oven. "The oven has cooled off some but it won't take long to get it revved up again." She fed a few sticks of wood into the firebox.

"How can you tell when it's hot enough?" Terpsichore asked.

"After you've used a woodstove for a while, you just know, like you know how much milk to add to your biscuits—it just feels right."

Gloria stood again on the chair. "Here's how you adjust the heat. You start with the damper wide open, that's handle facing up the smokestack, so the fire gets lots of air, then adjust down about halfway once it gets going. Not too far down, though. You do have to let the smoke escape, as your mother found out today." She laughed as she stepped off the chair.

Terpsichore felt disloyal about laughing at her mother, but Gloria's laughter was contagious. "She sure did! But although Mother doesn't know how to use a woodstove yet, she won the senior piano prize in her last year at St. Olaf College."

"Wow! So where's her piano?" Gloria asked.

"She sold it for food," Terpsichore said. "When the lumber mill closed down and Pop lost his bookkeeping job, we were just as poor as everyone else."

"So I guess up here, we all start out equal," Gloria said. "Same woodstove, same tent, same forty acres. Do you think we would have been friends if we lived in the same small town down below?"

"I think we'd be friends anywhere," Terpsichore said.

"Me too."

Bing! At the sound of the timer, the girls jumped and Terpsichore opened the oven to golden brown biscuits.

"You're a natural!" Gloria started to take off a biscuit to sample, but dropped it back on the cookie sheet and sucked her burned fingers.

"Here's a spatula," Terpsichore said. Together, the girls arranged the biscuits on two plates and carried them outside, where folks were still gathered.

"Nothing like a little fire scare to get to know your neighbors," Pop was saying.

Mother looked flustered. It was not the way she would have wanted to be introduced to Palmer society. But Terpsichore smiled at everyone. Perhaps now they would remember her as the girl who baked perfect biscuits.

CHAPTER 15

A Visit to a Place of Their Own

AFTER CHURCH SERVICES IN THE COMMUNITY CENTER, Pop took off his tie and slipped behind the sheet dividing Mother and Pop's part of the tent from the children's cots. He emerged in overalls. "The sun shines, kiddles! Get into your dungarees and get ready for a picnic on our own farm."

Terpsichore, Cally, and Polly pulled out the boxes under their cots to retrieve their dungarees and long-sleeved shirts. Once they had wriggled out of their dresses and into play clothes, they were ready for an adventure.

Mother hadn't bought pants yet, but she did change into her oldest cotton dress. While Matthew stood in his make-shift crib, banging on the sides to be let out, Mother made sandwiches, wrapped them in newspaper, and slipped them in a tote bag. She tied on her straw hat draped in mosquito netting, a hat she'd dubbed her "Matanuska veil." She scooped Matthew up in one hand and the sack of supplies in the other. "I'm ready, Harald."

"We're ready too," the twins chorused as they tied the chinstraps on their own netting-shrouded hats. Terpsichore followed suit. They all burst out of the cocoon of their tent to see where their new home would be built.

Pop took Matthew from Mother and lifted him up on his shoulders. As they headed out of the tent city, Terpsichore breathed in the scent of spicy spruce and wild roses. Wherever there was a clearing, spiky lupine, seas of bluebells, and purple fireweed bloomed. Even the mosquitoes were on good behavior, resting as the day warmed. For the first time since they left Wisconsin, Mother hummed.

After following the railroad tracks south for half a mile, they cut east on a new dirt road Pop had helped build. At the third survey stake, they turned off the dirt road to a stump-spotted trail.

Mother tripped over a sun-hardened mud rut. "This is a road?"

"It's just the first stage," Pop said. "The tractors and teams of horses will be in next week to pull stumps and level it out."

"Humph!" was all Mother said. She wasn't humming anymore.

After half an hour, they were still walking.

"Are we there yet?" That was Cally.

"I thought you said it was close to town," Mother said. "We must have walked two miles already."

"We're almost there," Pop said. "And our lot is closer than the ones that are twelve miles out by the Butte, or out by the lakes west of town."

"*Caw! Caw!*" The deep-throated, raspy call echoed from the top of a spruce tree. The raven sounded as unhappy about the human invasion of his forest as Mother sounded about being there.

Terpsichore raced ahead to find lot seventy-seven. How blissful to see the sun! How blissful to run without shoes pulling off in the mud! At each stake, two or three town-blocks apart, she checked the numbers. Seventy-one, seventy-three—seventy-seven! She waved back at the rest of the family. "I found it!"

Mother looked at the solid stand of timber. "So where does the house go, Mr. Johnson? I don't see enough cleared land for our tent, let alone a house and barn."

She turned to look along the land cleared for the road, where she had a sliver of a view of the Chugach Mountains. "At least when land is cleared we'll get to see the mountains." She pointed toward a prominent peak south of Palmer. "That," she said, "that is what I want to see outside my kitchen window. Does it have a name?"

"If it does, I don't know it," he said. "Maybe I'll name it after you. We'll call it Clio's Peak."

For a moment, as she squinted toward Clio's Peak, Mother smiled.

However, a scowl returned when a squadron of mosquitoes swarmed out of hiding. With a white-gloved hand, Mother reached up past Pop's shoulders to bat at the ones buzzing around the netting draped over Matthew's baby-sized baseball cap. "Bad mosquitoes," she said.

"Bad 'toes," Matthew said. "Bad 'toes bite!"

"We'll have a great view of the mountains after our turn with the sawyers and bulldozers," Pop said. "And we can face our tent right at those Chugach Mountains if that's what you want."

"And then we get our own horse?" Cally and Polly's words stumbled over each other's in their rush to be the first to ask.

"That's the plan," Pop said.

Mother raised her eyebrows. She didn't need words to say what she thought of the planning process in Palmer.

Pop turned to Terpsichore, who gazed back toward town instead of investigating their land. "Aren't you excited about getting our garden planted?"

"I am," Terpsichore said. "But I hope Gloria won't be too far away. We'll be so spread out when we all move out of the main camp."

"Once we get that horse and wagon," Pop said, "it will be easy to trot into town for errands and visits. You can see your friends then. And of course you'll see them at school."

"Whenever we're not buried in snowdrifts," Mother said. She scratched another mosquito bite on her leg. "Terpsichore, is it true that even some of the teachers wear trousers?"

"It is," Terpsichore said.

"Our teacher too," said Cally and Polly.

"Mr. Johnson, I can't believe I am saying this, but if I'm to survive this summer, I will need to order a pair of trousers," Mother said.

CHAPTER 16

Summer Plans

ON THE NEXT TO LAST DAY OF SCHOOL, ALL THE OLD notices on the bulletin board in the entry hall were replaced by a new notice and sign-up sheets:

Have Fun This Summer!

Boys' Baseball
Girls' Baseball
Boys' Basketball
Girls' Basketball
4-H—Animal Husbandry
4-H—Domestic Arts
4-H—Agricultural Science
Mixed Chorus
Band

At lunch break, students clustered around the bulletin board, signing up with their names and plot numbers. Gloria signed up for mixed chorus and tried to convince Terpsichore to sign up too, so they could do something together.

"It's my sisters who can sing," Terpsichore said. "But maybe the agricultural science group would be fun."

"You're kidding! You'd be in with a bunch of boys in overalls who want to see who can grow the biggest rutabagas."

"My dad and I had a good garden in Wisconsin," Terpsichore said.

"It would be fun to do something together, too," Gloria said. "Do you play basketball?"

"Do I look like I do? Ever heard of a four-foot, six-inch basketball player?" Terpsichore asked. "It would be nice to be on a committee that does something useful. What this town really needs is a library."

"I like to read too, but I don't think you'll get much support to build a library when folks are still living in tents," Gloria said.

"We don't need a building for a library," Terpsichore said. "We need books." She chewed on the inside of her lower lip as she thought. Just before the bell rang to go back to class, Terpsichore went back to her desk and carefully tore out the last page of her lined tablet. With Gloria hovering over her shoulder, she printed a heading and held it up for Gloria to read.

"Perfect!" Gloria said. "Let's pin it up!"

While Terpsichore held her sign-up sheet up near the bottom of the board, Gloria tacked it into place. They both stood back to admire their work, and then signed their names and plot numbers:

Terpsichore Johnson, #77

Gloria LeClerc, #101

They had just started an official Library Society.

By the end of the last day of school, there was one other name on the sign-up sheet:

Mendel Theodore Peterson, #91

It didn't register with Terpsichore that Mendel wasn't going to be moving twelve miles out of town near the rocky knoll everyone called the Butte. He had listed space number ninety-one—which was, as the raven flew, only five plots away from space seventy-seven.

CHAPTER 17

The Library Society Meets

ON SUNDAY AFTER CHURCH, TERPSICHORE, GLORIA, AND Mendel sat on folding chairs around a card table set up in the corner of the community center farthest from the isolation ward that had been set up for sick children behind a canvas wall.

"Burned any cakes lately?" Mendel asked.

"That was Mother, not me," Terpsichore answered. "Now that Gloria showed me how the damper works, I can bake a perfect cake. And perfect muffins and cornbread too. But let's get to library business.

"Since I've volunteered in both the public library and the school library back in Wisconsin, I should be the chairman of the society and one of you could be secretary and one of you could be the treasurer."

"Just a minute," said Mendel. "We have to vote. Besides, a girl can't be chair*man*. I nominate myself."

"Boys aren't men either. And you can't nominate yourself; someone else has to nominate you."

Mendel and Terpsichore glared at each other. "I'm certainly not going to nominate an annoying know-it-all!" Terpsichore said.

"And I'm not going to nominate a bossy girl!" Mendel said.

"Another reason," said Terpsichore, "you can't be chairperson; it has to be someone close to town, where we'll set up the library. You're clear out at the Butte."

"Not anymore," Mendel said. "We swapped with a family who wanted to be close to their old friends from Michigan who had plots at the Butte. We're right by the river now, on space ninety-one. We're closer to town than you are."

Terpsichore looked for sympathy from Gloria. She got it.

"I'm not sure this is proper parliamentary procedure either," Gloria said. "But why don't we say we're all candidates and vote?"

"Good idea," said Mendel as he tore strips of paper from his tablet and passed them out. He took his newsboy cap from his lap and placed it on the table. "Put your votes in here."

Terpsichore cupped her hand around her ballot while she deliberated. It might not be polite to vote for yourself, but if you were obviously the most qualified and if the whole committee was your idea, you should be the head of it. She bent over her ballot and wrote "Terpsichore Johnson" and placed it in Mendel's hat. Mendel and Gloria added their votes.

Gloria reached in and unfolded the first ballot. "One vote for Mendel Peterson." She held it up for inspection.

Terpsichore looked at the precise printing on the ballot. Mendel's for sure. He had voted for himself too.

Gloria passed the hat for Terpsichore to draw out the next ballot. "Gloria LeClerc," she read. From the bitty circle dotting the *i* that was Gloria's vote.

Terpsichore passed the hat back to Mendel. "Trip Johnson," he read.

"I didn't write Trip, I wrote—"

"Ha! I knew it!" Mendel bounced in his chair, pointing at Terpsichore and showing off his full set of braces. "You voted for yourself."

"You did too," Terpsichore said.

Gloria rapped her pencil again for order. "We all did, and we're getting nowhere. Let's think about who will do the best job of leading the committee."

"I have money-making ideas, and you can't have a library without money," said Mendel.

"I've actually worked in two kinds of libraries," said Terpsichore.

"And I can keep you two from wasting all our time by arguing," Gloria said.

In a second round of voting, Mendel still voted for himself, and Terpsichore and Gloria voted for each other.

A third round of voting. This time there were three votes for Gloria. She stood and curtseyed. "As your new chair*person*, I'd like to suggest that since Mendel has money-making ideas, he should be treasurer, and since Terpsichore knows about how a library works, she should be our operations manager."

Terpsichore nodded. *Operations manager* sounded almost as good as *chairperson*. Mendel shrugged. Treasurer would do.

"Operations Manager, what should be our first priority?" Gloria said.

"Just a minute," Mendel said. "I think our first priority should be to choose a name. 'Library Society' sounds like a bunch of snooty tea-sippers."

"You might not like the name, but at least I had the idea of taking action to start a library," Terpsichore said. "So what's your great idea?"

"Actually," Mendel said, "you just gave me an idea when you said you took action. How about the Library Action Committee?"

"Library Action Committee," said Terpsichore, trying out the words. The name did sound stronger. "I like it," she said.

"I like it too," Gloria said. "It's unanimous?"

Mendel and Terpsichore nodded.

"Okay, then. Back to the operations manager. How should we start?" Gloria said.

Terpsichore had already thought about it. "Even without money to work with, we could start Saturday story hours, like we used to have back in Little Bear Lake."

Gloria bounced in her seat. "I was in drama club, so I'd be good at that."

Terpsichore sighed. She'd been hoping to do the story hours herself. "My teacher used to let me read picture books to the first-graders when they came in to the library."

Gloria pursed her lips, thinking. "Did your family bring

any picture books? You could read to the little kids and I could read aloud in installments to the older kids. We could both have story hours." Gloria grinned expectantly.

Terpsichore grinned back.

Mendel apparently had no interest in the story hours. "We should get good stuff for the library, like a subscription to *Entomological News.*"

"What's that?" Gloria and Terpsichore chorused.

"To put it simply to the uninitiated, bug research," Mendel said.

Terpsichore grimaced. "Who wants to read that?"

"I do," said Mendel. "Think of all the new bugs I might find in Alaska Territory. I might even get one named after me."

"If I had something named after me, I wouldn't want it to be a bug," Terpsichore said.

Gloria rapped the table with her pencil. "Before we can buy anything . . . and by the way, I think a subscription to *Modern Screen* or *Photoplay* would be a lot more popular than the *Journal of Bugs.*"

"*Entomological News,*" Mendel said.

"Bugs," continued Gloria. "We have to have money. Mendel, since you're the treasurer, would you like to move that we should all try out ways of making money?"

"I move we make some money so we can start buying stuff for the library," Mendel said. "And if we can't get *Entomological News* right away, I think we should at least get *Scientific American.*"

Gloria tapped her pencil again. "I think I only heard the first part of that motion. Do we need a second and discussion or can we just say we'll do it?"

"Let's do it!" Terpsichore said.

Mendel stood. "And let's report back here in two weeks."

CHAPTER 18

Bottles for Books

T ERPSICHORE WAS SCANNING THE COMMUNITY BULLETIN board to see if anyone had answered her ad for babysitting when she was nearly knocked over by a boisterous dog. "Oof!" Terpsichore brushed the paw prints off her shirt.

"Come, Togo!" Mendel commanded.

"That's Togo? What have you been feeding her?" She crossed her arms over her chest to defend herself.

As if to prove how much she'd grown, Togo darted up to Terpsichore's shoulder to lick her hand. Then, tail wagging, she danced her way back to Mendel.

"She likes you!" Mendel said.

"I'm not sure I like her back," Terpsichore said, wiping her slobbered-on hand on her dungarees.

"Togo's going to help us earn money for the library, so I bet she'll grow on you."

Mendel rattled the handle of a rusted Radio Flyer wagon and held his dog still between his legs while he picked up the loose ends of two ropes he'd threaded through holes drilled into the front of the wagon and tied them to Togo's collar.

"So how's Togo going to help earn money for the library?" Terpsichore said. "Are you going to give little kids rides?"

"Togo isn't up to pulling a heavy load yet. She's going to start out with light stuff, like all the bottles I'm going to collect. See?" Mendel had painted a sign on one side of the box in the wagon: **Bottles for Books**. "I'm going to collect soda bottles and haul them to the general store for the two-cent refund."

"Nice sign," Terpsichore said, "but who's going to give you their empties when they could take them in for a refund themselves?"

"You haven't seen my winning ways in action." When Mendel smiled, the sun glinted so fiercely off his braces Terpsichore had to shade her eyes against the glare. Togo whined impatiently to get moving, but danced in place.

"Good dog, Togo." At the sound of her name, Togo wagged her tail so hard she almost tipped over the wagon. "A boy and his dog, earning money for the library—who could resist?"

"Good luck," Terpsichore said.

"Hike!" Mendel called, and Togo followed Mendel toward the CCC camp, the wagon rattling behind.

Terpsichore turned back to the bulletin board and pulled off her notice so she could read the tiny lettering of a reply. She grinned. A new mother, Mrs. Jarlsted, needed help with her first baby. She'd been secretly dreading the possibility that someone with seven obstreperous children would reply. One baby sounded like fun.

On the way to the store to find her mother, Terpsichore passed Gloria, who had set up an outdoor beauty salon next to where her father, who had once been a barber as well as a farmer, had set up a barbering station. "What's that goop?" Terpsichore asked, as she pointed toward a bowl of thick, clear liquid perched on top of an apple crate beside an oak chair. Mrs. LeClerc, Gloria's mother, was the first customer. She said, loud enough for passersby to hear, "Gloria does a much better job setting my hair than I could ever do myself. It's worth the ten cents to me to have perfectly styled hair for church tomorrow."

Gloria dipped a comb into the goop in the bowl and ran it through a strand of her mother's hair. "It's just water with a teaspoon of unflavored gelatin dissolved in it to make it thick." She meticulously wound the strand into a perfect snail shape and secured it with two crisscrossed bobby pins. As she continued her row of curls she said, "With two rows like this Mom will have a perfect ruff, just like our teacher, Miss Burgess."

As more families walked by, Mrs. LeClerc pitched her daughter's service. "I just love the way Gloria sets my hair. It looks as good as any professional job. And she's donating all proceeds to the new Palmer Library!"

Gloria leaned over to whisper directly into her mother's ear. "Good job, Mom."

Another woman got in line. "I guess if my husband can spare ten cents to get his hair cut, I can find ten cents to have my hair done."

Terpsichore pointed to the sign next to Gloria's styling station. "What does BYOBP mean?"

"Bring Your Own Bobby Pins," Gloria said. "But I can use my own bobby pins today if people promise to bring them back."

Gloria looked up from tying a folded bandanna around her mother's head to cover the pins. "Do you have any babysitting jobs yet?"

"Just one," Terpsichore said. "I guess most families have an older child or a neighbor to babysit for free. Ten cents an hour for babysitting one baby! Doesn't that sound like fun?"

When Terpsichore found her mother, she said, "Somebody answered my ad for babysitting. Could I go meet them?"

"Yes, but I'd feel more comfortable if I could meet them too. I'll go with you."

As Terpsichore and her mother found their way to the Jarl-steds' tent, she noticed several blank spots where tents used to be. "Will we be moving our tent to our lot soon?"

"Very soon," Mother said, "for better or worse. I hate the crowding in the main camp, but I'm not eager to leave what passes for a town to live in the woods."

When Terpsichore arrived with Mother at the tent in the second row, eleventh from the south end, Mr. Jarlsted was coming in from one of the tent city's community gardens. "Is one of you Terpsichore?" He pronounced the name with three syllables, Terp-si-core, which made both Terpsichore and her mother wince.

Terpsichore raised her hand. "I'm Terpsichore," she said, "with four syllables."

"With such a big name I expected someone bigger and older," he said.

Mother boosted Matthew up farther on one hip and extended her hand. "I'm Terpsichore's mother and I can vouch for her ability to take care of babies." She bounced Matthew to make him giggle. "Do you agree, Matty-boy?"

"Named him for the Matanuska Valley, did you?" Mr. Jarlsted asked.

"No," Mother said. "Matty is just a nickname for Matthew."

"Our little one is Edna." Mr. Jarlsted untied the tent flap and shooed Terpsichore and her mother inside. "Betsy? I have someone to help take care of little Edna for us."

"Thank goodness," Mrs. Jarlsted said. "Edna has me up half the night and I'm desperate for a rest."

Terpsichore knelt to look at baby Edna, swaddled in a flannel receiving blanket, her pink mouth making tiny puckered sucking movements even in her sleep. Watching Edna would be the easiest ten cents an hour she ever made. "Sure," Terpsichore said. "How many hours a day would you like me to come?"

Mr. and Mrs. Jarlsted exchanged a look over Terpsichore's head. "Two hours every couple of days ought to do it," Mr. Jarlsted said. "Can you start now?"

"Okeydokey. Mom?" Terpsichore said.

Terpsichore's mother rolled her eyes at the slang she had picked up in camp. "Yes, you may," she said, and headed back with Matthew to the Johnson tent.

Terpsichore made herself comfortable by the cradle and rocked it gently. "Don't worry, Mr. Jarlsted, I'll watch Edna every minute." She expected him to go back to the community garden but he did not.

He shifted his hat from hand to hand, working up courage to say something. "Since Edna is asleep, and you're earning money, I'd take it kindly if you could help take care of Edna in other ways besides just sitting there," he said. "You know about diapers?"

"I've changed lots of diapers," Terpsichore said.

"That's not exactly what I was getting at," Mr. Jarlsted said. "We had no idea a baby that little could go through so many diapers in one day. Mrs. Jarlsted and Edna have been home from the maternity tent for just a day and we're already down to just one clean diaper left."

"My mother could probably loan you a couple until you get them washed," Terpsichore said.

"That's just it," he said. "How do you wash diapers without a washing machine?"

Terpsichore didn't like the way this conversation was going, but it wasn't Edna's fault her parents didn't know how to wash diapers. "Mother has a system," Terpsichore said as she stood. "Do you have a five-gallon bucket and a plunger you don't mind getting holes in?"

"I was wondering about that plunger the neighbors gave her at the baby shower," he said. "From the way they tittered when Mrs. Jarlsted asked what it was for, I thought it was a joke. It's got holes drilled in the top and sides of the rubber parts, so it's about the most useless thing I can imagine. I tossed it out back."

"You'll use it a lot with a new baby," Terpsichore assured him.

Terpsichore followed him out behind the tent where a canning kettle, hoes and rakes, and unpacked boxes were heaped up. "Will this do?" He held up a dented bucket.

"It'll do to start with, but you might want to round up something with a lid on it so you don't get splashed with hot water."

Terpsichore didn't have to ask where the dirty diapers were. She followed her nose to another bucket heaped with sodden diapers near the back of the tent.

"My wife has a delicate nature. I don't know if she's up to handling . . . you know."

"She's going to have to get used to it," Terpsichore said. "Babies get diapers dirty and they have to get washed. Use a flat stick to scrape them into the chamber pot as you go, and then soak the diapers in a bucket like this, in water with baking soda until you're ready to wash them." She looked sternly at Mr. Jarlsted. "This has to be done every day."

"And this plunger, does this come into it?"

"Yes," Terpsichore said. "It's perfect for the mother with a delicate nature, because once the diapers have been scraped off, she won't have to touch the hot dirty water even once while she washes.

"Now," she said. "I'll show you how the plunger comes in

handy." For two or three minutes, she jabbed and poked the plunger into the bucket, agitating the diapers in the pre-rinse water. "While I'm doing this, you can heat a teakettle of water to wash these in," she said. "And bring your washing detergent."

Mr. Jarlsted obediently hauled a bucket of water into the tent to heat on the woodstove inside. By the time he came back out with a teakettle full of water, Terpsichore was draining off the pre-rinse water onto a row of flowers. She poured the boiling water over the diapers, scraped flakes from the bar of Fels-Naptha into the water, and began to attack the diapers again with a two-fisted grip on the plunger. "If Mrs. Jarlsted is too weak to do this by herself, you might want to learn to wash diapers too," Terpsichore said.

"Oh no," Mr. Jarlsted said, backing away. "You're doing such a good job of it I wouldn't want to interfere. I'll just watch so I can tell the missus how you did it."

Terpsichore brushed the hair out of her eyes with the back of her forearm and continued plunging.

"I'll just go check on Edna," he said. "Keep up the good work!"

If washing diapers wasn't earning money for a new library, she would have thrown down the plunger and walked home. This wasn't the job she expected, but she guessed it was worth it for some new books. If she got any better jobs, though, she wouldn't be coming back to the Jarlsteds.

CHAPTER 19

The Library Action Committee
Meets Again

AFTER CALLING THE MEETING TO ORDER AT 11:04 A.M., Chairperson Gloria LeClerc asked for committee reports.

Terpsichore read her report on library operations. "The Library Action Committee placed announcements for the new story times on the community bulletin board. By the second Saturday, Miss Terpsichore Johnson had fourteen in attendance for her picture book story time, which included *Angus and the Ducks*, *Raggedy Ann Stories*, and *Millions of Cats*. Miss Gloria LeClerc also reported eleven listeners for the second chapter of *Smoky the Cowhorse*, loaned to the committee by Cally and Polly Johnson."

Mendel stood to read his treasurer's report. "After just two weeks Mr. Mendel Theodore Peterson has collected one hundred thirty-seven soda bottles with his Bottles for Books drive, mostly from the CCC workers. The bottles were turned in to the commissary for two cents apiece, for a total of $2.74.

Miss Gloria LeClerc's beauty service has earned $2.90, and Miss Terpsichore Johnson has earned $2.40 with her diaper laundry business. She said there probably would be a big demand for diaper washing and asked if Mr. Peterson or Miss LeClerc wanted to earn money for the library by washing diapers too. Mr. Peterson and Miss LeClerc both declined."

Mendel sat back down. "With our $8.04 we could get a subscription to *Scientific American* and still have money left over for something fun, like *Amazing Stories*."

Gloria LeClerc opened the floor to general discussion, and called first on herself. "But how many people want to read *Scientific American*? If we want a magazine more people would read, I still think we should have *Modern Screen* or *Photoplay*."

Terpsichore said, "If somebody wants a ten-cent movie magazine she could get it herself. I think we should save up for something nobody could get on their own, like a set of *World Book* encyclopedias. And we need basic supplies, like date-due cards and a date stamp and ink pad. I wrote to Miss Thompson, the librarian in Little Bear Lake, and she sent me her old Demco library supply catalog and a *World Book* brochure."

Terpsichore took out a folded brochure from between pages of the Demco catalog and opened it up on the table. "See? The nineteen thirty-three edition of the *World Book Encyclopedia* has nineteen volumes. It has science stuff *and* it has articles about movie stars."

"But not as many pictures as *Photoplay*," Gloria said.

"True, but there's something for everybody in it," Terpsichore said.

Mendel leaned back in his chair and crossed his arms over his chest. "How much is it?"

Terpsichore cleared her throat. "Well, we have a choice of three bindings. The cheapest is the green cloth, which is sixty-nine dollars, but I think we should get the set with the blue buckram stamped with a leather grain. That's seventy-nine dollars." Terpsichore caressed the picture of the set bound in red. "The red binding is the prettiest, but that's eighty-nine dollars. I know that one's too much."

"They're all too much!" Mendel said. "This is an action committee, and I think we should have some action before we're all snowbound for the winter. There's too much competition for bottle collecting, and once it gets colder, who's going to want to walk around all day with wet hair in bobby pins?" He paused a moment to emphasize his last point. "And how long are you going to put up with poopy diapers?" Mendel asked.

Terpsichore wasn't sure either.

"Maybe we should think of the best ways to use the money we have," Gloria said.

"What's a library without a set of encyclopedias?" Terpsichore said.

"Forget the encyclopedias," Mendel said. "It's impossible."

"It's not impossible, just difficult," Terpsichore said. "President Roosevelt said we have to have faith that we can control our destinies." She leaned over the table toward Mendel.

"And I think we should have faith that we can somehow earn enough money for the encyclopedias."

Mendel leaned forward too. Their noses were almost touching.

"How about buying a *World Almanac* instead?" Gloria asked. "An almanac has lots of facts."

Terpsichore tucked her encyclopedia brochure back into the Demco supply catalog. Opening the catalog to one of the pages she had dog-eared, she said, "Could we at least order some supplies, like this date-due stamp and ink pad, library paste and india ink, cellophane mending tape, and these book pockets and date-due cards?"

Mendel slid the catalog around to where he could read it. "Paying fifty-nine cents for date-due cards is ridiculous. Three-by-five index cards would work just as well and they're a lot cheaper. And a pocket might cover up part of a magazine somebody wanted to read. Can't you just paper clip an index card to the front?"

Terpsichore thought about last year, when she'd helped her school librarian. She loved the feel of the wooden pen with the metal nib as she dipped it into the darkest of dark india ink. She loved the smell of library paste, the satisfying thump of a date-due stamp onto the ink pad, and the look of the date on an official date-due card.

Mendel slid the catalog back. "All this fancy-schmancy library stuff? I don't give a tinker's dam—"

"Don't swear!"

"D-a-m, not d-a-m-n. *Tinker's dam* isn't swearing. A tinker

111

used to use a temporary ridge of clay to help patch a hole in a pan or teakettle or whatever he was soldering back together to keep the solder where it was needed. When he was through, he scraped off the dam and it was useless. When I say something isn't worth a tinker's dam, I'm saying it isn't worth diddly."

"You—you insufferable pedant! I don't care about the origin of *tinker's dam*. It still sounds like swearing, and supplies aren't diddly!" Terpsichore scooped up her catalog and held it protectively against her chest.

"I joined this committee to get stuff to read, not to buy stampers and india ink so you can play library lady."

The meeting of the Library Action Committee was adjourned at 11:57, but before doing so they voted, two to one, that subscriptions would be ordered for *Scientific American* and *Modern Screen*, and approved the expenditure of one dollar for stamps, stationery, and envelopes for the operations manager's plan to solicit donations.

CHAPTER 20

Little Tent in the Big Woods

MANY FAMILIES HAD ALREADY MOVED TO THEIR PLOTS and now it was the Johnsons' turn.

A green army truck with half a dozen men riding in the back and a Caterpillar tractor pulling a flatbed wagon bumped and grumbled down the half-empty row F and stopped in front of the Johnsons' tent.

"They're here, Mother!" Cally and Polly slipped through the tent flap and tugged on Mother's skirt. "They're here!"

As the movers jumped off the back of the truck, the team leader called out, "Let's move it!" Pop took his place with the crew circling the tent. With one heave, the tent rose on its wooden platform and slid onto the back of the flatbed wagon.

Terpsichore helped load all her mint and vegetable starts onto the flatbed along with the tent.

When it was time to go, Mother and Matthew got in front with the driver of the truck, and Pop, Terpsichore, and the twins crowded into the open back.

The truck had just rumbled to a start when Terpsichore stood, gripping the side of the truck bed so hard her fingers were white. "Where's Tigger? Oh my gosh, I haven't seen her all morning! I have to find her!" She swung one leg over the side of the truck to jump off, but Pop pulled her down to sit.

"Terpsichore, we have to leave now. The crew has other families to move today, and I'm sorry but they can't wait on a cat."

"Tigger came all the way from Wisconsin to be with us. I can't leave her! How will she find us?" She pictured Tigger coming back from her morning hunt for breakfast and finding an empty tent site. She'd howl mournfully and wonder why Terpsichore had abandoned her.

"Cats and dogs are good about finding their people, and Tigger is a smart cat," Pop said. "And if she hasn't found us by tomorrow, we can come back and look for her."

Terpsichore's mouth trembled and her eyes blurred with tears. "Tigger trusts me. I told her I would never leave her and now I'm leaving!"

Pop scooped Terpsichore into his lap. "I promise I'll help you look for her, but we have to go."

Mother looked through the window of the back of the cab and motioned for Terpsichore to sit next to her, but Terpsichore shook her head.

"We'll help you look for her too," said Cally, patting Terpsichore's shoulder.

"Yes, we promise," said Polly, patting the other shoulder.

The sympathy just made Terpsichore cry louder.

• • •

At the Johnsons' lot, another crew was finishing clearing an acre for the tent and chore yard. Each time a fifty-foot tree fell and shook the ground, Cally and Polly clapped and yelled "Tim-berrr!" At first, Matthew howled and hid his face in Mother's shoulder, but Cally and Polly's enthusiasm was catching. Soon Matthew clapped and cheered along with the twins.

Mother pulled Terpsichore to her with the arm that wasn't holding Matthew. "Tigger would be terrified to be around all this noise and commotion," she said. "If we had brought her with us, she probably would have run off to hide."

"But at least she would know where we're going to live now," Terpsichore said. But Mother was probably right. Saws scraped and screeched as they removed limbs from each tree. Roaring Caterpillar tractors pulled logs to trucks headed to the sawmill to be squared off on three sides.

Laura Ingalls' father would have had to work weeks with his hand tools to do what the CCC crews could do in a day!

When there was enough land cleared for a barn, a house, and all the outbuildings, Pop helped the crew slide the tent off the flatbed truck to its new location.

Before leaving, the CCC dug the Johnsons a pit for their very own outhouse. Terpsichore held boards steady while Pop sawed and nailed. Most folks cut a crescent moon into an outhouse door for light and ventilation. Father cut out a *J*, for Johnson. Terpsichore still didn't like outhouses, but at least now they didn't have to share.

Terpsichore was happy for the long hours of sunlight. Before going to bed, she found a trowel and the mint plants she'd potted in nail kegs. She divided the clumps of mint and planted some along the road in front of the tent and some by each turning between the main camp and lot seventy-seven. Tigger had a good nose. She hoped the mint would help her find her way to her new home.

CHAPTER 21

A Farm of Their Own

FIRST THING IN THE MORNING, POP AND TERPSICHORE hitched a ride with one of the moving crews back to the tent camp. They called until they were hoarse, but no Tigger.

While they were in town Pop picked up their allotment of Orpington and Sussex hens and some lumber to build a coop. They found someone driving toward lot seventy-seven and piled the lumber and their crates of chickens in the pickup bed and rode home with their load.

While Cally, Polly, and Terpsichore took turns holding the boards steady, Pop sawed and nailed. It was a fine coop, with double-sided walls insulated with straw. When Pop showed off the coop to Mother, he said, "If we don't get our house built before winter we could always live here with the chickens."

She stomped off back toward the tent, yelling back over her shoulder, "You'd better be in jest, Mr. Johnson!"

Next, Terpsichore finished clearing roots and stones from a patch of ground next to the tent. She raked the ground smooth, and used a hoe to mark furrows for her vegetable starts. This first garden wouldn't be big by Alaska standards, but it was just as big as the garden she and Pop had in Wisconsin.

Mother came out of the tent holding Matthew's hand.

"Dig!" Matthew said. "Matty dig too!"

"Okay, you can dig too." Terpsichore gave him a little trowel and set him down several feet away from the ground she'd prepared for the garden. Mother helped her erect tripods out of scrap lumber on either side of the tent door.

"I love pole beans," Mother said as she reached up with twine to bring three poles together at the top. "Their flowers are as pretty as sweet peas. In a couple months they'll be almost as pretty as the roses by our old house."

She sighed and bustled away to check on Matthew, who had unearthed a pile of small stones that he was lining up in a row. "Mama!" he said. "Choo-choo! Go fast!"

Terpsichore smiled to hear Mother laugh, even though her heart was still heavy with worrying about Tigger.

"Your rock train won't go very fast," Mother said, "but maybe your father can make you a train that can."

Two days later came the day Cally and Polly and many of the colonists had been waiting for. The horses were arriving at the train station! The twins hopped from one foot to the other and took turns holding the ticket for a horse.

The ground began to vibrate and the train whistle sounded. With squealing brakes and clouds of steam, the engine slowed and stopped beside the platform. Terpsichore coughed at the bits of coal dust in the air. She hadn't wanted to come. She had wanted to stay by the tent in case Tigger came home.

From inside the cars came the sounds of shuffling hooves and anxious neighs. Railway workers heaved open the sliding boxcar doors, and one by one, they led horses down a ramp to the loading platform. Some horses skittered and balked at the ramp, others meekly stepped down.

"Which horse is ours?" Polly asked. The twins continued to hop from one foot to the other.

Cally and Polly already had a name picked out: Smoky, after the book *Smoky the Cowhorse*. Terpsichore couldn't count the number of times she had read it to them. The twins were determined to find a horse that fit the name. They saw black horses, chestnut horses, white horses.

Cally grabbed Polly's arm. "See him?" She pointed to a horse that was mousy gray with wisps and speckles of lighter gray across the back and flanks that looked like drifting smoke. His legs were darker gray, and he had a perfect white blaze down the center of his face.

"Smoky! Here I am!" Cally waved. Polly waved too.

Someone else grabbed his halter and started to lead him away, but Cally bolted from the platform. "Smoky, it's me!"

Polly and Pop sprinted after her, but Cally was already doing her own negotiation.

"This horse's name is Smoky. And I know I was meant to have him. Here, Smoky." She held out a half-grown carrot she had pulled from Terpsichore's garden.

The horse nickered, and with soft lips took it from Cally's hand.

Cally's eyes were wide, and she almost forgot to breathe.

"Looks like this horse is yours, all right," the man said. "I'll go pick another horse. Doesn't matter to me which one it is, as long as it can pull a plow."

"He's big," Polly said when she caught up with Cally. "Look at his feet! They're as big as dinner plates."

"I was almost afraid of him," Cally said, "but I read all the books at the Little Bear Creek Library about horses, and I knew Percherons were gentle."

"Can we ride him home?" Polly asked.

"He's big enough to carry all three of you girls, but let's let him get used to us first," Pop said.

Leading Smoky, the Johnsons trooped home. Cally and Polly were happy to have the horse they'd always wanted. Pop was happy that they had a horse so they could enlarge the garden. Mother was happy that they had a horse that could pull a wagon with all the Johnsons in it back and forth to town.

Terpsichore trailed farther and farther behind. How could she be happy without Tigger? As she passed each clump of mint marking the way to the Johnsons' new home, she called out "Tigger, Tigger!"

Finally, near the last clump of mint, a furry, orange-striped bundle bounded out of the woods and leaped to Terpsichore's shoulders, nearly knocking her over.

"Tigger! Tigger found me!" Terpsichore yelled. She trotted to catch up with the rest of the family as Tigger dug her claws into Terpsichore's sweater to avoid being bounced off.

Now all the Johnsons, including Smoky and Tigger, were home.

CHAPTER 22

Our Children Are Dying

MOTHER RETURNED FROM TOWN ONE DAY WITH NEWS that several of the children who hadn't yet moved out of the tent city were sick. Measles and scarlet fever were spreading easily from tent to tent.

On July 7th, Ingrid Soderlund died of scarlet fever. Oscar Eckert died on July 9th.

On the day of the funerals, the community center was packed elbow to elbow, but since the twins were singing, the Johnsons sat up front alongside the Soderlunds and Eckerts. The CCC workers had made caskets of red fir, scaled down for a four-year-old and an infant. Terpsichore breathed in the scent of candles and the wild roses surrounding the coffins. She tried not to think of the bodies inside, but there they were: two dead bodies just ten feet in front of her.

After the homily, Pastor Bingle boosted Cally and Polly to a bench just in front of the coffins. They squeezed hands and began to sing "Jesus Loves Me." Their pure voices wafted over the heads of the gathered colonists. As they sang the last two verses, the two verses the little kids usually didn't sing in Sunday school, Terpsichore could imagine Jesus hovering over the bodies, ready to carry them away to heaven.

Jesus loves me! Loves me still, though I'm very weak and ill;
  From His shining throne on high comes to watch me where
    I lie.
Jesus loves me! He will stay close beside me all the way;
  If I love Him, when I die He will take me home on high.

After the service, Ingrid's and Oscar's parents hugged Cally and Polly. "Thank you. It was perfect." They were too upset to say more.

Other adults, still dabbing handkerchiefs at noses and eyes, had the twins floating on praise. Mother kept a hand on Cally's and Polly's shoulders to make sure everyone knew the singing twins were her daughters.

"You little dears!" one grown-up said.

"It was just like listening to angels," another said.

One stranger noticed Terpsichore standing close to her mother. "You must be very proud of your sisters."

Terpsichore knew she was expected to be proud, so she smiled and nodded.

On the way to their wagon, the twins held hands and

pranced through the rain, perky with all the praise for their singing. Mother kept pace with them and Pop carried Matthew, holding his hat as an umbrella for him.

Terpsichore lagged behind, walking at a somber pace suitable for leaving a funeral, but as the rain increased from a mist to a serious downpour, she had an excuse to run. She passed the rest of the family, gradually increasing the distance between herself, her parents, and the twins. After the smoking stove, she had hoped that she would be known as Terpsichore, champion biscuit maker. She was still just the unmusical Johnson.

Back at lot seventy-seven, Pop shook out his coat, leaving a puddle by the tent opening. Terpsichore wrinkled her nose at the smell of the coal fire in the stove, wet diapers, and gray-green mold that bloomed in patches along the tent seams that never quite dried between sessions of rain. She shrugged off her wet coat and hung it on a nail.

Pop handed Matthew back to Mother, who worked his flailing arms out of his coat and placed him in his crib. Terpsichore shuddered. The packing box crib looked too much like another coffin.

Mother must have thought the same thing. "What if it was Matthew or one of the girls in those coffins? Counting the little girl who died of measles last month, that's three children dead now."

Terpsichore thought about what would happen if she died of scarlet fever or measles. There'd be a Terpsichore-sized coffin balanced on two sawhorses. The twins would sing again, of course. Maybe they would cry a little as they sang. Instead of being sorry Terpsichore was dead, the congregation would be sorry the singing twins had lost their sister.

Mother took down a brown bottle of cod liver oil from a shelf and shook it in Pop's face. "Our babies are dying and what does the colony administration do? Ship up a boxcar full of cod liver oil! What we need is a doctor, and a hospital, and I don't see any signs of getting them. We have to take the children home on the next ship out of Alaska."

At the words *cod liver oil*, Terpsichore's throat contracted and her stomach lurched. Just the rotten fish smell was enough to make you gag, but then there was also the slimy, sludgy texture. It was like swallowing slugs.

Pop reached toward the cod liver oil bottle to put it back, but Mother banged it back on the shelf herself. "This colony was President Roosevelt's idea." Mother hissed the words. "Well, it's nice for the six hundred CCC men who are getting paid to work here, but not so nice for a thousand people who are suffering because of the idiocy of whoever's in charge here.

"I'm not the only one wishing we could move back home," Mother continued. "Half the colony is planning to either go back home or strike out on their own somewhere else in Alaska." She put her hands on her hips, waiting for a response.

Pop guided Mother down to sit beside him on the bench and put his arm around her shoulder. His eyes paused briefly on Cally, then Polly, then Terpsichore. His calming gaze was as effective as a hug. "Your mother is upset because this project

125

hasn't gone the way we expected. I agree with her. I worry too, about how we're all going to get our houses built before snowfall."

Mother turned her head to blow her nose on one of Pop's large handkerchiefs. When she turned back she said, "I doubt if the people making reports to Washington, D.C., have admitted how fouled up it is here. Does President Roosevelt even know what we're going through, abandoned in the wilds of Alaska Territory?"

Terpsichore remembered that President Roosevelt said his projects were carefully planned, like building a ship, but the phrase she heard most often when people talked about colony administration was 'messed up.'"

Mother started crying again. "I heard the original plan was to wait a year to send up families, wait until houses and schools and a hospital were built. I feel like some idiot sent up a thousand people as casually as sending up a load of pipe fittings or paper towels."

Despite the snags, Terpsichore wasn't ready to give up on Alaska yet. She remembered the part in President Roosevelt's speech where he said people should let him know when work could be done better. She said, "Maybe we should write to the president and let him know what's going wrong here. Maybe all the colony administrators are afraid to tell him how messed up it is."

"Humph," Mother said. Her nostrils flared, dismissing Terpsichore's suggestion. "President Roosevelt must get a million letters a month with hard luck stories and complaints. Who's going to listen to us?"

Terpsichore tried again. "Maybe you could write to Mrs. Roosevelt."

Mother crossed her arms in front of her. "Mrs. Roosevelt gets boxes of letters too," she said.

Pop rubbed a thumb against the callused palm of the other hand as he watched the debate between Mother and Terpsichore. He'd worked long days turning their patch of stumps into a farm. How would he feel if all that work was for nothing? Terpsichore kept expecting him to help her convince her mother to write to the Roosevelts, but he didn't interrupt. Perhaps he thought Terpsichore had a better chance of convincing her mother to give Alaska a chance than he did.

"A telegram, then," Terpsichore said. "Everybody pays attention to a telegram."

"We don't have enough money for a telegram telling Mrs. Roosevelt all the things that are wrong here," Mother said.

"Don't tell her everything, then. Just pick the most important thing. Once we have her attention, we can tell her about everything else." Terpsichore blew her bangs out of her face in exasperation.

Mother shook her head. "Still, I'm a nobody. Why should Mrs. Roosevelt do anything because of what one person says?"

"Mother, you have to have confidence, like President Roosevelt said. You can figure out a way to get her attention. Make it dramatic, like what you said when we first got home. 'Our babies are dying.'" Terpsichore said the words like a heroine on a radio melodrama.

"Our babies are dying," Mrs. Johnson half whispered. Then she spoke more forcefully. "Our babies are dying . . . and we have no doctor or hospital."

"That's perfect, Mom!"

Mother shook her head, as if she could hardly believe what she was about to do to humor a stubborn daughter. She re-buttoned her coat. "Terpsichore, will you watch Matthew?"

"Can't I come?" Terpsichore said.

"I need you to watch Matthew so your father can get back to work in the field," Mother said. She nodded toward the crib where Matthew stood to watch the activity.

Terpsichore wished she could hover along the telegraph line following the telegram to the White House. She wanted to be in the room when Mrs. Roosevelt's secretary rushed breathlessly into Mrs. Roosevelt's office.

"Mrs. Roosevelt, I knew you'd want to see this telegram from Alaska right away!" the secretary would say. Then she would hand the telegram to Mrs. Roosevelt.

Mrs. Roosevelt's fingers would tremble as she read. "Babies are dying in Alaska? We have to do something!"

CHAPTER 23

The Power of a Telegram

THE NEXT DAY AND THE NEXT DAY AND THE NEXT, IT rained. Inside the tent, Matthew's diapers hung like damp white flags of surrender from a line strung from tent post to tent post.

The evening of the fourth day, Terpsichore was on her cot reading the funnies from a two-week-old Seattle newspaper. She even read the Joe Palooka and Buck Rogers strips she usually skipped.

Cally and Polly were on their bunks, listless after being cooped up in the tent for three days. "Raining again," Cally said.

"We know, Goofus," Terpsichore said.

From her upper bunk, Cally poked her finger on a point of the canvas roof where it met the side of the tent. "Ack!" she said, wiping her face.

Pop threw down his section of the newspaper. "How many times have I told you not to touch the canvas when it's raining? Didn't I tell you it would start a leak?" With a sigh, he got up to tug the bunks a few inches toward the middle of the tent to avoid the leak. Mother ducked under the diapers to retrieve a pot to catch the water.

"I want to go home," Cally whined. She flopped back dramatically on her top bunk.

"I want to go home too," Polly moaned. She flopped back on her bottom bunk.

"At least you've been inside. I was out in the mud all day." Pop ran his fingers through his damp hair.

"Does that mean you want to go home too?" Mother asked. Drops of water hit the pot catching the new drips. *Ping. Ping. Ping.*

Pop's hands coiled into fists, then relaxed. "No, not yet," he said. He sighed as he looked at Cally and Polly, wilted on their bunks; Terpsichore, trying to ignore everybody else and reading two-week-old funny papers; Matthew's damp diapers; and Mother.

Pop dug under the twins' bunk cots and came out with the checkerboard. "All right, who wants to play checkers?"

Cally let one arm dangle from the top bunk. "Bor-*ing*," she said.

Polly coughed weakly. "I think I'm too sick to play checkers."

Mother knelt by Polly's bunk to feel her forehead. "You don't feel hot," she said. "I think you're just bored too." She stood in front of Pop, who had gone back to halfheartedly trying to read the old newspaper. "I don't think Polly is sick now, thankfully," Mother said, "but what if she were sick? We don't have a doctor, let alone a hospital."

Pop folded his newspaper. "I know, Clio. I know."

From far down the tracks, a train whistle sounded. Two long, one short, one long, signaling approach to the Palmer Station. The wavering minor chord of the whistle that echoed in the valley suited everyone's mournful mood.

Terpsichore cocked her head toward the sound. "This isn't the normal daily run from Anchorage," she said. No one else seemed excited about an extra train, but Terpsichore's imagination came up with lots of possibilities. Another load of horses to pull the wagons that arrived last month, or a shipment of hammers . . . or maybe a letter from Mrs. Roosevelt! Whatever it was, Terpsichore was going to find out.

Raindrops had stopped plopping into the pan, and early evening sun brightened the tent. Terpsichore tugged her galoshes over her shoes.

"Where are you going?" Mother asked.

"I'm not staying in this tent with a bunch of grumps," Terpsichore said, looking at the twins. "I'm going to get Mendel and walk to the station to see why there was a special train." She slipped through the tent flap before her mother could object. Mendel's tent was on the way and they could go on together to collect Gloria if she wasn't at the train station herself by the time they got there.

They hung back as they approached the platform, where an engine with only one passenger car had stopped. Terpsichore waved when she saw Gloria.

"I heard the extra train too," Gloria said. "What's up?" The three edged close enough to hear what the men were saying.

"Who's that with Mr. Carr and Mr. Irwin?" Gloria asked, pointing. Mr. Carr, the camp commissioner, and Mr. Irwin, liaison to the colonists, were the only ones they recognized. A group of men and women conferred with each other, and some of them frowned as they looked out at the tents and muddy roads.

"I thought the colonists had been promised houses." That was the most distinguished man on the platform.

Mr. Carr took off his hat and wiped his forehead on the sleeve of his coat. "We've had a few snags in getting supplies in the right order, Mr. Fuller. Bound to happen in a project this big."

"We were sent here to build a hospital. How are we supposed to if we don't even have the proper equipment?" The man named Mr. Fuller had a voice loud enough for even the people at the back of the gathering crowd to hear.

Mr. Fuller shook his head. "Who the dickens is in charge here?" he said.

Mr. Carr finally said, "I guess I am, but it's too much for any one or two people to handle. There's wells to dig, roads to build, houses, barns, and a school to build, land to clear so folks can get a crop in . . ."

Mr. Fuller's mouth tightened. "I see," he said. "Well, we can't take care of all of that at once, but now that we have Dr. Albrecht here, and four nurses who've volunteered to transfer from Anchorage . . ." He paused to point to the smiling man

132

and four women in the group. "We'd better build them a hospital. Mr. Roosevelt was most emphatic after Mrs. Roosevelt showed him that telegram."

Terpsichore gasped. "Mrs. Roosevelt read my telegram!" She grabbed Mendel's arm on one side and Gloria's on the other.

"You sent a telegram?" Mendel whispered. Amazement made his eyes look even more owlish than usual behind his round-rimmed glasses.

"To Mrs. Roosevelt? Keen-o!" Gloria said.

"Not me exactly," Terpsichore explained. "My mother actually sent it, but I suggested that she send a telegram to Mrs. Roosevelt and helped her figure out what to say. Don't tell anyone, though. I want Mom to think it was her own idea."

Mendel held out his hand. "Good work, Terpsichore. My father always said it's amazing what you can get done if you don't care who gets the credit."

He called her Terpsichore! From Mendel, that was the best compliment she could hope for.

Terpsichore hugged herself as images ricocheted through her head so fast she could hardly focus on what Mr. Fuller was saying: Mrs. Roosevelt reading the telegram, President Roosevelt sending his friend to Alaska, sick children getting well, and grateful parents saying, "Thank goodness for Terpsichore Johnson, who got a hospital for Palmer." She had to pinch her arm so she could focus on Mr. Fuller again.

"I want you to know President Roosevelt takes your concerns seriously," he was saying. "As one of his trusted advisers and friends, he told me to get the next plane to Alaska. 'Get those people a doctor and a hospital, and see that it gets done immediately,' President Roosevelt said, and I don't intend to disappoint him. I'm leaving tomorrow and I want to see that hospital built before I leave."

The CCC man was burly, but his voice came out in a squeak. "Tomorrow? I still don't have enough hammers for each carpenter."

"Some of the colonists must have hammers," Mr. Fuller said. He turned from the men on the platform and shouted out to the crowd, "I'm depending on you to get the word out. Anyone with carpentry tools should report to the community center."

No one in the crowd needed to be told twice.

They had just started back when they saw Mr. Johnson with Smoky and the wagon. "I came looking for you as soon as I got the wagon rigged," he said. "I heard what Mr. Fuller said, so I guess I'd better go back for my hammer. Anyone want a lift?"

Terpsichore, Mendel, and Gloria piled into the back of the wagon.

At home, Terpsichore burst into the tent. "Mom, it worked! Mrs. Roosevelt read the telegram and she didn't just send a letter back. She had her husband send someone they knew to get us a doctor and a hospital. The doctor and four nurses are already here and Mr. Fuller—that's the guy the Roosevelts sent—is leaving tomorrow and he wants to see a hospital built before he goes and he wants everyone with carpentry tools to report to the community center!"

Mother put her hands to her chest and then patted her reddening cheeks. "She read the telegram! We're getting a doctor!"

Pop hugged Mother. "Good work, Clio! We're proud of you." Over Mother's shoulder, he winked at Terpsichore. She winked back.

In less than a minute Pop had found his hammer and headed to the community center.

The valley echoed that night with the sound of hammers, saws, and shouting, but no one complained. Each blow of a hammer, each whine of the steam-driven sawmill was a sign of hope. The president had personally sent help. The colonists had not been abandoned in the wilderness.

The saws and hammers were silent by two A.M. Twenty minutes later, Pop entered the tent.

"Still up?" he said when he saw Terpsichore sitting up on her cot.

"I think we all are," Mother said. "Why did everyone stop?"

Pop took his hat off and put it on Mother's head. "Because, Mrs. Telegram Writer," he said, "we finished! Come on, everybody, let's see what a difference six hours can make!" He scooped up Matthew, and everyone scrambled for clothes and shoes and raced to the wagon.

From all over camp, colonists swarmed toward the community center.

Dawn would not come for another two hours, but it was a new day.

There was the completed hospital, twenty feet by twenty feet. Peeking in through clean windows, Terpsichore saw beds with clean sheets, a stove, and floors still damp from mopping. The new doctor and four nurses were already tucking in their first patients, moved from the temporary isolation area in the community center.

How could this hospital appear without a magic wand, in only six hours? But it wasn't magic, Terpsichore thought. It was the power of colonists and CCC men working together with a goal and a plan. She had done what President Roosevelt said he wanted people to do: tell him when things could be done better. He listened, and sent help. If a small hospital could be built in six hours, with everyone cooperating, maybe everyone would have a house before snowfall.

Terpsichore looked at the faces of colonists around her. People were beginning to hope again.

CHAPTER 24

Living off Sea and Land

"Better go ahead and hit it," Mendel said. "You'll cut yourself if you try to clean a fish that's still flopping around."

Seeing the salmon helplessly flopping, Terpsichore felt its panic. "Don't let it suffer," she begged, as her father brought the rock down on the fish's head.

"This is going to be gory, Trip," Mendel said. "You'd better not look. Now, Mr. Johnson, you're going to want to cut the gills to start it bleeding out. Even when it's dead, the heart will keep on pumping out the blood. You don't want the blood to settle in the meat."

Terpsichore peeked just long enough to see her father wince as he cut the gills, and then she whirled away from the barbaric scene of fish murder. "La-la-la," she chanted to herself. She could still hear Mendel's instructions.

"Now wash it off in the river and take it over to this rock," Mendel said. "I'll show you how to clean it. Start in front of the anus—no, not right on it, because you'll let out the bacteria in the intestines."

Terpsichore took a few steps away, but still couldn't block out Mendel's words. "Cut along the middle of the belly," he said, "but not far enough to hit the organs . . . that's it, clear up to the gill covers . . . cut off the head—that's it, right behind the pectoral fin . . . pull off the intestine, scoop out the kidneys—just toss them in the slop bucket. Now saw off the fins and you're ready to fillet."

When Terpsichore turned she saw two bright pinkish orange slabs that no longer looked like a living fish, but like food you might get at the butcher.

"You're a natural, Mr. Johnson," Mendel said. "Give me the slop bucket and I'll wade out and let the river wash the guts away so we don't attract the bears."

In Wisconsin, the Johnsons had never had to kill what they ate. But Farmer Boy and his family had raised animals to eat. Terpsichore had just never had to think about all the steps between the cow in the field and the roast in the stove.

Once home, Mother consulted a mimeographed handout that she'd received at the monthly mothers' meeting on how to can salmon.

"Some of the women are going for the tin can method, but I'll stick to jars. It's what I know, and you don't have to buy an expensive sealer for the jars."

After a moment's squeamishness, Terpsichore nerved herself to touch the raw fish flesh.

"At least your father cleaned the fish before he brought them home, which is more than some men do."

Terpsichore picked up fillets in both hands and slipped them into the pan of water. "They're still slimy, though," she said.

"The vinegar in the water will cut the slime," Mother said. She pulled a fillet out of the water, cut it into chunks, and packed the chunks, skin side in, into pint jars.

Terpsichore followed her example.

"Leave about an inch of space at the top," Mother said, "and while I put the lids on, would you get some water?"

Terpsichore brought in a bucket of water from the washtub they used as a cistern and poured two or three inches of water into the pressure cooker. Then her mother put in the rack, settled each jar gently into place, and hoisted the loaded pressure cooker to the stove.

"Don't forget to open the damper," Terpsichore said.

Mother laughed. "I don't think anyone will ever let me forget that burned cake."

Once the canner had let off steam, they loaded in more coal until the pressure gauge went up to eleven pounds, then watched the gauge to keep the pressure there for one hundred minutes. It was long enough to get the next batch of fish ready to go.

"You know," Mother said as she cut up more fish, "I didn't mean for you to cook dinner forever, after Matthew was born. I just needed help when he was keeping me up all night."

"It's all right," Terpsichore said. "I like to cook."

Mother wrinkled her nose as she dropped another fillet into the vinegar water. "I don't even like fish. But if the government is charging colonists fifty dollars for a nonresident hunting license, I guess we'll have to settle for fish this winter."

"Next summer, though, when we've been here a year, Pop won't have to pay fifty dollars, right?"

"Right," Mother said, although she didn't sound one hundred percent happy. Maybe she was thinking like Terpsichore: If it was this hard to face a dead fish, what would they do with a dead deer?

Mother wrenched the next jar lid too tightly and had to loosen it up. Since her hands were slimy, she didn't touch Terpsichore, but nudged her shoulder companionably. "If you can think of twenty ways to cook pumpkin, do you think you can come up with twenty ways to fix salmon so it doesn't taste so much like salmon?"

Terpsichore nudged her mother back. "I'll work on it," she said.

Terpsichore and her mother took turns monitoring the gauge and putting in more fuel to keep it at a steady eleven pounds. One batch, two batches, three.

Pop snored. Cally, Polly, and Matthew finally slept. It was just Terpsichore and her mother, working far into the night. It was free food, Terpsichore kept thinking. It was free food.

Terpsichore was thrilled when a few days later Pop went in with Mr. LeClerc and Mr. Peterson on a smoker they could share. Smoking transformed salmon into chewy strips you could crumble into soup or gnaw on for a snack. It made salmon taste like something completely different.

The next shipment from Seattle brought cows. The twins named the Johnson cow Clarabelle. Mother was skittish at first around their new cow, but she was determined to learn to milk it. Her piano-playing hands made her a champion milker. Clarabelle produced more milk than they could drink, so Mother bought a butter churn and picked up pamphlets on making cheese from the Agricultural Office tent. With salmon, berries Cally and Polly had picked, their own egg-laying chickens, and cheese, milk, and butter from Clarabelle, gone were the weeks of nothing but pumpkin and sauerkraut. Gone were the days of relying on overpriced goods from the Palmer store. Terpsichore could make custards and muffins, bread pudding and berry cobblers, omelets and salmon in a dozen different ways. Matthew's favorite word now was "more!"

CHAPTER 25

Palmer Colony Makes News

ALL SUMMER, ARTICLES AND PHOTOGRAPHS ABOUT PALMER were appearing in newspapers and magazines from coast to coast. One woman got her picture taken with a pyramid of all the tins of salmon she had canned. A sketch artist drew a cartoon of a mother outside her tent with her washtub, laundry lines, and five children playing around her. A Baltimore photographer picked four boys to hold flowers and look sad at Oscar Eckert's grave.

"He should have picked us," Cally said. "We sang at his funeral."

"Those boys didn't even know Oscar Eckert," Polly said.

"I'm glad he didn't pick you," Mother said. "It's ghoulish, taking pictures at a poor child's grave."

And now there was news that Will Rogers, America's favorite actor, was planning to visit Alaska to gather material for his newspaper column.

• • •

On the morning of August 14th, an excited crowd gathered on the shore of the Matanuska River.

"I see it!" At the shout, five hundred heads turned skyward. Terpsichore clutched the batch of oatmeal raspberry cookies she'd wrapped in a dishtowel to protect them from the folks elbowing in at her prime position next to the ropes that cordoned off an improvised runway on the river.

"That's a Lockheed Orion model 9E Special fuselage," Mendel told her and Gloria. "But you can see that Wiley Post has rigged it with a Lockheed Explorer Model 7 Special wing. See? It's at least six feet longer than the regular Orion wing." Mendel was gratified to see several grown-ups' heads turned his way and nodding.

Mendel spoke louder once he knew he had an audience. "And hear that engine? I bet it's at least five hundred horsepower." He pointed toward the bottom of the plane as it landed. "And they've replaced the fixed landing gear with floats. Wow! Look at the size of those floats! They look like they were designed for a bigger plane and could cause a problem."

The plane slid along the river with a rooster tail of spray and came to a stop. First out was Mendel's hero, Wiley Post, who had flown around the world in only seven days, eighteen hours, and forty-nine minutes. He looked more like a pirate than a world-famous aviator, with his mustache and white eye patch. He stood on the wing and waved.

After Mr. Post jumped off the wing onto a short pier extending into the river, Will Rogers filled the doorway. One of the newsmen used a microphone to be heard above the crowd trying to get Mr. Rogers's attention. "How do you feel, Mr. Rogers?"

The crowd hushed for the first words of Will Rogers.

"Why, uh, why—wait'll I get out, will you?" Mr. Rogers said. "I came to look around, not report on my health." He joined Mr. Post on the pier and was quickly surrounded by colony administrators who would take Rogers and Post on a quick tour of Palmer before they took off again for Fairbanks.

The colonists had been gossiping about all the excuses the administrators were going to have to come up with to explain why families were still living in tents and why there were piles of sinks with no plumbing fittings, crates of electric meat slicers when there was still no electricity, and only twenty hammers for the CCC workers who were supposed to be building houses.

When the administration car returned after the tour, Terpsichore and her friends thronged back toward the river but were pushed toward the back of the crowd. How was she going to get Mr. Rogers the cookies? Rogers stepped over the rope farther down the line. "Mr. Rogers, Mr. Rogers!" she called.

Mendel and Gloria called too. "We have cookies for you, Mr. Rogers!"

One of the men just in front of them heard about the cookies. "We'll get Mr. Rogers those cookies, Missy. For Mr. Rogers," he said as he passed them along.

"Thanks!" Terpsichore bounced on tiptoe, trying to keep track of her cookies as they were passed from hand to helpful hand to the front. She relaxed when she heard someone say, "For you, Mr. Rogers, compliments of one of our colonists."

By then, Mr. Post was already in the cockpit and Mr. Rogers had clambered up to the wing of the plane again. Above the shoulders of the men in front of her, Terpsichore could see the knot of his tie, his broad grin, and his Stetson hat.

The sun had not yet set behind the mountains when Terpsichore, Gloria, and Mendel drifted back to their families' wagons.

Gloria exhaled in a swooning sigh. "Imagine, the most famous actor in Hollywood visited us right here in Palmer. Everyone back home will be so jealous!"

Mendel sighed too. "Who'd have thought a flying ace like Wiley Post would ever fly to Palmer? I got to see him, eye patch and all."

Terpsichore couldn't hold back a smile. "Do you think Mr. Rogers is eating one of my cookies right now?"

"Probably," Mendel said.

"You betcha," Gloria said.

The three linked arms and agreed: When Rogers wrote about his visit, everyone in the country would know where to find Palmer on the map.

But the excitement over Will Rogers was not over. After supper the next day, the Johnsons gathered with everyone else near downtown Palmer at Pastor Bingle's tent.

Pastor Bingle had a battery-powered radio with antenna wire stretched along a barbed wire fence. At news time, he

145

turned up the volume so everyone could listen to the broadcast from reporters following Mr. Rogers's travels. What would Will Rogers say about Palmer in his interview?

But instead of the lighthearted report they expected, a somber voice intoned the night's news without preamble: "Will Rogers and Wiley Post, cultural icons of Hollywood and aviation, are dead. They lost their bearings in the fog between Fairbanks and Point Barrow, above the Arctic Circle. They landed to get directions at an Eskimo village. The engine failed on takeoff, and the nose-heavy plane plunged into the lagoon. It is believed that both men died instantly. Colonel Charles A. Lindbergh may fly north to supervise the return of the bodies of Will Rogers and Wiley Post."

Mendel, who had sidled up to Terpsichore, was as pale as a winding sheet. "I was just being a smarty-pants, repeating what one newspaper article said about the floats being too big for the plane. Now I feel like I jinxed them." He reached under his glasses with one finger to brush away a tear.

Terpsichore patted him on the back. "You may be a smarty-pants, but you're not a jinxer. It was just an accident."

She let her hand rest on his shoulder as she thought about one of Will Rogers's most famous quotes: "I never met a man I didn't like."

Terpsichore knew it was a good attitude, but she was realizing that sometimes it took a while to know someone well enough to like him. To think that she hadn't liked Mendel at all when she first met him.

CHAPTER 26

A Box from Below

THE NEXT DAY BROUGHT GOOD NEWS. POP DROPPED THE box with a thud onto the table in the middle of the tent. "Special delivery for Miss Terpsichore Johnson!"

Mother leaned over the box to read the return address. "What would my mother be sending you?"

Cally and Polly fidgeted with impatience as Terpsichore cut each string and methodically folded the brown paper so it could be saved. Slowly, she lifted the flaps of the box and picked up a note addressed to her in Grandmother VanHagen's old-fashioned script.

"What's under the note?" Cally and Polly's hands darted toward the box, but Terpsichore batted them away.

"The note will explain everything," Terpsichore said. She read aloud:

Dear Terpsichore,
I'm proud of you for attempting to bring civilization

to Alaska Territory. All the books have bookplates with
my name on them so you can round them up again
when it's time to come back home to Wisconsin.

With love and affection,
Grandmother

"With love and affection," Terpsichore repeated to herself. Whenever they visited Grandmother in Madison, Terpsichore had felt like Grandmother paid more attention to the twins. But maybe it was just because the twins always demanded Grandmother's attention, while Terpsichore hung back. But now, when Terpsichore had asked for Grandmother's help, she had given it right away.

Mother leafed through an old *New Yorker* that Grandmother had packed on top of the books for her. "Well, the news is old but I'll at least have new short stories to read." She laid the magazine on the table for later. "What did Grandmother mean about bringing civilization to Alaska?"

"I wrote to Grandmother and the Girl Scouts and the Red Cross, asking everyone for books so we could have a library. Grandmother was the first to send something." Terpsichore's voice trailed off as she excitedly sorted through the books in the box. Grandmother had sent a wonderful selection! All together there were thirty-six books, a good start to a library.

Mother picked up a copy of *Anne of Green Gables*. "My old copy! See, there's my mother's writing on the title page: *To Clio, from Mother and Father, Christmas, 1911.* I remember that Christmas; I was ten then, the same age you were when we gave you your copy."

Terpsichore glanced up and grinned. "Good tradition, Mom!" She picked up a copy of *A Daughter of the Snows*, by Jack London. "This is perfect reading for Alaska, isn't it?" She opened it to the title page. "Here's an odd inscription: 'From Nate to Happy, with love.' Who were they?"

"I don't recognize either of those names," Mother said. "Grandmother must have bought the book secondhand, which isn't like her." She put the book in Terpsichore's stack of grown-up fiction.

"Where are you going to put the books?" Mother asked.

"I thought we could keep them here," Terpsichore said.

"This isn't the most convenient place for everyone," Mother said. She probably meant it wouldn't be convenient for her to have people barging into the tent at all hours, and Terpsichore could see her point.

"The community center?" Pop offered.

"These are Grandmother's books," Terpsichore said. "We have to make sure each person signs for the book, so we can get it back again."

Mother said, "I'll ask Pastor Bingle if his family can find someplace in their tent for them if the library's only going to be open a few hours a week. His tent's near the middle of town and it's a little bigger than ours."

That evening, Terpsichore began her first task as operations manager of the Palmer Library. She turned to the first page of the composition book she planned to use as her accessions log. Which book would have the honor of being number one? She finally decided to enter the first batch alphabetically by title and wrote in her best handwriting:

No. 1, Anne of Green Gables, *Lucy Maud Montgomery, on loan from Mrs. Thalia VanHagen, August 16, 1935.*

After Terpsichore and Gloria's story time that Saturday, Gloria and Mendel piled into the wagon to come home with the Johnsons and see the beginning of the collection for the library.

Gloria shuffled through the fiction stack. "Do we get first dibs on reading new books?"

"Why not?" Terpsichore said. "That should be one of the privileges of being a committee member."

Mendel sorted through the nonfiction without finding anything he wanted to read. "What's our next step, Trip?"

"Madam Operations Manager, or Terpsichore, if you please. I've logged in each book and started making catalog cards. While I finish those, one of you can write up the circulation cards and paper clip them to the first page, and one of you can make the spine labels and tape them on. You can ask me what Dewey number to use for the nonfiction."

"I have the neatest printing. I'll do the circulation cards," Mendel said.

Gloria cut a tidy rectangle from plain white paper, wrote the first letter of the last name of the author, aligned it neatly a half inch from the bottom of the spine, and taped it on. "Like this?" she asked.

Terpsichore scrutinized Gloria's work. "Perfect!" she said.

Like the parable of loaves and fishes, when Terpsichore put out the first batch of labeled books from her grandmother to share, more books appeared from nowhere, slipped under the flaps at Pastor Bingle's tent or at the Johnsons'.

Box after box of books arrived after Grandmother's. Some were from places Terpsichore had written to, and others were from places her grandmother must have contacted: women's book clubs, assistance leagues, and churches. Grandmother should almost be an honorary member of the Palmer Library Action Committee!

Terpsichore pulled the latest five boxes of books out from under her cot to show Gloria and Mendel.

"Hot diggity!" Mendel said. "We allotted you a dollar for postage stamps and see what we got! Good work, Operations Manager."

Gloria was sorting through copies of *Movie Mirror* and *Screenland*. "Keen-o! Some of these magazines are only a few months old!"

Terpsichore's heart hardly had room for itself in her chest. Instead of whining about not having a library, she had taken action. Well, she and her friends had taken action. "You guys are the best!" she said.

Gloria stood. "Absolutely-tootly the best Library Action Committee ever!"

Mendel stood too. "I second that sentiment!"

CHAPTER 27

Sixth Grade in the New School

On August 19, the first day at the new Palmer school, Terpsichore met Gloria by the front entrance. Gloria twirled to show off her new yellow slicker with metal toggles like you'd see on a fireman's jacket. She paused with her back to Terpsichore to show off what she'd done: She'd spelled out G-L-O-R-I-A in four-inch-high letters with white first aid tape.

"Do you like?" Gloria asked. "I got the idea from a photograph in one of the *American Girl* magazines the Girl Scouts shipped up. By the end of the day, everyone will know my name. And that's not all I got. Here, hold my lunch and satchel for a minute."

She unclasped the toggles on her raincoat. "My first straight skirt and a matching sweater set."

Terpsichore sighed. It was what she had wanted too, but her mother said it was too expensive, even with her father now working part time at the lumber mill. Some folks were running up debt, ordering willy-nilly from the Sears and Montgomery Ward catalogs, but not the Johnsons.

"What did you get for school?" asked Gloria.

Her mother had made her a navy blue corduroy skirt with an elastic waist and a double hem, so she could still wear it if she grew another six inches this year like she had the last. With it, she wore a plain white shirt with a Peter Pan collar and a red paisley bow her mother had made from a scrap in her sewing basket. She had black kneesocks with the tops folded over a rubber band to keep them up. Before she left home, she had felt grown-up, wearing a skirt and blouse instead of a puffed-sleeved dress like the twins. She wilted when Gloria frowned.

"It looks like a uniform for a kid in an orphanage," Gloria said. "But don't worry, it's not totally hopeless. First off, that Peter Pan collar is too goody-goody, especially with that bow." Gloria untied the bow and retied it like a loosened man's tie, unbuttoned the top button on Terpsichore's shirt and lifted the back of her collar. "There! Almost like Katharine Hepburn. She likes simple clothes too, so maybe that's your look."

Terpsichore wrinkled her nose and flinched when Gloria spit on her fingers and took a wisp of hair from one side of Terpsichore's forehead, shaped it into a coil, and stuck it to her forehead.

The first bell from the school tolled.

"Whoopsie doodle," Gloria said. "We'd better shake a leg."

The final bell rang just as Terpsichore and Gloria were hanging up their coats on the hooks at the back of the room.

The sixth-grade classroom smelled like new wood, paint, and floor polish. Mendel was just hanging up his coat too.

"Isn't that your girlfriend?" Terrible Teddy poked Mendel and snickered.

Mendel locked eyes with Terpsichore, but only for an instant. "Nah," Mendel said, turning away. "I was just helping her out with her library project. I wanted to make sure she got some decent stuff, like *Amazing Stories*, not just girly stuff like Nancy Drew."

"*Amazing Stories*—yeah, that's keen," Teddy said.

"Kids back home called me Metal Mouth," Mendel said. He strained to make his voice several tones lower than usual. "I've started drawing a comic strip with a hero called Metal Mouth with braces that act as a radio antenna, so he can receive secret messages from Buck Rogers. I'm also training my dog Togo to be a sled dog."

Terpsichore was relieved that Mendel had again dispatched that rumor of being her boyfriend before it spread. He was nicer than she had thought he was at first, but she was still happy that he was making other friends to listen to all the stuff about mosquitoes and spiders she didn't want to hear.

The teacher rang a crystal bell. "You're in alphabetical order, class. The As start in this front corner by the flag and the Zs are in the back corner."

Terpsichore found her place, and Gloria and Mendel were behind her. As she lifted the desktop to put away her tablet and pencils, she ran her hand over the underside of the lid. No stale gum wads or carved initials. She quietly closed the lid, sat up straight, and folded her hands. For the first time ever, she had a spanking new desk. She would try to keep it nice for whoever sat there next year.

After everyone had found their places, the teacher rang her bell again. She was as fresh as the school. Unlike Miss Burgess, this teacher was dressed more like Terpsichore, in a plain dark skirt and white shirt. Her collar lay flat, and Terpsichore self-consciously folded her own collar down in the back.

"Good morning, class. I'm Miss Zelinsky, and you are my very first students. I graduated from Eastern Montana State Normal School in Billings, so I know about hard winters and I'm excited to be here with you in this brand-new school.

"I'll warn you now. In this sixth-grade classroom you'll be expected to work hard, but we'll have fun, too. Twice a week, you'll have music class with me, and when I go across the hall to Miss Olafson's class for their music lessons, she'll come in to you for art. The school will also be putting on a musical just before school lets out in June."

Terpsichore heard impatient rustling from the seat behind her and could almost feel the wind on the back of her neck from a waving hand.

"Miss Zelinsky, Miss Zelinsky, what musical are we putting on, and when are the tryouts?" Gloria asked.

"*The Wizard of Oz*," Miss Zelinsky said. "There'll be a part for everyone who wants one. Tryouts will be after Christmas. Terpsichore, I've already heard about your younger sisters, and I hope they will perform. There will be non-performing roles too—the artists among you can make backdrops, anyone handy with a hammer can make props, and we'll need seam-stresses for costumes."

Miss Zelinsky didn't mention needing anyone who could cook salmon a dozen different ways.

"But only one person can be Dorothy, and that will be me," Gloria whispered from behind her.

On the way home, Gloria talked on about what a good Dorothy she hoped to be.

Terpsichore interrupted Gloria's bubbly rambling with an awkward hug. "Thanks for being such a great friend."

"Ditto," said Gloria. "But what made you say that now?"

"I knew from the day I met you that you loved acting more than books, but you helped me most of the summer with the library."

"But that's what friends do, isn't it? Help each other?" said Gloria. "And I had fun too, with the story hours."

"Anyway, thanks. You'll make an amazing Dorothy! Now that you and Mendel have helped me, I think I can keep on with the library project, even if you both get busy. We can still be good friends even if sometimes we're doing different things, can't we?"

"You said it!" Gloria said.

Every Saturday from ten to two for the last two weeks of August, Terpsichore took charge of the little library. Soon, every kid who liked to read was calling her "library girl."

At the end of August, a box arrived from Demco Library Supplies in Wisconsin. The box was full of supplies: india ink, a wooden pen with metal nibs, mending tape, real circulation cards, an ink pad—even a date-due stamper with metal ratchets to change the month, day, and year. The note on Demco letterhead read:

For our pioneering librarian from Demco's home state of Wisconsin.

Terpsichore doubted they knew the "pioneering librarian" was eleven years old.

CHAPTER 28

Popcorn Wars

It was movie night at the community center. Terpsichore and Gloria sat cross-legged on the floor near the front of the audience as the projector whirred into action and the words "Hearst Metrotone News" flickered against the sheet hung on the wall.

The newsreel shocked everyone to silence. In the background was their own Matanuska River. In the foreground was a two-seater plane, ladder set up against the open door. Will Rogers waved good-bye to the hundreds of people gathered to watch him take off.

Terpsichore could barely swallow. "It's hard to believe that two weeks ago Will Rogers was here."

"He wasn't waving good-bye just to Palmer, but to his fans all over the world," Gloria whispered, still staring at the screen.

After the newsreel flickered off, the community center remained quiet.

As the feature film started—*State Fair* with their lost hero,

Will Rogers—someone tried to lighten the mood. "If I just had a bag of popcorn, I could imagine I was back home in Minnesota," he said.

After hearing that, Terpsichore hardly paid attention to whether Janet Gaynor, the actress playing Will Rogers's daughter, was going to fall in love with the newspaper reporter. Instead, she ran calculations in her head. If she sold popcorn at ten cents a bag, and the popcorn and the bags cost her three cents—she'd have to check prices—she might net seven cents a bag. If she could sell fifty bags, she'd clear $3.50 in just one week and it would only take six months to save enough for a whole set of *World Book* encyclopedias.

The following week, Terpsichore was ready. With a Shirley Temple movie like *Bright Eyes*, the community center would be packed. Terpsichore got her father's permission to put small brown paper bags and popcorn kernels on their tab at the general store. She took over the kitchen all afternoon, popping batch after batch in a pan on the stove and measuring two cups into each sack. She folded the tops over twice and loaded them into Mother's laundry baskets. Mother and Matthew sat with Pop on the seat of the horse-drawn wagon, and Terpsichore sat in the back with Cally and Polly, holding the baskets steady so none of the popcorn would spill.

Terpsichore stood just inside the entrance to the community center. She was shy, but her sisters and Gloria were not. They called out, "Popcorn, get your popcorn! All profits to the Palmer Library!"

"Selling popcorn—crackerjack idea!" Gloria told Terpsichore. "I bet we could sell twice as much and I could help you make it."

"That would be keen," said Terpsichore. "If we sell a hundred bags a week, we'll have those encyclopedias by Christmas!"

The next Saturday, Gloria went to Terpsichore's and she and the twins helped Terpsichore pop and package one hundred bags of popcorn. An hour before the movie started, Pop helped load the wagon with bags of popcorn heaped into packing crates and laundry baskets.

At the community center, Terpsichore led them toward what she considered to be her station just inside the door. But Mendel was in her spot.

"Get your popcorn, fresh hot popcorn!" Mendel already had a card table set up with his pile of popcorn bags.

Terpsichore dropped her basket with a thud and shoved past the line of people waiting to buy popcorn from Mendel.

"You stole my idea. You knew this was how I was raising money for the library." Terpsichore could feel her cheeks beginning to redden.

"I'm not on the library committee anymore, and I need to raise money too," Mendel said, avoiding her eyes.

"Well, selling popcorn was my idea . . . you're a copycat!"

"You weren't the first person in the world to sell popcorn at a movie, so it's not like you invented the idea." Maybe Mendel did feel a little guilty, because his cheeks started to redden too.

"But I was the first person to do it here!" Terpsichore said.

Gloria, Cally, and Polly shoved through the line to stand beside Terpsichore and back her up with fierce nods. "Trip was here first," the twins said.

Mendel was outnumbered, but he stuck out his chin and said, "Well, you weren't first today."

A curious crowd paused at the doorway to watch the showdown before taking their seats.

Terpsichore would not be weak and girly in front of Mendel and all these people. "You're a dirty rotten thieving claim-jumper."

Gloria, Polly, and Cally echoed, "Dirty rotten claim-jumper."

Mendel pointed behind them toward their stacks of popcorn bags. "There's the real claim-jumper."

A kid stooped over Terpsichore's laundry basket heaped with bags of popcorn and held up a bag in each hand. "Hey, guys, free popcorn!" Within seconds, almost half her popcorn was gone.

Terpsichore dashed back through the people entering the community center to protect her inventory. "That's ten cents!"

Mendel continued shouting like a sideshow barker. "Popcorn, fresh hot popcorn! Get your popcorn here!"

Terpsichore glared at Mendel and shouted even louder, "Best popcorn in the valley! All profits to a new library!"

In between customers, Mendel and the girls traded epithets:

"Spoilsport!" That was the girls.

"Crybabies!" That was Mendel.

"You should be set out on an iceberg!" That was Terpsichore.

A stranger, too old to be a colonist or CCC worker, greeted Mendel. "What are you earning money for, young man?"

"A real dog harness," Mendel said. "I'm training my dog to be a sled dog."

"Come see me when you have the harness and I'll help you," he said. "Ask anyone out at the Butte where old-timer Crawford lives."

Terpsichore was trying to think of another insult when the old-timer turned her way. "Here's another enterprising popcorn seller. What are you saving money for?"

"I'm saving for a set of encyclopedias for the new library," Terpsichore said, "not for something for myself." She glared again at Mendel.

"Well," the man said, "I guess I should buy a bag of popcorn from you too."

"Who was that, Trip?" Cally asked.

"It's Terp-sick . . ." Terpsichore's rebuke about using her nickname trailed off as her eyes followed the strange man as he carried his two bags of popcorn to find standing room at the back of the audience. "I don't know who it is. Somebody who likes popcorn, I guess."

Gloria looked up from counting money. "Even with Mendel stealing your spot and wise guys making off with free popcorn, we collected four dollars and eighty cents for the library!"

"Yay, our team," the twins cheered.

CHAPTER 29

More Popcorn

ON THE RIDE HOME FROM THE MOVIE, TERPSICHORE looked anxiously at the Chugach Mountains. When it rained in the valley, it snowed higher up in the foothills. The wind had howled through Palmer the night before, blowing every gold and red leaf from the alders and cottonwoods, leaving the trees stripped bare as skeletons.

Throughout the next week, the stove burned constantly, partly to warm the tent, and partly to process the last of the beans and tomatoes and peas from the garden and berries foraged from the wild. The kitchen table was covered with jars. The tent was filled with steam.

Pop had built shelves and more shelves in the root cellar so they could store jars where they wouldn't freeze. The floor of the root cellar was heaped with bins of potatoes, turnips, beets, onions, carrots, parsnips, and rutabagas.

They wouldn't starve this winter. Terpsichore's garden had yielded some of the largest vegetables she had ever seen. Pole beans grew as long as her forearm. And one pumpkin grew so big her father couldn't budge it. After he split it open, she got inside it with a shovel to scrape out the seeds. Some she toasted, to eat. But she cleaned the biggest ones, spread them out on layers of newspaper, and brought them down to the shelves in the root cellar. In a month they'd be ready to put in envelopes, ready for next spring. If a pumpkin could grow as big as a washtub without any special attention in Alaska Territory, how big could a pumpkin grow with proper care? Next year she would try Farmer Boy's recipe for champion pumpkins. Next year, she would grow the biggest pumpkin Palmer had ever seen.

No one knew quite what to expect of an Alaskan winter. They'd been told it wasn't much worse than the northern Wisconsin winters they had left behind, but Mother didn't seem to believe it.

After the week of canning, Terpsichore took over the kitchen on Saturday, making more popcorn.

"No fair. Mendel stole my idea for popcorn," Terpsichore muttered.

"You'll just have to make your popcorn better than his," Mother said.

"Popcorn is popcorn, isn't it?"

"Does his have butter?"

"I love hot buttered popcorn," Cally said.

"Me too," said Polly.

"How could I serve hot buttered popcorn in the cold community center?" Terpsichore said.

"You could drizzle warm butter on each bag of popcorn as you sold it," Mother said.

"How are we going to keep the butter warm in the cold?" Terpsichore asked.

"I have an idea," Mother said. "Your father made fun of me for packing my mother's silver serving dishes, but I packed them anyway." Mother got down on her hands and knees, pulling boxes out from under the cots to read the labels. "Sheet music, records . . ." Mother paused at the box of records. "Records were another thing it was probably foolish to pack, but I couldn't stand to leave them behind. Even though I don't have a way to play them here." She patted the box like it was a beloved pet. She shook her head. "What was I looking for?"

"Something for the butter," Terpsichore said. She felt sad for her mother. Terpsichore now had boxes of books to partly replace the library she had left behind in Wisconsin, but how could Mother replace her music?

Mother shifted more boxes. "Ah-ha! My mother's silver." In addition to the felt-lined wooden chest that held twelve place settings of wedding silver and a box with a silver sugar and creamer set was another box with two sizes of silver chafing dishes.

She held up a small silver chafing dish and fit a can of Sterno into the cup made for it. "Let this and my homemade butter be my contributions to your library project."

Gloria came in time to help bag up the last batches of popcorn, and Terpsichore and her family arrived early to beat Mendel. Her father set up a borrowed card table and

Terpsichore smoothed out one of her mother's linen table-cloths over it. She peeled back the top on a can of Sterno, set it in the heat cup under the chafing dish, and lit it. Soon her mother's homemade butter was melting in the chafing dish and she was ready for business.

Mendel wandered over to see what his competition was up to. "Well, la-di-da—aren't you the fancy one. A linen table-cloth and the family silver to sell popcorn?"

Terpsichore mimicked her mother's formal voice. "One can't relinquish all vestiges of civilization just because one is in the Territory of Alaska."

Mendel went back to his own station and still sold pop-corn—especially after he lowered his price to seven cents.

Gloria and the twins got in the spirit of rivalry.

"Hot popping corn's our favorite treat! Pour on the butter, now let's eat!" The twins singsonged and hopped, partly to draw more attention to Terpsichore's booth, and partly to stay warm—and it worked!

The girls drew in a crowd and Gloria helped by calling out, "Hot BUTTERED popcorn! All profits to the new Palmer Library!"

Terpsichore was awhirl, taking money and opening each sack to drizzle in a teaspoon of warm melted butter.

Not playing favorites, old-timer Crawford bought a bag of popcorn from Mendel, and one from Terpsichore.

That night Terpsichore held her own, even with Mendel's seven-cent competition.

Two weeks and two movies later, Mendel strolled over

to Terpsichore's booth after both had sold all their popcorn. "Popcorn business is all yours now. I have all the money I need for Togo's harness. Still friends?" He held out his hand.

"What do you mean—still?" Terpsichore hesitated, then sighed and held out her hand too. "You haven't acted like a friend lately, but I'll accept your handshake as an apology," she said. "Good manners don't cost a cent and are the cornerstone of civilized life." Mother would be proud.

The next Saturday movie was dull without having anyone to shout insults to across the aisle. This time the old man bought two bags of popcorn from Terpsichore. "Got so used to eating two bags a movie, have to support my habit, especially since it's for the library." He started for a chair, but then came back. "Which group of colonists did you come up with?"

"Uh . . . the second group; we're from Little Bear Lake, Wisconsin."

"Not Madison? You're almost the picture image of somebody I used to know from Madison. She would also have brought out a silver chafing dish to serve popcorn in Alaska . . ." He squinted at Terpsichore's face. "And there's something about your stubborn chin and eyes that don't miss anything that remind me of her."

Terpsichore couldn't help fingering her chin. How was a chin stubborn?

"Are you any relation to the Olmsteads?" he asked.

"My grandmother's last name was Olmstead before she got married. She's from Madison."

"Hmmm," he said, "that might explain it." He munched popcorn as he headed toward the chairs.

Terpsichore leaned over the table toward the retreating old-timer. "Explain what?" she asked. But the mysterious man was already too far away to hear.

CHAPTER 30

Gone with the Wind

Even Tigger seemed to be getting ready for an Alaskan winter, putting on an extra layer of insulating fat, but then she surprised Terpsichore with two kittens. Cally named the orange one Willa, and Polly named the gray one Rogers.

Later that week, as the wind shrieked through spruce trees and bare limbs of cottonwoods, Terpsichore huddled in her cot and pulled the blankets up over her ears, trying to muffle the sound. Moments later, Tigger led her two new kittens under Terpsichore's blankets. Terpsichore wished she had ten more cats to keep her warm.

The tent canvas whipped in the howling wind that threatened to fly them all away to Oz, like Dorothy and Toto. Outside, the washtub clanged and rattled across the plowed field. Wind thrust itself under the narrow space between the wood platform and canvas walls, and whipped Matthew's drying diapers off the clothesline.

At a crack like a gunshot, Matthew stood in his crib and howled.

"What's that?" Cally and Polly whimpered.

"Probably a tree that couldn't stand up to the wind," Pop said.

Terpsichore coughed and pulled the blankets over her head. She flinched each time a tree snapped. She didn't think any trees were close enough to hit the tent and crush them, but she wasn't sure.

The next morning the wind had quieted from a shrieking howl to a dull roar. Pop peeked out the screened window. "It might be Friday, but with so many trees down and blocking roads, I doubt there will be school today. I think I see the washtub by the edge of the woods," he said. "I'll untangle it from the shrubs and see if I can find Smoky and Clarabelle."

"They didn't get blown away, did they?" Cally and Polly pulled over a chair to look out the screened window too, but didn't see the animals.

"A one-ton horse won't get blown away," Pop said. "Clarabelle and Smoky probably just took shelter in the woods." He pulled on his jacket and tied his hat on with a scarf. "But I'll check on Smoky and lead Clarabelle back to the shed for milking."

"Check on the chickens too, Pop!" Terpsichore said. She didn't have to worry about where Tigger and her kittens were. They had never left her bed.

All the rest of the Johnsons crowded up to the window as Pop leaned into the wind to fetch the washtub and whistle for Smoky and Clarabelle. The animals emerged from the shelter of the woods, where they had kept each other company during the night.

"Uh-oh," Terpsichore said. "The outhouse blew off its foundation and tumbled clear over to the fence between us and the Ellisons next door."

Mother sighed.

The chicken coop still stood, but when Terpsichore went to collect eggs, there were none. Maybe terrified chickens didn't lay.

By the end of the day, Pop and Mr. Ellison from the neighboring farm had braved the wind to put the outhouse back on its moorings and replace shingles on Mr. Ellison's shed.

Outside the general store on Saturday morning, everyone traded stories with their neighbors about the wind damage.

"Our outhouse too!"

"Our woodpile got tossed around like toothpicks!"

"The henhouse roof kited right off to who knows where!"

"My washing—nearly every stitch of clothing we own but what was on our backs."

Someone made a show of looking at the grain calendar on the wall inside the general store. "Just checking," he said. "I thought maybe the wind had skipped us over a couple months and we had blown clear into January." He put his nose within an inch of the calendar. "Nope! Still October."

"If this is October, what will January be like?"

"If we don't get our houses by the next big blow, you won't find me here. I won't have blown away—my family will have packed up and left on the next boat south."

Terpsichore anxiously picked her way over felled tree branches and scattered garbage toward Pastor Bingle's tent. There was a note safety-pinned to the Bingles' tent flap: "No library service today."

Terpsichore knocked.

Mrs. Bingle pulled aside the tent flap with one hand, still holding a broom in the other. "Hello, Miss Terpsichore."

"Did the storm hit your tent too?" Terpsichore asked.

"It did. The wind blew seventy-five miles an hour, I hear. Thank goodness none of us was hurt, but everything smaller than a breadbox went flying. Your books and magazines I'd set out, all your filed date-due cards, everything was hurled around, including some of our glasses and dishes. There's still broken glass in here or I'd invite you in."

Terpsichore peered into the tent. "Where are all the books now?"

"Don't worry, they're safe," Mrs. Bingle said. "Pastor Bingle thought that if the rest of the winter's going to be like this, your books would be safer in the new school building instead of a tent, so he got the key to the school and put the books in the hall outside the principal's office."

Terpsichore sped toward the school to see for herself that all the books were safe.

Both doors to the school were locked, so she trudged back to the general store to rejoin her family.

"No library today?" Mother asked.

"Pastor Bingle moved all the books to the school after the wind storm hit their tent," Terpsichore said. "And the school is locked, so I'll have to wait until Monday to get all the books back in order."

On Monday, Terpsichore packed her acquisitions log along with her homework. She wanted to take inventory to make sure every book was accounted for. The books were right where Mrs. Bingle said they would be, just outside the principal's office.

"Good morning, Terpsichore," Miss Quimby, the principal, said. "Isn't this a grand surprise? Pastor Bingle moved the little library from his tent to the school for safety. The teachers and I had just been talking about how we'd like to start a school library, and here we are.

"Miss Fromer came in Saturday afternoon to look over the collection. She took classes in library science at the University of Washington, so she'll be our librarian. She plans to train some of the eighth-graders to check books in and out during lunch hour. I understand you've been helping Pastor Bingle with the library, so I'm sure she would make an exception about using eighth-graders and let you participate in the training."

Terpsichore's hand went to her pounding heart. "I already know how to shelve and check books in and out. And those books weren't Pastor Bingle's to give the school; they belong to the Palmer Library Action Committee, a group I started."

The principal flushed while Terpsichore continued.

"Some of those books are my grandmother's and she wants them back if we move back to Wisconsin next fall. And I wrote letters to the Red Cross and Girl Scouts to get donations." Terpsichore dropped her satchel and dragged out her accessions log and opened it to the first page. "See? This list shows where each book came from. And it was the Action Committee that earned money for supplies and our first magazine subscriptions. Mendel collected bottles, Gloria had a hair salon, I washed diapers, and we sold popcorn. We did it all ourselves."

"I had assumed that Pastor Bingle had solicited donations . . ."

"It's not just grown-ups who can do things, you know." Terpsichore clenched her hands so tightly her fingernails bit into her palms.

"I appreciate your efforts, but it's time for a professional to take over. Miss Fromer has had the proper training to run a library."

Terpsichore jutted her chin, that stubborn chin, according to Mr. Crawford. "Then I'll take back all of Grandmother's books, and the ones from my mother," she said, daring the principal to say she couldn't.

Terpsichore pulled some of her books from the various boxes where they'd been packed higgledy-piggledy after the wind had scattered them. She put as many as would fit into her satchel.

"I'll be back for the rest," she said.

CHAPTER 31

The Committee Meets

EVERYONE ELSE WAS ALREADY SEATED WHEN TERPSICHORE edged through the door and dropped her overloaded satchel on the floor beside her desk.

Thud! It was only books, but it sounded like a tree felled in the forest. Shock waves traveled the floor, shaking the rows of desks and making every set of eyes turn in her direction. She turned slowly to meet all those eyes. Terrible Teddy opened his mouth to make a rude comment, but one blast of her basilisk eyes made him clamp his mouth shut. Even Miss Zelinsky, who normally would have chided her for being late, just raised her eyebrows.

She felt a splotchy blush spreading from her cheeks, down her neck, and advancing to her chest, over her heart. At roll call, instead of a chipper "Present!" she croaked "Here." Miss Zelinsky was watching her too closely for her to be able to pass notes to Gloria and Mendel. She'd have to wait for first recess to gather the troops.

Finally, the minute hand of the clock clicked from 10:29 to 10:30. Desktops clapped shut over schoolwork and students lined up to go outside. It took two eighth-grade boys to shoulder the doors open against the wind.

Gloria's yellow slicker whipped against her legs, and fierce wind cut through Terpsichore's jacket. Gloria grabbed Terpsichore's hand. "What is it?"

"We have to get Mendel too," Terpsichore said.

The good thing about a friend is that she doesn't need to wait for answers to questions before helping. Terpsichore and Gloria darted into a cluster of boys and pulled Mendel away from his new buddies, which surprisingly included Terrible Teddy. "Come on, Mendel, we need you," Terpsichore said. "Emergency Library Action Committee meeting."

"What's the emergency?" Mendel asked.

"The school is taking over all our work!" Terpsichore said.

Mendel jerked his arms away from the girls' grasp. "Look," he told them, "I already quit the library committee, okay? It was something to do during the summer, but now that school has started, I don't have time."

Gloria linked arms with Terpsichore. "All right then. Be that way. We don't care. We girls can take care of it ourselves."

"Gotta go," Mendel said, and strode off to join his buddies.

Terpsichore and Gloria huddled on the side of the school building. Terpsichore shouted over the howling wind. "After the storm blew our books all over his tent, Pastor Bingle moved everything we collected to the school, and now Miss Quimby wants to keep the books here permanently and put Miss Fromer in charge."

Gloria leaned toward Terpsichore's ear. "Is that such a bad idea?" Gloria shouted. "If the books are here, kids could check them out whenever they're at school instead of just on Saturday." She pulled back to read Terpsichore's expression. Terpsichore was not convinced by this argument. Gloria persisted. "It will be a lot easier for some kids. Don't you want everyone to have books? I thought that was the idea of a library."

"But it's ours," Terpsichore said, "our library." She realized she was still shouting, even now that the wind had abruptly stopped.

Gloria finger-combed her hair back into place. "Look, we got what we wanted, a library. What does it matter where the books are or who runs the library now? I'm just as happy to have Miss Fromer do all the work."

The next day, Terpsichore dumped nearly twenty dollars in dimes and nickels on Miss Quimby's desk. She followed the money with the well-worn *World Book* brochure. "Here's the money I earned selling popcorn to buy a set of encyclopedias. Since you're taking over the library, you can figure out how to get the rest of the money."

She didn't stay to see the look on the principal's face.

Terpsichore was glad she was alone in the tent after school.

Cally and Polly must have been with Mother and Matthew somewhere. Her father was at work at the mill. She took out the box that had her date-due stamper and her inkpad, nibbed pen and india ink, mending tape and spine labels. She took out the date-due stamper and stamped the back of her hand. Then she stamped a row of dates on up her forearm. She stamped each page of her arithmetic homework.

She looked up when Mother, Matthew, and the twins came home.

"I just got back from the school," Mother said as she set Matthew down. He toddled over to Terpsichore's cot and grabbed the stamper. Terpsichore grabbed it back. "That's mine," she said. "It's not a toy."

"Matty's toy," he said, trying to grab it back.

Terpsichore held the stamper over her head.

Her mother sat on the cot next to her. She looked at Terpsichore's arm, with the row of dates marching up to her elbow, but did not comment on them. "Miss Quimby sent a message to me," she said. "She said you threw money on her desk and were rather rude. That's not the way you were brought up."

"It was nineteen dollars and seventy cents! She should have been happy to get it."

"It didn't sound like you were happy to give it, though."

"Of course I wasn't happy. I worked hard for that money and I worked hard to get a library started and now the grown-ups are taking it over, like kids don't know how to do anything right by themselves."

"I think there's room for you in the reorganized library, but you might have to apologize to Miss Quimby and show Miss Fromer that you are a responsible young woman and—"

"Me apologize? They should apologize to me. They took everything over without even asking!"

"From what I heard, that was a misunderstanding. Miss Quimby is new here and didn't know about your library committee. When Pastor Bingle brought over the books, she assumed that the library was something he had started, and that he was turning the books over to the school where they'd be safe."

The wind howled again that night and Terpsichore did not sleep well. On the way to school the next morning, she worked out what she would say. She knocked timidly on Miss Quimby's door. "I'm sorry if you thought I was rude," she said. "I was upset. Starting the library committee was the biggest thing I'd ever done, and when all the books got moved to the school it was like no one was giving us credit for all our work."

Miss Quimby stood and came around from the back of the desk to sit in a chair next to Terpsichore so they were eye to eye. "I apologize too. We didn't know how the library got started. It must have been a shock to see all the books here. Miss Fromer and I have decided we will call the collection the Palmer Action Committee Library. And of course you don't have to share your grandmother's books, but I hope you will."

Terpsichore's next stop was the eighth-grade classroom. She opened her satchel and put her shoebox of library supplies on Miss Fromer's desk. "Um . . . here are the supplies the Demco Company sent." She pulled down her sleeve, covering up the blue ink that hadn't completely washed off that morning.

"Thank you, Terpsichore," Miss Fromer said. "It was very generous of you to donate the money you'd raised for the encyclopedia fund. Maybe you can help us come up with ideas on how to raise the rest. I always thought that a dictionary, an almanac, and a set of encyclopedias were the heart of a reference collection. It sounds like we think alike on that."

Terpsichore felt her jaw unclench.

"Miss Quimby said you used to volunteer in your school and public libraries back in Wisconsin too. Could I convince you to pair with some of the eighth-grade volunteers to teach them during training?"

Terpsichore suppressed a smile. A sixth-grader teaching eighth-graders?

As Gloria would say, "Keen-o!"

CHAPTER 32

Sleeping in the Hayloft

ONE MORNING IN LATE OCTOBER, TERPSICHORE WOKE TO eerie quiet. The roof of the tent sagged, and Tigger, Willa, and Rogers purred softly from under the covers when she stirred. She slid out of bed and tiptoed in wooly-stockinged feet to untie the tent flap and see what kind of morning they had that day. Eight inches of snow blanketed the field and weighted down the slender branches of the spruce and cottonwoods.

Mother joined Terpsichore at the tent opening and, in a barefooted stomp, returned to the cot where Pop was still half asleep.

"This is it, Mr. Johnson," Mother said. "We get our house now or we're moving back to Wisconsin!"

Pop stood up and wrapped his scarf around his neck. "You're right, Clio. We have to get out of this tent and into a house. I'm going to harness Smoky and pay a not-too-friendly call on Mr. Irwin in the administration office. I'll stop by the

LeClercs' and the Petersons' and some other neighbors and see if they will back me up."

"Can we go too, Pop?" Terpsichore asked.

Pop looked at Cally and Polly, huddled under the blankets on their cots, and Matthew's red, dripping nose, and Mother, standing with her hands on her hips.

"Well?" Mother asked.

"Maybe it would help our cause," Pop said. "Bundle up."

Mr. Irwin's office tent also sagged with the weight of snow. Pop rapped on the tent support. Terpsichore heard Mr. Irwin's chair scrape back from his desk as Pop, Mother, Cally and Polly, the Petersons, the LeClercs, and a few others crowded into the tent.

Pop started off. "Your contract with the CCC that says they have to do all the building is ridiculous. If you want this colony to succeed, let us work with the CCC to build our own houses and barns."

Mother continued the argument. "The next telegram to Mrs. Roosevelt will tell her that hundreds of children are freezing to death because you won't let us work on our own houses." Cally and Polly shivered and put on their best winsome waif expressions.

Mr. Irwin sighed. "This snow has me starting to think the same way. I'll meet with the head of the CCC to tell them we can't wait any longer. We'll deliver building supplies to every family still in a tent. We'll keep our crews felling timber and working the heavy equipment, and you can organize your-selves into teams to get houses built and your families under cover."

"Get us the wood and nails and we'll do the rest," Pop said, and everyone else agreed.

When word got out, it was like that wonderful night when their hospital got built in hours.

Trucks rumbled back and forth with supplies. Mr. LeClerc had built his own log house back in Minnesota, so he super-vised. Mr. Peterson was good at finish work, like putting in windows and doors.

Pop had been kidding last summer about living in the chicken coop, but he wasn't kidding about building the barn before the house.

"What do you mean," Mother said, "we're getting the barn before the house? A cow and a one-ton horse need shelter more than your own children?"

"There will be plenty of room in the barn for us while the house is being built," Pop said, "but would you want the cow and the horse sheltering in your kitchen if we built the house first?"

Mother threw up her hands at such convoluted logic.

Ten days later, they had a barn. It was oblong, with two horse stalls, six cow stanchions, and a hayloft. So far they just had Clarabelle and Smoky, but more cows and another horse would come later.

The girls explored. The barn still smelled of freshly cut

wood, not manure and livestock. They were unanimous: "We want the hayloft!"

"It's going to be cold up there," Pop warned. "The woodstove that was big enough to heat the tent can't warm the whole barn."

Mother couldn't climb the ladder to the loft with Matthew, so Pop wrestled bales of hay to the side of the main floor farthest from the animals and walled off a little bedroom for them. The CCC men and Pop moved the woodstove from the tent into the barn.

The luxury of space after being cooped up together in the sixteen-by-twenty-foot tent for over five months was delicious—a whole loft to themselves! Pop marked off two bedrooms with more bales of hay, and for the first time since Wisconsin, Terpsichore had her own space. Hearing Cally and Polly on the other side of the two-bale-high partition, though, whispering and giggling, she felt left out. Cally and Polly always had each other as best friends. Sometimes she wished she had a twin too. Her teeth chattered and her toes were numb. Pop was right; it was cold. She dragged her bedding to the other side of the hay bale wall and snuggled into a communal pallet with Cally and Polly. They slept together like puppies in a basket.

In another two weeks, when the roof, floors, and outer walls were done, they moved into a house complete with a closet for a chemical toilet. No more chamber pots and trips to the outhouse in the snow! There were also rumors that the new hospital would be getting electricity soon. Would they be getting electricity next year too? Simple comforts, like the plumbing and electricity that they had taken for granted in Little Bear Lake, seemed like luxuries when they'd been without them for so long.

They spent days with putty knives, poking oiled ropes of oakum into every crack between the flat inside edges of the logs. If oakum could keep the water out of a ship at sea, it should keep out the wind that came howling down the valley.

Once the oakum was in, Pop hammered sheets of plywood over the inside walls and painted everything white, the only color the general store stocked.

The main floor, including Mom and Pop's room, had seven-foot ceilings. Upstairs was cozier, with ceilings sloping down to within two feet of the floor. Now that the twins had their own room, Pop separated their bunk bed so that both cots rested on the floor. Terpsichore had a room all to herself, with no company but Tigger, and a window near the floor, which she could look out of from her cot.

After eating dinner and washing dishes, the family huddled around the woodstove. Cally and Polly played teacher with Matthew, quizzing him on his letters using blocks that Pop had sanded smooth and painted. They laughed and clapped whenever Matthew got a letter right, and Matthew laughed and clapped too.

When Terpsichore started to pile up pillows on one end of the settee, Matthew raced to the lowest row on the bookshelf to pick out the three picture books he wanted her to read to him that night.

He put them on Terpsichore's lap one at a time. "Tip read," he said. "This book, this book, and this book." He snuggled onto Terpsichore's lap with a contented sigh.

The kerosene lamp over the dining room table barely gave enough light for Terpsichore to read by, but she had memorized all the words long ago when she was just a little older than Matthew was now. She felt the warm weight of his back against her chest and bent her head so her cheek brushed the side of his forehead.

Pop shifted his chair so he could see his whole family: Mother, who was at the kitchen table now, writing her weekly letter to her mother; Cally, Polly, and Terpsichore, all reading their books; and Matthew, who had fallen asleep in Terpsichore's lap.

"Home sweet home," Pop murmured.

Mother looked up from her letter-writing. "At last," she said.

CHAPTER 33

The Old-Timer Comes to Call

THREE DAYS BEFORE THANKSGIVING, WHEN MOST FOLKS were snowbound, someone knocked on the door. From outside came the happy yips of half a dozen dogs. Mother opened the door to a middle-aged man with a beard. He held a bundle under one arm, and despite the icy snow, he snatched off his toque before bowing. "Mrs. Johnson, I presume?" he said.

"Yes, but who—" Mother started.

"It's the popcorn man," Terpsichore said, racing to the door.

"Come in," said Pop. "It's too cold for introductions in an open doorway. Terpsichore, you seem to know him."

"It's Mr. Crawford, my best customer at the popcorn stand," Terpsichore said. "And he used to live in Wisconsin, just like us."

"Nathaniel Crawford, ma'am," he said, extending his hand toward Mother, then to Pop. "You can call me Nate. I dropped by to see if you knew how to cook a moose," he said.

Mother was taken aback. "A moose?"

"My gun overreached itself and I have more moose than the dogs and I can eat. It seems a shame to waste a good moose roast on the dogs when they're just as happy with the scrappy pieces." He presented Mother with the bundle, but when she sagged with the weight of it, Pop took it over.

"This is very generous," Pop said. "How'd you decide to share your bounty with us?"

"I could tell from your daughter's popcorn business that you folks have the real enterprising spirit," he said, "and I want to encourage people like that to stay. With Thanksgiving coming up, I thought you might appreciate a change from the canned salmon I know most of you new folks are living on. I brought a moose roast, but of course the real Alaska delicacy is jellied moose nose."

Cally and Polly gagged. Mother was too polite to make gagging noises, but her face blanched.

"Maybe roast moose heart with lowbush cranberry stuffing?" Mr. Crawford had the kind of eyes that twinkled when he made jokes, and they were twinkling now.

Cally and Polly gagged again.

"Hmm," Mr. Crawford mused. "Maybe not . . . How about cranberry moose pot roast?" He tapped the roast Pop was holding. "You cook it like a regular pot roast in a Dutch oven for about three hours, but if you have a couple cups of lowbush cranberries, you could throw them in too, along with a cup or so of stock and a couple chopped onions."

Terpsichore committed the recipe to memory.

"Will you be able to join us for Thanksgiving?" Pop asked.

"Since you're providing the meat, the least we could do is invite you to share it with us."

Mr. Crawford's eyes crinkled and he bowed again. "I was hoping you'd say that."

By Thanksgiving morning, Mother had thawed the roast and put some through the meat grinder for Matthew. Terpsichore cooked the roast, made two pumpkin pies, and helped Mother with all the side dishes. The twins covered the picnic table with Mother's biggest white linen tablecloth, then set out the silver candlesticks and the Royal Copenhagen china.

Mr. Crawford arrived wearing a clean but inexpertly ironed white shirt, a heavy tweed sports jacket, and a bolo tie with a carved ivory eagle holding the two ends of the tie together at his throat.

If Mother had expected an Alaska old-timer to eat with his fingers, she was pleasantly surprised. While they waited for their stomachs to settle between their dinner and dessert, Mr. Crawford told them about how he had come to Alaska.

"I first came north when they discovered gold in Nome. I suppose you've heard of Wyatt Earp and Jack London . . . Well, I can't say I was best buddies with them, but I did meet them. Wyatt had the most luxurious saloon in Nome . . ." He cut off with a nod to Mother. "Not that I frequented it much, but that place was the first wooden two-story building in town and everybody had to see it when it opened.

"Then when the Lucky Swedes found gold just north of here at Hatcher's Pass, I came south to the Matanuska Valley.

I wrote my sweetheart from Wisconsin to come north now that I had enough gold to provide for her properly, but by then she was already engaged to someone else. It was a hard life for a family in those early days, so I didn't blame her for not wanting to come up." He stopped to sigh. "She was partial to her big-city comforts and concerts."

Mother sniffed and said, "I can understand that!" She lifted her chin with a "so there" look toward Pop.

"And you never married?" Terpsichore asked.

"No, Miss Terpsichore, I did not," he said. He fiddled with his napkin and wiped his mustache even though nothing was there. "You have an unusual name," he said.

Mother spoke. "It started with my mother. Her name was Thalia, for the Muse of Comedy."

The old-timer's face froze for an instant, and then—Terpsichore could tell even with his beard—a slow smile traveled from his lips to his eyes.

"My mother named me Clio, for the Muse of History, and I kept up the tradition by naming my girls for Muses too: Terpsichore, Calliope, and Polyhymnia. Cally is the twin with a dimple in the left cheek and Polly is the twin with a dimple in the right cheek."

The twins obligingly smiled to show their mirror-image dimples.

Mr. Crawford studied his plate, and then looked up. "Is your mother planning to join you in Palmer now that you're settled? Your father too, of course."

"My father died just after the stock market crash, and

Mother is content—except for missing us, of course—living in Madison. In fact, I'm afraid you may have overestimated our fitness for Alaska. We may move back to Madison ourselves if it doesn't work out here."

Pop snorted. "If I take an accounting job your mother says is mine if I want it."

"An accountant?" Mr. Crawford asked. "How could you be happy as a chair-twirler after you've seen Alaska?"

Mother, to avoid what might become an argument on the relative merits of farming in Alaska and accounting in Wisconsin, interrupted. "How about some of your pumpkin pie, Terpsichore?"

Terpsichore cut generous slices of pie for everyone and passed a bowl of whipped cream. "I made the pie myself, right down to growing the pumpkin from seeds I brought from Wisconsin."

"It looks good, Miss Terpsichore," Mr. Crawford said.

"I was going to make a pecan pie too, but the syrup at the store was too expensive and there aren't any sugar maples here. There's a chapter in *Farmer Boy*—"

Mr. Crawford held up his hand. "You should taste my birch tree syrup. I don't know if I make it like that farmer boy of Miss Terpsichore's, but this spring I'll show you how to tap the birch trees. I've discovered Alaska has everything you need for a good life."

Mother shook her head.

"Alaska grows on you," he said. "You see if it doesn't."

CHAPTER 34

Christmas 1935

IN DECEMBER, THE SUN BARELY CLEARED THE MOUNTAINtops by ten in the morning, and set again before Terpsichore walked home from the bus stop. Sometimes, the wind blew snow into enormous drifts against the sides of barns and houses, and neighbors helped each other digging out. Every evening, Terpsichore made her way out to the chicken coop to rub glops of Vaseline into the combs and wattles of each chicken so they wouldn't get frostbite. She had to protect her source of eggs.

A week before Christmas, the whole family trooped out to cut the spruce tree the family had scouted out months before. Presents started appearing under the tree. Terpsichore was ready. She had bought Shirley Temple paper dolls for the twins—her only store-bought present—and made bookmarks with summer wildflowers she had dried and ironed between layers of waxed paper for her mother, a felted yarn ball for Matthew, and a knitted ear-warmer for her father.

Pop tantalized everyone with the promise of a big surprise at Christmas, and although there were little presents wrapped in funny papers under the tree for the children, he had nothing there for Mother.

While other families had been ordering whole dining room and living room sets of furniture from the Sears and Montgomery Ward catalogs, Terpsichore's father had been firm: They would not run up debt to buy anything not necessary for survival. If her father had gone against his no-unnecessary-debt rule, what had he bought?

On Christmas morning, everyone opened gifts of knitted sweaters or mufflers from Mother.

Pop had made a wooden train set for Matthew—an engine and three cars with wheels that turned and doors that opened. He bought books for Cally and Polly: *Doctor Dolittle's Return* for Cally, and the latest Nancy Drew mystery, *Message in the Hollow Oak*, for Polly.

Terpsichore's present was also shaped like a book. She peeled off the cellophane tape holding the paper closed and as soon as she saw the cover, she jumped up, clutching the book to her heart. "*Little House on the Prairie*! I didn't know Laura Ingalls Wilder had written another book!"

"It just came out," Mother said. "Your grandmother wrote to tell me she had read a newspaper article about it and we knew . . ."

She didn't get a chance to finish, because Terpsichore was smothering Mother and Pop in hugs. She wanted to go upstairs and read more about Laura right away, but she was still curious about Pop's surprise.

Now that all the other presents were open, Pop grinned and said, "I'll be right back."

Terpsichore, Cally, and Polly huddled at the window and huffed on the glass to melt peepholes in the frost. Pop tromped the path to the barn that he shoveled every day. He left the barn door open, disappeared for a moment, and reappeared at the barn door with a large shipping crate balanced on the rims of a wheelbarrow.

Still clutching her book, Terpsichore raced to be first to the door. "What is it, Pop?"

"What is it, Pop?" echoed the twins.

"What on earth?" said Mother.

Pop laid the box carefully on the table. Matthew toddled over and banged on the sides of the crate with his palms.

"This present's for everyone, but mostly for you, Clio," he said, and kissed the top of Mother's head. "Close your eyes for a minute while I take apart the box." He took out a crowbar, claw hammer, and large serrated knife he'd stowed in the broom closet. Terpsichore resisted peeking, even at the mysterious creaks and squeaks of nails being pulled out of the crate and the rasp of a knife on cardboard.

"Ta-da!" he crowed. "You can all open your eyes now."

Mother turned and approached the object on the table. Her hands hovered over the black enamel finish on the playing arm. A smile widened as she looked up at Pop. "A Victrola," she breathed.

"Well, you had to leave your electric record player behind because we won't have electricity up here for a while, but you still hauled up all those heavy records."

Mother broke off Pop's next words with a kiss, then bustled to the closet by the front door to drag out a tattered cardboard box too heavy to lift. She undid the flaps and took out records to spread them on the floor around her. "What shall we play first?"

"Something Christmasy," chimed the twins as they knelt on the floor beside their mother to find the record album they wanted.

Cally and Polly took turns paging through the sleeves in the storage album Mother had labeled CHRISTMAS. "'Silent Night,'" Cally crowed, "the one with Bing Crosby and Paul Whiteman!"

Mother continued sorting, intent on finding something else. She took out another album of records bound together like a book. "We can start with 'Silent Night,'" she said, "but then we're playing Handel's *Messiah*."

With no rugs or curtains yet in the house, Bing Crosby's mellow voice gently echoed on bare walls and floors. The music cocooned Terpsichore and warmed her like a quilt. The Johnson house was insulated with drifts that shut out the rest of the world. They would have a silent Christmas night.

Mother replaced the Bing Crosby record in its sleeve and reverently placed the first record for Handel's "Hallelujah" chorus on the turntable. At the opening hallelujahs, her father joined in to sing the bass part, the twins sang first soprano, and Terpsichore sang alto with her mother so the strength of her mother's voice would guide her own voice toward the right pitch. As they sang, voices blending in joy, she treasured the feeling that she was part of something bigger than herself. Together they created a sound that no single voice, no matter how perfect, could create on its own.

With yet more snow, Terpsichore didn't know if Mr. Crawford would be able to make it to dinner, but at three o'clock, she heard the bells on his sled and the enthusiastic clamor of his dogs. She opened the door to let him in. "We're so happy you got here!" Terpsichore told him. "Come on in."

"It's the popcorn man!" Cally and Polly each took a hand to lead him on into the house, but Mr. Crawford stayed just inside the door.

"Need to take care of my dogs first," he said. "Who wants to help?"

As Terpsichore started to follow Mr. Crawford, her father interrupted. "I've heard sled dogs can be dangerous."

"Not these dogs," Mr. Crawford said. "I treat them like family. In fact, they are my family. The only thing Terpsichore would have to worry about is getting her face licked off."

Terpsichore bundled up, but Cally and Polly stayed by the woodstove.

"I hope I'm not being too forward," Mr. Crawford said, "but can I invite myself and my dogs to spend the night in the barn? They could easily run the twelve miles home—it only took them an hour or so to get here, but I'd rather run them in daylight."

"Don't even think about running home tonight," Pop said. "We'll move the settee in front of the woodstove for you, and Clarabelle and Smoky won't mind the company of your dogs in the barn."

Mr. Crawford herded the dogs into one of the empty stalls, removed their harnesses, and checked their booties. Pop and Terpsichore found buckets for thawed water and broke open a fresh bale of hay for the floor of the stall.

"Guess who I saw in town?" Mr. Crawford said. "It was Mendel with that dog of his. Mendel was on skis and Togo was pulling him into town so he could load up his backpack with supplies. Looked like they were both having fun."

"At least Togo was doing something besides scaring cats," Terpsichore said. "Do you think Togo will grow up to be as helpful as your dogs?"

"She's off to a good start," Mr. Crawford said. "You know," he continued, "as I get older, I'm beginning to think living in town has its advantages: movies, hospital, more friends . . . It gets lonesome on the far reaches of the Butte."

He looked up from removing the booties on a dog that, true to prediction, wouldn't stop licking Mr. Crawford's whiskers.

Terpsichore leaned over to pet the dog and giggled when it licked her face too. Its tongue was softer than a cat's. "I promise to save you scraps from dinner," she said.

"They'd like that, Miss Terpsichore," Mr. Crawford said. He stood and watched his "family" explore the confines of the stall and settle down in a cozy heap.

After dinner, Mr. Crawford pushed back his chair. "This dinner is the best Christmas present anyone's given me in years. And now I have something for you. Knowing this family's penchant for books, I hope it's something you'll enjoy.

"Before my first winter here I wrote down to Shorey's Book Store in Seattle and had them send me up a crate of books to stave off cabin fever." He opened a leather rucksack and drew out several books: Robert Service poems, Jack London stories, *Ben-Hur*, and *A Connecticut Yankee in King Arthur's Court*. "Let me know when you've finished these and I can loan you some more."

"Thank you, Mr. Crawford," Mother said. "You've been so good to us." She reached over to look at the Twain book. "My mother used to like Twain." She replaced the book in the stack. "I wonder what she's doing this Christmas, without us."

"Maybe she could come up and visit," Mr. Crawford said.

"She may be here at the end of summer to take us home with her," Mother said. She sighed and ran her fingers over the embossed cover of *A Connecticut Yankee*.

"Maybe she'll surprise you," Mr. Crawford said, "and decide she'd like to live up here with you in Alaska, instead of taking you back to Madison."

"She'd never adjust to a life like this," Mother said. She turned to Terpsichore and the twins. "Can you imagine your grandmother hauling water for her bubble bath? Or living without a radio or her piano? I still have a hard time picturing her now without a cook and chauffeur."

Mr. Crawford was subdued. "It sounds as if your mother married well."

"It depends on what you mean by that," Mother said. "My father did well with the railroad until the crash. We had a fine house, but I'm not sure they were happy in it."

"Sometimes we don't know what we want most until the chance of getting it has passed us by," Mr. Crawford said.

What Terpsichore wanted most was to stay in Alaska, and she wasn't going to let any chance to make that happen pass her by.

CHAPTER 35

The New House in Town

BY LATE APRIL, PILES OF MELTING SNOW TURNED THE ground to muck so hungry it would suck your boots off. The old-timers called this season *break-up*, the time when the frozen river cracked open and began to move again. Mother called it a mess, and Terpsichore agreed. By late May the ground would dry out enough to plow. That's what the optimists said, anyway.

Meanwhile, Pop laid out planks between the house, the barn, the henhouse, and along the side of the road to the school bus stop so the girls and Mother could avoid the mud and come home with the number of shoes they started out with.

Mother insisted that Matthew play in the house or barn. Pop agreed. "Don't want the mud to suck Matty down to his eyeballs!" He reached over to tickle Matthew on his tummy.

"Eye-balllls, eye-balllls!" The word made Matty giggle more than the tickle.

But this season brought good things too. True to his word, Mr. Crawford took the Johnsons into their woods to tap the birch trees before they budded out and the sap turned sour. For two weeks, Pop and Terpsichore hauled home five-gallon buckets full of sap. For hours, each batch steamed up the kitchen with a sweet smell that made everyone hungry for pancakes. Terpsichore was already planning a birch syrup glaze for salmon and chicken, and a dollop of syrup on the morning oatmeal and in mint tea.

One sunny day, when the snow remaining on the mountaintops etched a jagged line against a densely blue sky, Pop came back from town with something held behind his back. "Special delivery for Clio Johnson!" he said. With a flourish, he held out something wrapped in burlap and twine.

Mother approached cautiously. "It looks like a bundle of sticks."

Pop jingled the metal tags on each bundle with one finger. "Come this summer you won't say that," he said.

Mother leaned down to read the tags. "Sitka—that's some kind of *rugosa*, I think." She looked up at Pop.

He grinned. "Right as usual, Clio."

"*Nutkana*—is that a rose too? And a *rubrifolia*. Three roses!"

"I said you'd have roses in Alaska, and here they are. I read the nursery catalog at the store, and these roses are all supposed to be good in Alaska. In fact, the *nutkana* is the rose that grows wild along the roadsides here."

Pop held the prickly sticks out of the way as Mother moved in for a hug.

On one of the Johnsons' Saturday trips into town for supplies and for the story hour Terpsichore still gave twice a month at the library, she noticed someone had chopped down trees and graded dirt on a plot of land not far from the school. "Who's getting ready to build in town?" she asked.

"I hadn't heard about anyone building there," Pop said.

"I'll find out," Terpsichore said. While the rest of the Johnsons were in the general store, Terpsichore tromped through the mud to the big colony map by the post office that identified everyone's parcels. The mystery parcel, which looked like about five acres, was surrounded by colony land, but was in a different color. Who owned that land?

Terpsichore balanced on the loose boards serving as a sidewalk over the mud to the architect's office where two other men were looking at plat maps.

"Mr. Crawford?" one of them said, as he read the name on the plat map.

The other one shrugged. "Nobody I know."

But of course Terpsichore knew. It looked like Mr. Crawford was going to build in town, just as he said he might last Christmas.

Terpsichore raced back—as fast as one could race through the muck—to the construction site. This time Mr. Crawford himself was there.

"Are you building a house, Mr. Crawford?" she asked.

He slid off the papery brown covers of a couple of spruce tips and popped them in his mouth like popcorn. "You guessed right, Miss Terpsichore. I bought that land when I first moved down from Nome, then decided I wanted to be farther out. But now I plan to spend at least the winters in town, and eventually year-round if things work out right."

"What kind of things?" Terpsichore said.

Mr. Crawford smiled but changed the subject, pointing out where various parts of the house would go. "The kitchen will face east, toward sunrise, and I'll have a study, bedroom, dining room, a bathroom with a claw-foot tub, and maybe an extra room just in case I think of another use for one. What else do you think a house needs?"

"Mother misses a real bathroom, a water pump right in the kitchen, a generator for electricity, a windmill by the well to bring up water, a music room—one with a piano of course—separate bedrooms for all the children . . . Well, I guess you don't have children."

Mr. Crawford patted Terpsichore on the head. "No, Miss Terpsichore, I never had children, but if I did I'd have wanted a kid just like you."

All the way back home, Terpsichore felt a lightness on top of her head, right where Mr. Crawford touched it, right where the soft spot was on a baby's skull. Even though she wasn't musical, someone would like a kid just like her.

Pop wasn't one to have to keep up with the neighbors, but when he saw the look on Mother's face when she heard that Mr. Crawford had ordered a claw-foot tub, Pop started enlarging the tiny corner room that had the chemical toilet. He also ordered a real bathtub. Without running water they would have to heat water on the woodstove, then carry buckets of it to the tub. It would be a tub, though. One Mother could soak in for an hour. He dug a gravel-lined ditch for the water to drain into. He made a washstand for a pitcher and basin and laid a linoleum floor. It looked like a real city bathroom even if there was no plumbing.

When it was done, the whole family circled around the bathroom door to admire the result. "I thought you were against running up more debt, Mr. Johnson," Mother said. "If we leave in a few months it's a waste of money." She pretended to be mad, but her mouth twitching toward a smile showed she was pleased.

"I admit we had lots of problems at first, Clio, but look what progress we've made already! We have a school and a hospital and plans for churches . . ."

"Won't we want to stay?" Terpsichore asked.

Cally and Polly nodded in agreement with Terpsichore.

"Only if *I* vote to stay," Mother said. "You haven't changed the bargain, have you?" She narrowed her eyes at Pop. "Or are you just trying to sway my vote."

"Of course I am." Pop smiled.

CHAPTER 36

An Announcement

As Gloria had predicted, she got the part of Dorothy in *The Wizard of Oz*, and Miss Zelinsky, after hearing the twins sing at church, made sure they got to lead all the first-, second-, and third-graders in the Munchkin songs. Mendel was working on special effects. Since Terpsichore couldn't sing, dance, or make houses fly in a cyclone, she volunteered to make cookies to sell at intermission. If she wanted to take proper care of her pumpkins, she didn't have time for rehearsals.

Every school lunch hour and recess, Gloria handed Terpsichore her rumpled mimeographed copy of the script Miss Zelinsky had written for *The Wizard of Oz*, based on the book and using some of the songs from the old Broadway production. Huddling on the non-windy side of the school building, they would go through another scene.

Terpsichore gently tugged on a section of Gloria's hair,

which was now halfway to her shoulders instead of a wavy bob. "Your hair is getting so long!" Terpsichore said.

"My hair wasn't long enough for two ponytails like Dorothy, so I started letting it grow as soon as Miss Zelinsky announced the musical," Gloria said. "I knew I'd get the part, and all the great actors prepare for a role by getting into character."

"If you want to get into character as a Kansas farm girl, maybe you ought to help me in my pumpkin patch," Terpsichore said.

"I get into character enough on my parents' farm," Gloria said. "You were kidding, right?"

"Yes, kidding!" Terpsichore said. "Where do you want to start?"

"Where she meets the Scarecrow?"

"Okeydoke," Terpsichore said, and found the page.

Gloria had underlined all her parts with red pencil, so Terpsichore's job was to feed Gloria her lines, to say the lines of dialogue just before her next words.

Between helping Gloria with her lines during the day and listening to the twins rehearse their songs in the evening, Terpsichore would have nearly the whole play memorized herself, even if she didn't have a part.

"So," Miss Zelinsky said one morning, "I have a few announcements to make. I know September is a long way off, but I wanted to get the word out now. If you hear of

anyone who wants to buy a spinet piano, please let me know."

Gloria raised her hand. "But why are you selling your piano?"

"Well, that's the other part of the announcement." Their teacher held her left hand in a shaft of sunlight so the tiny diamond chip could be seen even at the back of the room. "I'm getting married this September and moving down to Washington State. My fiancé has a piano too, so I won't need mine."

Terpsichore, Gloria, and every other girl scrambled out of their seats to coo over Miss Zelinsky's ring.

While the other girls continued to titter and congratulate Miss Zelinsky, Terpsichore just thought about the piano. A spinet wasn't as nice as the piano Mom had sold a year ago, but it was a piano, and since it was small, it would fit in their living room. Would a piano help make her mother vote to stay?

Terpsichore broke into the other girls' questions about what kind of dress Miss Zelinsky was going to wear for her wedding. "How much are you asking for the piano?"

Miss Zelinsky was still blushing over her announcement and attempting to quiet the class, but she stopped long enough to answer. "I'm asking seventy-five dollars."

Giving up on regaining order, Miss Zelinsky dismissed class for an early recess.

Terpsichore ran up to her teacher's desk. "Please save the piano for me. I don't have the money now, but I know I can raise it."

"How could you earn that much money in four months?"

"Give me a chance." Terpsichore all but knelt and clung to Miss Zelinsky's skirts. "Please?" Her voice trailed off in a squeak.

"All right. But my fiancé is coming up for the fair and taking me home the next day, so I can only give you until the last day of the fair, September fifth. If you don't have all the money that day, I'll need to sell it to someone else."

"Thank you, thank you! I know I can do it!" She didn't know just how she would do it, though. Not yet. It would take a grown-up all summer to earn that much money. Other kids were babysitting now. Other kids were selling popcorn at the movies. What could she do that no one could copy? What could she do to earn that much money?

CHAPTER 37

The Pumpkin Plan

POP FLIPPED THROUGH THE INFORMATION BOOKLET ABOUT Palmer's first fair. "I heard the officials are sending copies of this booklet to every state in the union. We'll probably get lots of tourists coming up to see how many of us have lived through the winter without getting eaten by a polar bear or turning into Popsicles."

His voice trailed off as he read a page midway through the booklet. "They're offering prizes for almost anything you can think of," he said. "I might enter the woodworking division with my rocking chair, and, Clio, you should enter some of your fancy knitting."

He looked up, eyes wide. "Whooey! There's going to be a twenty-five-dollar prize for the biggest vegetable grown in the valley!"

"Let me see that!" Terpsichore snatched the catalog so she could read for herself. Twenty-five dollars was a third of the way to a piano. What could grow bigger than a pumpkin in one summer? Last year she'd grown large vegetables willy-nilly, in raw soil. If she got pumpkins twice as big as the ones she'd grown in Wisconsin by just throwing seeds in the ground, how big could one grow in soil that had been enriched with compost? And how big would a pumpkin grow if she pruned off all but one pumpkin on a vine and fed it milk, like Almanzo did in *Farmer Boy*?

Terpsichore shoved the catalog back toward her father and wandered over to the warming shelf above the stove. She had planted her largest pumpkin seeds into Mason jars filled with compost-enriched soil to cocoon them. She poked the dirt in each jar with a finger. Too wet and they'd develop white mold. Too dry and the seed would never germinate. One of those seeds needed to grow a pumpkin big enough for Cinderella to ride in. One of those seeds needed to grow a winner.

She pictured herself walking up the steps to the stage to shake hands with the mayor and collect the twenty-five-dollar prize. Wouldn't everyone be surprised that the winner of the biggest vegetable growing contest was not an old-timer, but a soon-to-be twelve-year-old girl?

"Grow big, you guys," she whispered, using her finger as a magic wand as she tapped each jar in turn. "I believe in you."

"Who's been using my emery board?" Terpsichore's mother asked. She held up the board. Nearly all the rough emery was worn off. "This was my last emery board, and I know it still had a lot of use left on it last week."

"It wasn't me," Pop said.

Mother huffed. "Well, somebody not only used it, but completely ruined it." She stared at the twins, but they just shrugged and went on playing with the kittens.

Terpsichore could feel Mother's eyes drilling a hole in her back as she turned each jar to see if there were any signs of a root breaking through the seed.

"Terpsichore?"

"It wasn't me," Terpsichore said as she turned to face her mother. "I mean, it was me, but I didn't use it on myself." She held out her ragged fingernails as evidence. "It was for my pumpkin seeds. I filed all the surfaces except the pointed end. It helps the water penetrate and makes it easier for the leaves to split open the shell."

Mother cracked her mangled emery board and hurled it to land on the seed catalog on the table.

"See what Alaska's doing to our daughters? A normal girl would be using an emery board on her fingernails, finally taking pride in her appearance and preparing for womanhood. Instead, our daughter is in overalls and obsessing about pumpkin seeds."

Terpsichore fingered the straps on the overalls she usually changed into as soon as she got home from school. She liked her overalls. They protected her legs from mosquito bites.

Pop picked up the emery board and straightened it out. "There isn't anything wrong with being a dedicated farmer. Your own mother lived on a farm before she married Mr. Van-Hagen. I lived on a farm until I went off to college."

"That's the point," Mother said. "You went to college to

get off the farm and better yourself. Now we're backsliding into the life people were living generations ago." She ticked off months on her fingers. "May, June, July, August, and then harvest just after the fair in early September. Thank goodness we have to live here only four and a half more months, and then I can vote to go back to civilization."

Terpsichore turned back to her jars of seeds. "Four and a half months," she whispered. "You have just four and a half months to grow into the biggest pumpkins Palmer has ever seen."

Every morning, Terpsichore checked in on her plant nursery first thing. When the seeds sprouted she transferred the jars to the south-facing windowsill in the kitchen so the leaves could soak up sunlight. When the plants were an inch high, they unfurled their first real pumpkin plant–shaped leaves.

In the sunshine of early May, Terpsichore and her father pounded sticks and strung string to mark off where each crop in the kitchen garden and potato field would be planted. "I figure I need a plot about twenty feet by twenty feet for each pumpkin," she said. "And I should grow at least two pumpkins so I have a backup."

"If we're going to eat, we have to grow a lot more than two pumpkins in a space that big," Pop said.

"This isn't just about food to eat," Terpsichore said. "This is about winning twenty-five dollars at the fair."

"What are you planning to do with twenty-five dollars?"

"It's a secret," Terpsichore said. "But it's not just for something for me. It's for everybody. You too. Please-please-please?"

Pop laughed. "You're hard to say no to, Terpsichore. But you're my practical daughter. Certainly you can see we can't sacrifice eight hundred square feet of prepared land to two pumpkins."

"But what if something happens to just one pumpkin? There's blossom end rot, damping-off disease, and voles, and moose, and beetles. I need at least one backup." Terpsichore pointed to the scrubby back section where the tree stumps had been cleared but the soil was still riddled with rocks and shrub roots. "I'll work that back strip myself, and won't take any of the land that's already set to plant."

Pop wrinkled his brow in doubt. "I don't think you know what you're getting yourself into, but if you're willing to finish clearing that back section yourself . . ."

"Thanks, Pop! I can do it, you'll see!"

A raven cackled from somewhere in the cottonwoods. When Terpsichore spotted the bird, she shook her fist at it. "I'll do it, you raven, just watch me!"

Terpsichore loaded a shovel, hoe, and rake into a wheelbarrow that she pushed to the half-cleared land. She wouldn't think about how many blisters she would have by the time she cleared and fertilized it all. She'd take it one square yard at a time.

After school each day, Terpsichore left Gloria and her sisters to their *Wizard of Oz* rehearsals and ran home from the bus stop to change into her overalls, check on her pumpkin plants, and clear another few yards of ground for the pumpkins' new home. After roughly clearing the land, she lugged wheelbarrow after wheelbarrow of compost to her pumpkin patch. In mid-May, past the danger of frost, she placed her crate of pumpkin starts and a trowel in the wheelbarrow and wheeled them out to their new home. "You're going to love it here, little guys."

She turned slowly, taking in the mountains on three sides of the valley. Hatcher's Pass and the rest of the Talkeetna Mountains were to the north, and the Chugach Range guarded the south and east. The colonists had started calling the tallest peak just a few miles south of Palmer "Pioneer Peak."

Two hundred families had come north to meet the mountains of Alaska, and great things were bound to happen. She felt it, right down to her toes firmly planted in Alaska soil, that this was where her family was meant to be. She hoped that Mother would come to think so too.

With Tigger supervising, Terpsichore created two mounds, each three feet across with a trench around it to collect excess water during the summer rains. She dug two small holes in each mound, and gently turned each jar upside down to free the seedlings. "Okeydokey, in you go, little guys, right up to your first set of leaves." She patted the soil tenderly around each plant and returned with a bucket of water and compost slurry to give her pumpkins their first meal in their new home.

She didn't tell them that only one plant on each hill would be allowed to live. She didn't want to discourage any of them from trying to grow the biggest they could be.

CHAPTER 38

The Play's the Thing

FROM INSIDE THE HOUSE, MOTHER'S PITCH PIPE ANNOUNCED the start of another rehearsal session. The twins had long since memorized the words to all their songs for *The Wizard of Oz*, but now Mother was coaching them on interpretation.

"Hold on to the last note in that phrase," Mother said, "and see if you can get a little warble into it. See, like this." Her voice floated out across the greening fields to where Terpsichore and Pop were taking advantage of the long hours of daylight to work in the fields.

Pop stopped to ease his aching back as he looked back toward the house. "It's good to hear your mother singing again, isn't it?"

Terpsichore nodded as she passed Pop with another sloshing bucket of water for her pumpkins. "It is," she said. She paused when she heard another voice. "Who's that?" she asked.

Pop shrugged.

"It wasn't Mother. It wasn't the twins."

As soon as she heard the words "Just a simple girl of the prairie," she knew. That was from Gloria's first song, so Mother must be coaching her too.

Then she heard Mother, the twins, and Gloria's voices join in on "Home, Sweet Home," the number that Miss Zelinsky had substituted for the finale from the original Broadway show. "Home, Sweet Home" was a song even Pop and Terpsichore knew, so they sang along as they hoed and watered.

For the whole last week of school, mothers baked cookies and more cookies for the bake sale to raise money for the school band. Terpsichore baked too, after working in her pumpkin patch.

On the day of the play Terpsichore made the twins' favorite dinner, fried salmon burgers, but Cally and Polly were too bouncy to sit down and eat.

Mother draped a sheet over the twins' freshly ironed dresses from Easter. "Showtime!"

They all piled into the wagon and Smoky trotted them into town. The gymnasium was filled with every folding chair and bench that Palmer could round up. The twins went backstage to change into their dresses, and the rest of the Johnsons found places as close to the front as they could get. After hearing the twins rehearse, hearing Mendel's description of the special effects, and memorizing Gloria's copy of Miss Zelinsky's script, Terpsichore thought she knew what to expect.

She knew the house on stage was really a painted sheet stretched and stapled over a wood frame, but she oohed along

217

with everyone else when Gloria stepped through a flap door in the pretend house and started her first number. The applause had barely stopped after Gloria's song when the chorus began singing, sliding up and down scales that sounded like howling wind, and Gloria dashed back through the doorflap.

The audience gasped when the house jerkily rose from the stage and swung back and forth, as if hurled by a cyclone. From her vantage point near the left side of the audience, Terpsichore could see that Gloria had slipped backstage with Mendel and Terrible Teddy in the wings. The boys hauled on the rope in the block and tackle rig that hoisted the house. The audience gasped again when the house crashed back down on the stage and Terrible Teddy howled like a wolf, pretending to be the Wicked Witch of the East, who had been caught under the house.

As soon as the audience settled down, the twins and all the rest of the primary-grade Munchkins skipped on stage. Matthew stood on his chair and waved. "Hi, Cally! Hi, Polly!" Mother shushed him, but Pop chuckled.

Later in the production, Mendel and Teddy—maybe not so terrible if he was willing to help Mendel—made papier-mâché monkeys fly and a hot-air balloon rise. Terpsichore was sure Mendel was the brains of the special effects, but he had also found a use for Teddy's brawn to make the special effects work.

Near the end, when Gloria-as-Dorothy clicked her heels three times and chanted, "Take me home to Aunt Em," the crowd erupted into applause. The whole cast and crew, including Mendel and Teddy, gathered on stage to sing the final song. Almost everyone knew it, so the gymnasium echoed with the words:

> *"Home! Home!*
> *Sweet, sweet home!*
> *There's no place like home!*
> *There's no place like home!"*

As the curtain closed, Terpsichore followed Mother, Pop, and Matthew through the crowd to find the twins. So many people surrounded Gloria that Terpsichore had to jump up and wave to get her attention. Mr. and Mrs. LeClerc stood at her side, and Gloria, smiling so hard her mouth must have hurt, held an armful of wild roses and bluebells with a red ribbon tied around the stems.

"Terpsichore, we're leaving," Pop called.

Terpsichore blew a kiss in Gloria's direction and sidled through the crowd to the rest of the family. She got there just as Mother bent down to hug the twins. "You were perfect Munchkins! I wish my mother could have seen you."

CHAPTER 39

Drink Your Milk

NOW THAT SUMMER HAD COME, TERPSICHORE WAS relieved that Miss Fromer had taken over the library and organized other volunteers to take turns checking out books and giving story hours on Saturdays. Terpsichore was only responsible for one Saturday a month, so she had more time for her pumpkins.

Her greedy vines grew as fast as Jack's beanstalk, gulping and eating everything she fed them. After the first couple days of hauling water from the well, three hundred feet from her pumpkin patch, Terpsichore's palms were raw, even when she cushioned the wire bucket handle with a towel. Once she finally reached the pumpkin patch, she leaned over, straining against the weight of the sloshing buckets to dribble the water evenly as she stepped carefully along each of ten or fifteen side vines on each plant. She trained the vines to keep them from tangling, spreading them out like the tentacles of an octopus. Feeling like a villain, she ripped out all but the biggest plant on each hillock.

Each of those two remaining vines grew a foot a day. Each vine sent down extra roots every six inches to soak up water and nutrients. Each leaf, top and underside, had to be inspected regularly for attacks by rodents or bugs.

By the Fourth of July, the plants were flowering. The male blossoms opened first, with inch-tall stamens topped with bright golden pollen. The female blossoms opened next, with lobes to receive the pollen. Terpsichore could have left fertilizing each female flower to the bees, but she was taking no chances. She picked the biggest male flowers, and tapped the stamens over the female flowers.

By midsummer, she had to decide which pumpkins she would allow to live and grow. "Sorry, little guy, you're just not going to be the big one." She left only three baby pumpkins each on the main vines of her two remaining pumpkin plants.

When the six pumpkins reached the size of a basketball, she had to make the final decision of which two to keep. If all six continued to grow, each would be big, but not gigantic, and she needed gigantic to win. Those two pumpkins had to get the royal treatment if one of them was to be a winner, and she knew just how she was going to do it.

It was five o'clock in the morning. Terpsichore entered the barn, holding a pitcher in one hand and two battered pie tins in the other. Smoky nickered a greeting, probably hoping it was Cally or Polly with a morning treat of oats or a baby carrot from the garden.

Rhythmic burbles echoed tinnily as streams of milk hit her mother's milking bucket. Terpsichore stood at the entrance of Clarabelle's stall for a moment, waiting for her mother to notice her. "My pumpkins need some milk," she said. "May I have some?"

Mother halted the stream of milk flowing from Clarabelle's udder and lifted her forehead from Clarabelle's flank. "You want milk for what?" she said.

"In *Farmer Boy*, Almanzo grew the blue ribbon–winning pumpkin by feeding it milk."

Mother straightened on her stool and all but rolled her eyes in skepticism.

"It's true, Mom. That book is based on real life."

"And I suppose you're going to talk to your pumpkins too," Mother said.

"Yep," Terpsichore said. "I'll be talking to them nonstop if it makes them grow bigger. They won't get a word in edgewise," she joked.

"I always thought that was an old wives' tale. But, who knows?" Mother said with a shrug. "Maybe talking works. Hearing people talk helps babies thrive, so maybe it works with pumpkins. It couldn't hurt." She smiled at Terpsichore and turned back to her milking.

"So I can have some milk?" Terpsichore asked. She held out her pitcher.

"How much do you need?"

"Maybe about half a pitcher or so every day," Terpsichore said.

"Every day? That's going to cut down how much butter I can make to sell." Mother put on her *We have to be sensible* face.

"Isn't there buttermilk left when you make butter? Maybe the pumpkins would like that as well as whole milk." Terpsichore's mouth puckered at the memory of the sour taste of buttermilk. Maybe she could do everyone a favor by feeding the buttermilk to the pumpkins instead of having to drink it. Even Cally and Polly would thank her.

"Okeydokey." Mother strangled on the word and slapped her hand over her mouth. "I can't believe I said that," she said. "Before long I'll be talking like an uncouth person from the back of beyond." She made a wry face and patted Clarabelle's side. "And I guess that's just what I've become."

"Is that so bad?" Terpsichore dropped her pie pans to timidly pat her mother's back. Her mother wrapped both arms around Terpsichore and drew her closer.

"I don't know why you want to win that twenty-five dollars so much. But apparently you want that money for something as much as I want back our old house, my piano, my mother . . ." Mom pressed her lips together to hold back the rest of the list of things she missed in Wisconsin.

Terpsichore's throat ached with the effort of tamping down her urge to blurt her whole plan to her mother. She wished she could convince her that although Alaska wasn't Wisconsin, it could be good here too. And her mother didn't have to give up her music to live in Alaska. She had a plan to get her mother a piano. And one part of that plan required milk.

Mother turned over Terpsichore's hand, tanned to the color of strong tea and as callused as a stevedore's. "Look what Alaska is turning us into," she said. "Well, I know how hard you've been working to grow those monster pumpkins. You can have all the buttermilk you want if it makes you happy."

The next day after churning butter, Terpsichore headed out to the field with a half pitcher of buttermilk, a paring knife, the pie pans, string, and an ice pick. Tigger trotted behind. Standing in the middle of eight hundred square feet of pumpkin vines, she beamed. All this growth from two seeds! It was magic, Alaska magic. No wonder folks dreamed big in Alaska!

Well, she was going to help Alaska magic along with advice from *Farmer Boy.* She set her supplies down on a level patch of ground and knelt beside one of her pumpkins. "I guess it's time for you to have a name. Since I'm going to feed you like Almanzo fed his pumpkins, do you like the name Almanzo?"

A breeze fluttered the leaf closest to the pumpkin, which was now as big around as one of the tires on Grandmother's Pierce Arrow.

"I'll take that as a yes," Terpsichore said. As she turned to pick up the knife she caught Tigger dipping a paw into the pitcher to lick off a taste of buttermilk.

"No, Tigger, that's for Almanzo!"

She didn't have to scold Tigger away from the buttermilk a second time. The cat backed up, shaking her head and working her tongue in and out of her mouth, trying to get rid of the taste.

Terpsichore picked up the paring knife. "This is a knife, Almanzo, but don't be scared. I'm just going to make a tiny slit, like a little mouth so you can drink this buttermilk."

Tentatively, she poked at the stem a few inches from the pallet where Almanzo rested. "It'll just be a little prick, Almanzo . . ." Wincing, she jabbed the stem, making a half-inch slit. "See, that wasn't so bad, was it?" She patted Almanzo reassuringly.

"Now I'm going to feed you milk and watch you grow into the biggest pumpkin Palmer has ever seen." With the ice pick, she wedged one end of the string into the vine and put the other into the pan of buttermilk. She watched as the buttermilk slowly wicked from the pie plate to Almanzo. "Now wasn't that worth it? Milk will help you grow big and strong."

With more confidence, she approached her other pumpkin with her supplies. Kneeling, she said, "I guess I need to name you too. How about Laura? You saw it didn't hurt Almanzo, so I expect you to be brave."

She cut a slit in Laura's stem, wedged a length of string into the slit, and placed the other end into the milk. "There now, isn't that good? You're in a race now. One of you is going to win."

CHAPTER 40

Changes Coming

EVER SINCE FOLKS HAD MOVED OUT OF THEIR TENTS AND into roomier houses, families had taken turns having church at their houses. It was the Johnsons' turn. The good part about your turn to host church was that people left behind most of the food that wasn't eaten during the social hour after services. The bad part was that for the whole week before, Mother nagged Terpsichore and her sisters to pick up their rooms, not to track dirt into the house, and to keep the shedding cats outside. Mother poked a mop at the cobwebs on the ceiling, washed windows, and re-washed all the teacups on the shelves.

Saturday night, Mom and Pop moved the table, settee, and chair to the side to open up the living room. Everyone had a turn in the claw-foot bathtub, and Mother put Cally and Polly's hair in rag curlers. She sorted through her records, finally settling on a Bach organ recital and a recording of hymns sung by her college choir.

Standing in the middle of the room in her nightgown, Mother turned slowly to inspect the result. "We'll pass," she said, "as long as no one lifts the linen tablecloth to see that we're still eating off the picnic table we had in the tent."

"It's church, not a military inspection," Pop said.

"Humph," Mother said. "Nosy women can be more critical than any drill sergeant."

There were just over two hundred houses now in Palmer, and all had been built to one of five slightly different house plans. In the seven months since the last house was built, however, families had gradually put their own touches on each one. During Pastor Bingle's sermons at each neighbor's home, Terpsichore would try to imagine the lives that family had left behind in Wisconsin, Minnesota, or Michigan from the clues of their old belongings. She could also walk into any other house and know which catalog that family had ordered their couch or dining room set from.

The Johnsons' house was one of a kind, and Terpsichore liked it that way. Pop had made their simple settee, and Mother had covered a cushion for it with a flowered tablecloth. To go with the table, Pop had made benches with backs, so you could always squeeze in one more when they had company.

Their furniture was rough-hewn. But the Johnsons also had brought nice things from their old home, like her mother's Royal Copenhagen teapot, silver candlesticks, and damask tablecloth. She was happy her parents didn't do things just like everybody else. It made her proud to be a Johnson.

On Sunday morning, Gloria's father pulled a borrowed pickup as close as he could get to the front door without running over Mother's flower garden. Gloria and her mother slid out one side door and Gloria's father out the other. Pop came out to help unload the planks and nail kegs they set up as makeshift pews.

Chatter among the arriving families quieted at the sound of Pastor Bingle's bus. The motor sputtered, then stilled, and a dozen more people followed Pastor Bingle into the Johnsons' house, pushing aside the mosquito netting that hung in the doorway.

Mother stood next to Pop to greet families as they came in. As Mother predicted, their eyes darted from one corner of the room to the other, taking in things like the chair rails and baseboards Pop had added to the basic plywood walls.

Terpsichore cranked the handle on the Victrola, opened the doors beneath the turntable for maximum volume, and gently placed the stylus on the recording of Bach's Prelude and Fugue in D Minor. At the majestic thunder of the opening notes, a baby wailed and Mr. Carlsen dropped the mug he'd brought for the after-service social hour. As he bent to pick up the pieces, Terpsichore guiltily shut the doors on the Victrola to mute the sound. She liked the sound of the pipe organ loud enough to rattle her rib cage, but apparently not everyone shared her preference.

Mother strode from the door to where Terpsichore stood beside the record player. "Let's have the hymns instead—"

"You wanted the organ first," Terpsichore said.

"I changed my mind," Mother said.

Terpsichore lifted the record by the edges and slipped it back into its sleeve and replaced it with the recording of her mother's old choral society. Everyone was looking at her as she adjusted the doors under the turntable so the hymns would come out at moderate volume. The room sighed in relief at the more familiar opening to "In the Garden."

After the service, the men helped stack the planks they used for pews in the back of the pickup and the women moved the table back to the center so they could set out the food they'd brought for the social hour. Mrs. Bingle complimented Mother on how homey they'd made their place. "I see you have several stacks of sheet music, Mrs. Johnson. Do you play an instrument?"

"I studied piano and voice at St. Olaf College before I married. And before moving here I taught piano."

"Why did you give it up?" Mrs. Bingle asked.

"I had to sell the piano before we moved," Mother said. "And sadly I haven't played since."

"You must miss it terribly. You know, perhaps I shouldn't tell you this . . . My husband should be the one to make the official announcement. Can you keep a secret?"

From halfway across the room, Terpsichore's ears pricked to attention on the word *secret*. She picked up a plate of her pumpkin cookies and started passing them out, gradually working her way closer to Mrs. Bingle.

Mrs. Bingle guided Mother toward the corner by the bookcase and leaned in toward Mother.

Terpsichore, with her back to her mother and Mrs. Bingle, so it wouldn't look at all as if she were eavesdropping, offered the cookies to everyone nearby. She listened with one ear to everyone asking for her recipe and listened with the other ear to what Mrs. Bingle was saying.

"The Presbyterians down below have offered a fifteen-hundred-dollar loan to the Palmer church council to begin construction on a real church. Pastor thinks that if all the groundwork gets done this summer before the ground freezes and if he gets enough volunteers, the church can be finished over the winter when the men aren't needed in the fields. The church can be dedicated in time for Easter services next spring."

"That does sound like good news," Mother said cautiously. "Why did you think I should know now, before Pastor Bingle announces it?"

"So you can start thinking about putting together the music program for the first service. And you can help select a portable organ. I play enough to accompany the hymns, but I'm not a real musician. And, of course, once we have a real church we'll need someone to direct the choir. You said you studied voice?"

"Yes, but there's a big difference between singing and leading a choir," Mother said. "And I'm not even sure we'll still be here when the church is dedicated. Right after the fair, as soon as harvest is in, I get to decide whether we stay on in Palmer or we move back to Wisconsin."

"You'll want to stay," Mrs. Bingle said. "Alaska grows on you."

"We'll see," Mother said. "Everybody keeps saying Alaska will grow on me, but I'm not so sure I want to be grown upon."

CHAPTER 41

Invasion of the Squash Bugs

AFTER CHURCH, TERPSICHORE DRAGGED GLORIA AND
Mendel back to her pumpkin patch to show off Almanzo and
Laura. Gloria followed Terpsichore reluctantly, making sure
she kept to the rock-edged path that led through the potato
field back to where the pumpkin vines stretched in luxury.

Gloria surveyed the eight hundred square feet of leafy
green. "You got all this from two seeds?"

Terpsichore preened. "They're the descendants of my biggest pumpkin in Wisconsin," she said. "But with seventeen
hours a day of sunlight, they're growing even bigger than back
home. To get two giant pumpkins, I thinned each plant down
to one pumpkin." She swept her hand over the swath of green.
"All of these leaves are soaking up sunlight and the roots are
soaking up minerals and water. And all of that is feeding just
one pumpkin on each plant."

"Sort of like hundreds of worker bees all bringing back
pollen and nectar to feed one queen," Mendel said.

Terpsichore thought her pumpkins were more impressive than bees, but Mendel saw everything in terms of bugs.

Gloria bent down to ground level and lifted a couple leaves. "What pumpkins?"

Terpsichore grinned and pointed to the back of her plot, twenty feet away. "Look back there!"

"Glor-i-osky!" Gloria breathed as they neared Laura.

"Holy tomato!" Mendel said. "That's really just one pumpkin?"

Terpsichore patted Laura proudly. "Gloria and Mendel, meet Laura. Laura, these are my friends Gloria and Mendel."

Gloria snorted. "So are we supposed to shake hands now?"

"At least say something nice. They like to be talked to," Terpsichore said. "Or give Laura a hug; I think she likes that too."

Mendel bowed. "Pleased to meet you, Laura. That shade of green is most becoming on you."

"Good pumpkin, good pumpkin," Gloria said as she patted Laura like a dog that had obeyed a command to sit.

"Now come meet Almanzo. He's even bigger. I just measured him and he's already twelve feet around."

Placing each foot carefully between sprawling vines, Terpsichore led Mendel and Gloria to where Almanzo sat regally among leaves as big as umbrellas. "What kind of compost did you use?" Mendel asked. "Fish guts would have made a great slurry, but I guess you couldn't use guts because then you'd attract the bears. Do you really think talking to them makes a difference? We should do an experiment and talk to one group of plants and not the other. Maybe it's not really the talking that does the trick, but the CO_2 that you breathe out at them, because plants need the CO_2 . . . Hmmm."

"Eek! Ugh!"

Mendel's musings were interrupted by Gloria, who was trailing behind because she was bending back each leaf she passed to avoid getting any leaf stains on her church clothes. "There are yucky bugs on these leaves!"

At the word *bugs* Mendel started a high-stepping sprint over vines and leaves to see what Gloria had discovered. Terpsichore followed, one hand over her mouth, afraid of what she might find.

Mendel took a small collecting jar and a magnifying glass out of the pocket of his Sunday trousers and squatted down to leaf level.

Terpsichore wrung her hands as she waited for the verdict. Was it a relatively harmless roly-poly pill bug, or something worse?

Mendel swept one of the bugs into a collecting jar and capped it. "*Anasa tristis*, I'd guess," he said.

"Is that bad?" Terpsichore said.

"Very bad," Mendel said, without looking up. He examined the underside of a leaf with his magnifying glass. "And they've started laying eggs by the thousands."

Terpsichore steeled herself to look over Mendel's shoulder. He gave her the magnifying glass so she could see for herself. Clusters of reddish eggs stuck to the underside of the leaf. She traded the magnifying glass for the collecting jar and squinted at the evil bug inside.

"What's an Anna-whatsis?"

"*Anasa tristis*," he corrected. "The *tristis* is Latin for sad or stinky. One common name is stinkbug, but the other common name is squash bug, and they'll start sucking the life out of these leaves, and Laura and Almanzo could die."

"Yikes!" Terpsichore said. "What'll I do?"

"The only way to get rid of them is to pick off the bugs one by one and drown each in a bucket of soapy water. And the eggs have to be squished."

Gloria clutched her skirts close to her legs to keep them from coming into contact with any infected leaves. "I think my mom is probably looking for me," she said. "I hope the bad bugs don't hurt your pumpkins." She leaped over vines toward the main road.

Terpsichore raced through panicked calculations. Fifteen vines times two plants, that's thirty vines. Each vine was roughly twenty feet long, and had leaves roughly every six inches . . . That was over a thousand leaves to inspect.

Mendel must have read her mind. "If you haven't noticed them before, they probably haven't taken over the whole field." He stepped between leaves to inspect the next vine over. "Some here," he said. Then he followed the vine along another six feet and bent down to check again. "And here." At another six feet he checked a circle of leaves around him. "These seem to be clear, so you might have just a few dozen leaves that have been affected. The bugs like moist dark places. Do you have any shingles left from construction?"

"I think there are some in the kindling pile," Terpsichore said.

"Scatter the shingles among the vines. At night, many of the bugs will congregate on the underside of the shingles and then you can dump the shingles in soapy water. You'll get rid of dozens at a time."

"But what about the eggs?" Terpsichore pictured thousands of eggs turning into leaf-munching squash bugs. She clenched her fists, remembering the calluses formed from hours clutched around bucket and wheelbarrow handles. It was war against the squash bugs. Every last one of them had to die.

"The eggs are a different problem," Mendel said. "You have to get them before the nymphs hatch out. Are you squeamish?"

"Not as bad as Gloria," Terpsichore said. Looking back toward the house, she didn't even see Gloria anymore. She was probably at home already, washing her hands and inspecting her skirt to make sure there were no bugs clinging to it.

Mendel demonstrated. Holding one hand on the top of the leaf to stabilize it, he pressed fingers of the other hand against the eggs. "You'll have to press just hard enough to squish the eggs, but not hard enough to damage the leaf." He looked up to see if Terpsichore understood.

Terpsichore choked at the thought of having to squish

bug eggs bare-handed. Her hands would be covered with red slime and nymph bodies.

Mendel stood and reclaimed his collecting bottle. "Ask your mother for an old diaper. You can put it over the eggs so you won't have to touch them. Can I have one leaf with the eggs on it, though? I'd like to watch them hatch."

Terpsichore's eyes widened, and darted toward Laura and Almanzo. "You wouldn't let them near—"

"No, I promise they'll meet a watery end in a soapy bucket. I just want to take notes on their life cycle and document how much damage they can do. I'll report my findings to the agricultural agent so he can put everyone else on the lookout for them so they won't damage other people's crops."

Terpsichore tried to smile. "Okeydokey," she said. Her voice shook. She had always thought Mendel was wasting his time studying bugs, but what he'd learned about bugs might save her pumpkins.

"I'll help you get started," Mendel said.

Two hours later, the shingles were scattered among the vines, the bucket was full of the floating corpses of mature squash bugs and nymphs, and thousands of eggs had been squished before they had time to hatch.

When they had finished, Terpsichore shook Mendel's hand, ignoring any egg slime that might be on his fingers. "Thanks, bug boy!" She grinned to show she meant "bug boy" to be a compliment.

Mendel grinned. "I prefer the term *amateur entomologist*," he said.

"Don't be modest," Terpsichore said. "You're a master entomologist."

Tomorrow morning, Terpsichore would dunk shingles with sleeping squash bugs into soapy water before they had a chance to lay more eggs.

Laura and Almanzo would be safe. At least for now.

CHAPTER 42

A Recipe for Success?

THE FIRST DROPS WERE TENTATIVE PLOPS, AS IF THE CLOUDS were just testing their ability to rain. Random plops became a steady thrumming, and then a torrent. Terpsichore sat up in bed and pulled aside the quilt that shut out the midnight sun. She couldn't see Almanzo and Laura beyond the potato field, but she imagined a thousand sets of roots along the vines greedily sucking up pure rain.

She leaned back on her pillow, smiling and listening to the first serious rainfall in a month. She rubbed her thumbs across the calluses on her palms. Tomorrow, and the next day, and the next, she would not have to haul water from the well. Without the chore of hauling water, she could catch up with the library.

By morning, the sky was blue again and steam rose from the damp earth. Terpsichore sped down the straw path to her pumpkins to see how they had enjoyed the rain. With three weeks to go until the weigh-in at the fair, Almanzo and Laura were already as tall as Cally and Polly, and were sure to be the biggest entry in the contest. The twenty-five dollars was almost as good as hers. But even with twenty-five dollars for the biggest vegetable, she would be fifty dollars short.

She leaned against Laura. How would she raise the rest of the money she needed to buy the piano? Some kids were making root beer to sell at the fair. Mendel had been mounting butterfly specimens to exhibit, and Gloria and her mother were going to make pies and cookies to sell. Was there something Terpsichore could sell to tourists before Miss Zelinsky sold the piano to the next person who wanted to buy it? Thinking about leaving the money-raising to the last days of the fair gave her stomach cramps.

After breakfast, she headed to the teachers' dormitory on the other side of the tracks to collect the key to the school from Miss Fromer. Once inside the school, she locked the main doors to the school behind her. The halls still smelled like the floor polish that the CCC workers had used to wax the floors after school let out. Even though there was no one to hear, she tiptoed to the shelf-lined workroom that housed books waiting to be processed for the library.

When she opened the door to the workroom she was dismayed by how far behind she had become in the weeks she had been tending pumpkins. Dozens of boxes of books had arrived from groups down below and were stacked up higgledy-piggledy all over the room.

She shoved boxes right and left to clear a path between the shelving and the door. As she shuffled boxes, she read some of the return addresses: the Wisconsin branch of the American Red Cross, a Lutheran church in Minneapolis, and women's book groups in Chicago, Seattle, Denver, and New York. With a serrated knife, she cut the twine securing three of the boxes and started sorting books onto mostly empty shelves. She put children's books and magazines on one wall, grown-up fiction on another wall, and intermixed nonfiction on another. Some boxes were full of boring stuff, like old school textbooks, but even among those she found one book on bugs and butterflies Mendel would like.

Sunlight beamed through the windows above the shelves. As the sun rose toward noon, the room got hot, which brought out the musty smell of the old books. She quickly shelved duplicates of best-sellers of a few years ago, but lingered on a book from the last century on elocution, which had drawings of the gestures to make to signify surprise, wonder, horror, and sadness. Gloria would get a laugh from that one. She'd also want to see issues of movie magazines that were only a few months old.

When she came to half a dozen cookbooks, she sat down on one of the boxes and flipped to the index of each book to see if there were any ways to use pumpkin and salmon she had never tried. All the books had pumpkin pie and variations of the recipes she had developed herself, but there were a few new ideas, like pumpkin gingerbread, pumpkin butter that sounded like it would produce something like jam, and pumpkin bread pudding. Reading the recipes set her stomach to rumbling.

Terpsichore thought of all the strange recipes she'd collected since they moved to Palmer. She had developed a dozen unique ways to fix canned salmon. And there was Mr. Crawford's recipe for jellied moose nose that she hadn't been brave enough to try yet. With all those recipes and a few more local specialties, she could make a souvenir cookbook tourists might buy. She stood, squinting into the window at the sky that was beginning to cloud over. She wasn't seeing sun and clouds, though; she was seeing tourists thronging to her booth to buy copies of her cookbook. If she sold enough, she could buy the piano for sure.

She turned away from the window. She could only sell recipe books if she could print them. How could she make enough copies? Maybe Miss Quimby would let her use the mimeograph machine in the office. She was grateful now that Mother had made her apologize to Miss Quimby so they were on good terms again.

She would have to decide which recipes to include. Mendel had perfect printing, and had run the office mimeograph machine for the teachers, so he could help run copies. Gloria could help her design the cover, and she knew Pop would help get the pumpkin to the fair.

She finally had a plan to raise all the money for the piano. But she wouldn't know if either part of her plan worked until the last day of the fair, when Miss Zelinsky might sell the piano to someone else.

CHAPTER 43

Tragedy

Terpsichore let out a howl that could probably have been heard in Anchorage. Mother dropped her hoe in the patch of beets, picked up Matthew, and came running. "What's wrong?" she said. She dropped Matthew so she could examine Terpsichore's hands and check her feet to make sure Terpsichore still had all her fingers and toes.

At seeing Terpsichore's tears and moaning, Matthew screwed up his face and howled. "Tip sad," he said. He reached out to Terpsichore to pat her, like Mother did when he was sad.

Mother put her hands on Terpsichore's shoulders and bent down to Terpsichore's eye level. "Tell me, what is it?"

Between hiccoughs, Terpsichore got out, "It's 'Manzo, 'Manzo." She dropped to her knees in the mud that had formed in the last two days of rain and hugged Almanzo, leaning her cheek against his ribbed side and mixing her tears with the last drops of rain.

"Almanzo . . . your pumpkin? You're crying about a pumpkin? You nearly scared me into heart failure!"

"But Almanzo was the biggest," Terpsichore said. "He was already three inches bigger around than Laura, but with this last rain he must have soaked up so much water that he grew so fast he . . . he . . ." Terpsichore couldn't bear to say it.

Mother ran her fingers around the top of the pumpkin, and then walked around to the back where her fingers felt a fissure down the side. The skin had burst, exposing the flesh beneath.

Terpsichore continued to sob. Mother pulled her up out of the mud. "I know you've worked hard all summer on these pumpkins, but you still have another pumpkin. And think of all the pumpkin muffins you'll be able to make."

Terpsichore looked up, her forehead wrinkled and her mouth in a scandalized *O*. "Eat Almanzo?" She'd cooked pumpkins before, but never one she had talked to and named.

"Terpsichore, it's a pumpkin. People grow pumpkins to eat. If this is how you react to eating pumpkins you've grown, how on earth are you going to face eating a piglet if we get pigs, or a lamb?"

Matthew started to chant, "This little piggy . . ."

Terpsichore howled even louder. "Not a piglet! Not a lamb!"

"Why did you think we raise animals here?" her mother asked. "We'd better go back to Wisconsin before you have to face the hard facts of farm life."

"Wisconsin? Noooooo." If Mother had thought she was

244

already crying as hard as a person could cry, Terpsichore proved her wrong.

Mother gave up on consoling Terpsichore, picked up Matthew, and strode back to the kitchen garden. Terpsichore was alone again with her pumpkins.

"I'm so sorry, Almanzo." She kissed the gash in his side as if to make it well, but she knew no Band-Aid could fix Almanzo. Once a pumpkin was split, it would stay split, and be disqualified from the competition. She wiped her nose on her sleeve and took a deep breath.

With feet slowed by mud and dread, Terpsichore picked her way between her two champion pumpkins. Would Laura also be split? She ran her hands along Laura's skin as she slowly circled her last giant pumpkin. Laura was intact.

It was all up to Laura now. Terpsichore was glad school wasn't starting this year until after the fair, so she could devote full time to her only remaining pumpkin. "If I hear of frost coming, I'll cover you with a horse blanket. If it rains, I'll stand here with an umbrella, I'll talk to you at least an hour every day, and when I run out of things to say, I'll read to you. I'll read all the most inspiring stories: the chapter of *Farmer Boy* when his pumpkin wins first prize at the fair, the part in *Black Beauty* when he's rescued by Farmer Thoroughgood, and "Jack and the Beanstalk," with the stalk that grows to the sky . . . Well, not the last part." Terpsichore remembered just in time how Jack chopped down the beanstalk at the end. Laura was too young and innocent for such violence.

CHAPTER 44

The Deadline Looms

By the end of August, evenings were already getting chilly enough for a fire. Terpsichore sat with a tablet and a pencil, doodling possible names for her cookbook. Tigger occasionally roused herself from half napping on Terpsichore's lap to bat at the end of her pencil.

What to Do with a Two-Hundred-Pound Pumpkin?

Jellied Moose Nose and Rhubarb Pie?

Cabbage Patch Soup and Eskimo Ice Cream?

The Best Souvenir of the First Palmer Fair?

None of the titles sounded right.

She leaned back against the pillows she'd stacked against the wooden arm of the settee and stared out the window at Pioneer Peak for inspiration. Polly sat cross-legged on the braided rug in front of the woodstove, leaning over to stroke Willa behind the ears. Willa sighed and stretched in kitten bliss. Cally sat with Rogers on her lap. With one hand she petted Rogers just enough to keep him purring, but her attention was firmly on the Sears catalog, open to a page of horse equipment. Rogers meowed a complaint when she stood, dumping him to the floor.

"Smoky is going to need a blanket before winter, and I found the perfect one for him." She walked over to the table to show the page to her father.

Pop sat at the kitchen table, making lists of all the supplies that would be needed to build the new church. He sketched, scribbled figures, and erased, figuring and refiguring. He looked up, grinning. "Yankee doodle dandy!" he said. "Guess how many peeled logs we'll need to build the new church?"

"But Pop," Cally said, "see this blanket? This is exactly what Smoky needs. Can we order it?"

Pop crossed the room to rub Mother's neck. "Don't you want to know how many logs we're going to need for the new church?"

"But what about a blanket for Smoky?" Cally persisted.

Pop dropped his hands. "Doesn't anyone want to know how many logs we're going to need?"

Terpsichore closed her tablet. "Okeydokey, Pop. How many logs *will* it take to build the new church?"

Pop smiled at Terpsichore. "If all the logs are at least twenty feet long and at least eight inches in diameter, it will take a thousand . . . give or take a few," he said.

"Wow, a thousand," Cally and Polly said.

"That's nice," Mother said. "But I thought work on the walls and roof wouldn't start until late this fall, and you know, we might be gone by then."

"Clio, you said you'd wait until after the harvest fair to give your vote. Who knows what might happen between now and then?" Pop said.

"I'd almost forgotten that we might not stay," Cally said sadly. She closed the catalog and put it back on the bookshelf.

"Me too," Polly said. She snuggled Willa against her neck, and Willa licked Polly's face in return.

"Well, I most emphatically have not forgotten," Mother said. "And neither has your grandmother."

She put down the old sweater she was unraveling into a ball of yarn to reuse, and took the latest letter from her mother from her apron pocket. She read one line from the letter:

"'I'll be up by the last week of August to bring you all home to Madison. I so look forward to having you here with me!'"

Mother laid the letter on the kitchen table. She was smiling, but nobody else was.

"If we move back to Grandmother's house, we won't get to take Smoky," Cally said.

"And not even Tigger and Willa and Rogers," Polly said.

Terpsichore slipped off the couch to confront her mother. "That's not what you said before! You said you'd wait until after the fair to vote!"

"What difference does a few days make? Once she gets here, I know she won't want to stay very long."

Terpsichore wrung her hands. "But you said you'd wait until *after* the fair!"

"You did say you'd wait to vote until after the fair," Pop said.

Terpsichore put her hands together in thanks to her father for sticking up for her. "Yes, Mom, you never know what might happen at the fair."

Terpsichore led the twins upstairs so they could talk privately. Both twins sat on Cally's cot in their bedroom. Terpsichore sat cross-legged on the floor beside the bed. "I don't want to leave Alaska," she said.

"We don't either!" the twins chorused.

"I have a plan that I hope will work," she said. "And maybe you both could help. One of the things Mom misses most is her piano. Miss Zelinsky is selling hers, and if I can earn seventy-five dollars by the end of the fair I can buy it for Mother."

"How can you earn that much money?" Cally asked.

"I plan to win the twenty-five dollars for the biggest vegetable at the fair."

"But that's not enough," Polly said.

"I know, but I also thought of something I can sell at the fair—a book of my Alaska recipes. If I can sell one hundred cookbooks at fifty cents apiece, I'll have enough to buy the piano from Miss Zelinsky by the last day of the fair."

"How can you make a cookbook?" they asked.

"Mendel has tidy printing, and he's going to write out all the recipes. Gloria has drawn a picture for the cover. And we'll make copies on the mimeograph machine at school. My giant pumpkin will help bring people to the booth, but once they get close, how else can we get attention for the cookbook?"

"You need a jingle too, like on the radio," Polly said.

"Pumpkins . . ." Cally started. "Polly, do you remember the song we learned in class last year, the one about the pies with crazy stuff in them?"

"'The Pumpkin Pies That Grandma Used to Bake'?" Polly said.

The two began to sing:

> *"My grandma was a wizard*
> *At baking pumpkin pies;*
> *The things you would find in them*
> *Were surely a surprise!"*

"Only we can change the 'grandma' to our sister," Cally said.

"And the things that get baked into the pies to things that are more Alaskan . . ."

"Like ice skates or dogsleds . . ."

"Like salmon and snowflakes . . ."

Cally and Polly slid off the bed to hug Terpsichore from both sides. "If we could keep Smoky and the cats *and* have a piano again, it would be perfect!"

"It sure would!" said Terpsichore.

"Leave it to us," the twins said.

CHAPTER 45

Laura's Moving Day

Two days before the fair, Terpsichore borrowed her mother's tape measure. She and Gloria tiptoed into the field, as if afraid to wake Laura from her beauty sleep.

Gloria's arm looked spindly compared to Laura's stem. "That stem must be as thick as a lumberjack's arm," Gloria said.

"Let's see just how big she is today." Terpsichore took a carpenter's pencil from the side pocket of her overalls and made a light line on the skin of her pumpkin at the widest point, careful not to press too hard and make a dent in Laura's hide.

"Here," she said. "Hold the end of the tape here while I walk around with the rest of it."

Gloria held the tape while Terpsichore walked around Laura, careful to keep the tape level all the way. "There's two hundred . . ." Terpsichore said, "two hundred and seven! And she'll probably grow another four inches tonight."

"Mr. Hopstadt next to our place claims he's going to win for his cabbage," Gloria said. "I think he's been training the outer leaves to stretch out sideways as far as they'll go without cracking."

"But that's just stretching across empty air; that doesn't count."

"Maybe, maybe not," Gloria said. "Did the contest rules say they'd judge size by leaf-span or weight?"

Sweat broke out on Terpsichore's forehead and trickled down under her bangs. "The rule book didn't say," she said.

"Don't worry," Gloria said.

Gloria wanted to be an actress, but she wasn't convincing Terpsichore not to worry.

"How are you going to get it to the fairgrounds?" Both girls turned to see Mendel stepping over withering pumpkin vines.

"Pop said he'd help," Terpsichore said. "And he's going to borrow a truck and get some of his friends to help too."

Mendel laid both hands against the pumpkin, braced his feet in a giant step, and threw his whole weight into a push. The pumpkin did not budge. "Just as I thought," he said. "This pumpkin is going to take more than brute strength. It's going to take mechanical assistance. I'll rig something up tonight and meet you tomorrow morning. What time should I be here?"

"Thanks, Mendel! If you can make a house fly across the stage, you can figure out a way to move a pumpkin. I know you can! Seven tomorrow?"

"I'll take care of it," Mendel said.

• • •

The next morning, Terpsichore walked out to Laura with an old towel draped around her shoulders. One hand clutched a bucket of water. The other hand held a hacksaw behind her back. After hiding the hacksaw under a shriveled pumpkin leaf, she swabbed Laura with a sponge and rubbed her down with the towel. Terpsichore stood back to admire the result.

"You're a beaut!" she said. How could anyone disagree? Laura had turned a classic yellow-orange, a little lopsided, but just enough to give her character. Terpsichore squinted, imagining wheels, a door, and Cinderella peeping out the window on the way to the ball. With a sigh, Terpsichore stepped forward to lean her cheek against Laura's burnished side and stretch her arms out to hold as much pumpkin as she could in a hug.

"This had to come eventually," she whispered. "I'll make the cut as quickly and painlessly as I can."

Hands shaking, she picked up the hacksaw from where she'd hidden it. "Don't be afraid, Laura. It'll be kind of like a baby getting its umbilical cord cut so it can go out into the world. You're going to get a ride in the truck to the fairgrounds so everyone can see you. Everyone will admire you, and say what a beautiful pumpkin you are. And best of all, you'll win the money that will buy the piano that will make Mom want to stay. That's a good thing, isn't it?"

Terpsichore hadn't thought this step out well. Even with her belly snugged up against Laura's side, the stem was an arm's length away, and at shoulder height, she couldn't get full strength on the blade. The first timid pass with the end of the saw barely dented the surface of the prickly stem.

She lowered the saw in defeat.

"Let me," Pop said.

Terpsichore turned, and surrendered the hacksaw to her father, who had followed her out to the field. "Thanks," she said.

With her father's height and longer, stronger arms, he severed the stem in a few decisive passes with the saw. He pulled the loose vine away from the pumpkin's side.

Terpsichore felt the comforting weight of her father's hand on her shoulder. "You did a mighty fine job with this pumpkin," he said. "I'm proud of you, Terpsichore."

"Do you think she'll win?" Terpsichore asked. She looked up at his face to see if he was telling her what he believed or what she wanted to hear.

"I can't imagine anyone's growing anything bigger," he said. He looked like he meant it. "Mr. Crawford has a pickup and we can get a couple guys to help load her in." He lifted his hand from Terpsichore's shoulder to point to the edge of the vegetable garden. "Not sure how I'm going to get the truck here without running over some of the vegetable patch, though. We could run it through the chard or the spinach or the kale . . ."

Terpsichore's mouth convulsed at the thought of kale. "I vote for kale," she said.

Pop laughed. "Me too."

Both turned at the sound of Mr. Crawford's truck. And

just behind Mr. Crawford was Mendel with a tractor with a forklift. Terpsichore waved. "Hooray!"

"The whole crew's here," Pop said. "I think we're ready."

Mendel pulled out an armload of supplies from the floor of the forklift. The tractor driver and Mr. Crawford slid a heavy beam out of the back of the pickup, carried it up next to Laura, and went back for another.

Mendel set down a heap of four-inch webbing, block and tackle, and a heavy iron hook. "I've worked it all out with Mr. Crawford," he said. "We'll lift the pumpkin with a net of webbing and set her down in the back of the pickup. It's sort of like the way they hoisted livestock on and off the *St. Mihiel*."

Terpsichore watched her father and Mr. Crawford erect a tripod over Laura, wrap her in a harness of heavy webbing, and hook the top of the webbing to the iron hook at the end of a length of chain.

Terpsichore wrung her hands as, with a rattle and a clank, Laura began to rise.

She gasped in relief when gently, as gently as putting a baby in its crib, the hoist swung over the back of the pickup and Laura was laid on its nest of straw and quilts.

Terpsichore clambered up on the back to ride with Laura to the fairgrounds.

CHAPTER 46

The Great Weigh-In

Terpsichore and Gloria stood in the back of the pickup as it approached the weighing station by the train depot. Mr. Crawford couldn't get through the mass of people to get the pickup in line, so he pulled over at the edge of the crowd. Wheelbarrows were lined up with Laura's competition. Pumpkins weren't the only things that grew big in Alaska.

They listened to all the weigh-in results. "Seventy-five pounds!" Gloria said. "That rutabaga weighs almost as much as I do!"

"That may be big for a rutabaga, but it's no match for a giant pumpkin," Terpsichore said.

"You said it! But vegetables sure grow big in Alaska! That zucchini is as big as your brother! And it's taking two people to lift that cantaloupe!"

Gloria's voice dropped to a whisper as she grabbed

Terpsichore's arm and pointed to an approaching pickup truck. "Uh-oh! That's the man I was talking about."

Terpsichore watched as two men crawled out of the truck and lifted the cabbage out of the back. It had a leaf-spread wider than a tall man's arm span.

Terpsichore held her breath as the cabbage was weighed. "Only forty-five pounds," she said. "It is wide, but only the center weighs anything. The rest is just leaves stretched out to look big." She could breathe again.

The one other pumpkin was big, but no match for Laura. It was only ninety-eight pounds.

The judges were almost ready to call an end to the weigh-in when Terpsichore yelled out from the back of the pickup. "Hey, I've got a pumpkin too, but I need to clear a path to the scale because it's too heavy to lift."

Pop and Mendel held back the crowd as Mr. Crawford edged the pickup toward the loading dock. Terpsichore fought back the urge to cover her eyes as Pop and Mendel and one of the judges positioned the padded forklift under the edge of Laura to move her from the back of the pickup to the scale on the loading platform.

"Hello, old-timer. Is this your pumpkin?" a judge asked.

"I'm just the delivery boy," Mr. Crawford said. "Here's the grower."

"You? And your name, young lady?" the judge asked.

Terpsichore climbed up to the loading platform with Laura. "Miss Terpsichore Johnson," she said. "Lot number seventy-seven."

"Terp what?"

"Terp-sick-oh-ree," she said, speaking directly into the judge's microphone. "And my pumpkin's name is Laura."

The crowd laughed, then went silent as everyone watched the red arrow on the scale zip past fifty pounds, eighty pounds, one hundred pounds, two hundred pounds, and came to a quavering rest at two hundred and ninety-three pounds.

Terpsichore flushed as admiring oohs and aahs echoed through the crowd. Laura had surely won.

The judges conferred for a moment and one of them shouted out, "We have a winner! A two-hundred-ninety-three-pound pumpkin!"

The man with the cabbage stormed up to the platform. "Just a minute here! This contest was for the biggest *vegetable* grown in Palmer, and pumpkin is not a vegetable, it's a fruit. And why are we bothering with a weigh-in anyway? Big means measuring tape big, not how much something weighs."

Terpsichore scrambled off the loading platform to confront Mr. Cabbage Man. She barely reached the snaps on his overall straps, but her voice was just as loud. "If it's not animal or mineral, it's vegetable! And my pumpkin weighs more than your cabbage. It's bigger!" She put her hands on her hips in a so-there attitude.

Mr. Cabbage Man leaned over so he was eye to eye with Terpsichore. "The rules said the prize goes to the biggest." He stood and stretched his arms out like an eagle in flight. "My cabbage's leaf spread is pert-near six feet."

"But my pumpkin weighs over two hundred pounds."

Mr. Cabbage Man didn't back down. "Rules say ve-ge-ta-ble and rules say biggest, not heaviest," he said. He looked over his shoulder to make sure the judges were listening to his defense of his cabbage.

Terpsichore looked toward her cheering section. Mom, Matthew, and the twins were all at the apple pie booth that was earning money for new textbooks for the school, so it was just Pop, Mr. Crawford, Gloria, and Mendel. Pop raised his eyebrows and pointed to his chest, silently asking her if she wanted him to take over her defense, but Terpsichore shook her head. This was her pumpkin and her fight. Mendel was riffling through the rule book, probably trying to find another argument for her.

Mr. Cabbage Man trotted out his final argument. "Besides," he said, pointing to his cheering section, which consisted of eight stairstep children who all had his pointed nose and lank, sawdust-colored hair, "my wife died of pneumonia last winter and I have eight children to feed. What would you do with the money, buy a Shirley Temple doll?"

Terpsichore shook her head, but she was biting her lips shut against bawling and could not answer.

At first the crowd had been sympathetic toward Terpsichore, harassed and out-talked by a grown-up. But when the crowd turned toward the man's children, they chorused "Awww," and Terpsichore knew there was no point in pursuing her fight.

The judges huddled over the rule book.

Then the head judge stepped toward the microphone.

"After serious deliberation and careful reading of the rules, we have decided the prize goes to the biggest—not heaviest—true vegetable, the cabbage, with a circumference of two hundred and twenty-six inches!"

Mr. Cabbage Man's supporters applauded. But many in the audience muttered in disapproval. The judge wiped his brow and held up his hand. "But we decided that this young lady's pumpkin deserves recognition too, so she will be awarded a blue ribbon for best in category and a five-dollar prize." He smiled anxiously, hoping this acknowledgment would placate everyone. It did not. Several clusters of folks trickled away, muttering their disagreement. "The little girl should have won . . . just a technicality."

Terpsichore forced a smile, held her head high, and strode to the podium to collect her ribbon and five dollars.

CHAPTER 47

The Interview

Pop hugged Terpsichore. "A blue ribbon for best in category! That's great, Terpsichore."

Mendel and Gloria also tried to cheer her up, but Terpsichore could not be cheered, not after working so hard and losing. "But only five dollars. I needed twenty-five." Her grandmother would arrive later today, so it was beginning to look like the Johnsons would be back in Madison, Wisconsin, within a week unless Terpsichore could find a way to make up for the other twenty dollars she did not win.

Only a few yards away, a journalist from the *Anchorage Daily Times* was interviewing Mr. Cabbage Man and his eight children. While the man posed with his arms outstretched behind his cabbage, showing just how big it was, the photographer took his picture. Fame was only for the winners, not the runners-up.

But maybe not. Now the reporter headed toward Terpsichore.

"Terpsichore, maybe he'll take your picture too!" Gloria finger-combed her hair and made sure her collar was at its best rakish, propped-up angle.

Mendel positioned himself next to the pumpkin and spread one arm proprietarily across the top.

The reporter held out his hand to Pop. "I'm Scoop Swanson, *Anchorage Daily Times*."

"I'm Mr. Johnson, the proud father of this champion pumpkin grower, Terpsichore Johnson."

"That's some moniker, little lady. And it looks as if you grow pumpkins even bigger than your name." He took out his notebook. "Terpsich . . . something . . . that was one of those Greek goddesses, wasn't it?"

"Terpsichore was the Muse of Dance," she told him. "That's T-e-r-p-s-i-c-h-o-r-e."

"You grew this pumpkin all by yourself?" The reporter flipped his notebook to another page and took his pencil from behind his ear.

"Pretty much," Terpsichore said. "I started the seeds, made my own compost from the chicken coop droppings, and watered nearly every day."

"But I helped battle the squash bugs," Mendel said.

"And this champion pumpkin grower also has a book of her own Alaska recipes for sale tomorrow when we get the pumpkin back to the booth!" Gloria said.

"Whoa," the reporter said. "Let's start with the pumpkin grower herself. Mind if I take some pictures?" He looked to

Pop for approval. Pop nodded yes and stepped out of the range of the camera.

"You don't mind, either, do you, Laura?" Terpsichore reached out to rub her stem end.

"Laura?"

"I named her after Laura in *Little House on the Prairie*. The man she grew up to marry, Almanzo Wilder in *Farmer Boy*, grew a prize-winning pumpkin."

"Any secrets to growing the prize-winning pumpkin?"

"Well, I started the seedlings indoors, and when it was safely past frost I transplanted them outdoors. I thinned the seedlings to the strongest and pruned each vine to the biggest pumpkin so all the energy could go to producing a giant. I lost Almanzo, that was my other giant, when he soaked up so much water he split, but I saved Laura from squash bugs . . ."

"With my help," said Mendel.

"Yes. With Mendel's help," Terpsichore agreed, "and I carried a hundred gallons of water a week from the well and fed her compost and talked to her every day . . ."

"Talking, huh? What do you say to a pumpkin?" the reporter asked.

"Sometimes I just complimented them on how big and healthy they looked, or read the chapter in *Farmer Boy* when Almanzo's pumpkin won the blue ribbon, to inspire them, you know? And I explained what I was doing when I started feeding them buttermilk . . ."

"Now, just a minute." The reporter pulled his glasses down

on his nose and looked skeptically at Terpsichore. "How do you feed a pumpkin buttermilk?"

She leaned way over Laura to point out a tiny slit in the stem. "See? That's where I poked the string that wicked the buttermilk from a pie pan to the stem and on into Laura. And it worked. Just like it did for Almanzo."

The reporter shook his head as he wrote down what Terpsichore said. "Buttermilk feeding and talking . . ." He looked up again to ask, "What were you planning to do with the money? If you're anything like my little sister, you were saving for new school clothes, right?"

Terpsichore huffed indignantly. "It wasn't for anything for me. It's something for my mother, so she'll want to stay in Alaska. But it's a secret."

"Won't you tell me?"

"A secret is a secret. Can't you just print what I said: that it's something for my mother so she won't vote for us to move back to Wisconsin."

"So you like it here, huh?"

"Yes! And the rest of the family all wants to stay. Pop's worked hard to make us a home here and my sisters have a horse named Smoky, and my cat Tigger and her kittens like it in Alaska, and I can have a big garden, and my friends are here and . . ."

"Readers will want to know: what do you plan to do now with . . . Laura?"

"I hope she'll attract customers to our booth. I'll be selling my Alaska cookbook there tomorrow, with recipes for birch bark syrup, lots of pumpkin and berry and salmon recipes, of course, and even jellied moose nose."

"Jellied moose nose? I've heard of it, but does anyone really make it?"

Terpsichore grinned. "I haven't tried it either, but according to an old-timer friend from the valley, it's quite a delicacy."

The reporter hunched over his notebook, making notes before he looked up again. "How much are you selling your recipe books for?"

"Fifty cents," she said.

Gloria and Mendel, who had impatiently remained quiet for the last couple of minutes, both piped in:

"With covers by Gloria!"

"And elegant calligraphy by Mendel Peterson!"

"Do you want your friend to stay in Alaska?" The reporter turned to them, ready to record quotes.

"Absolutely-tootly," Gloria said.

"Without question," Mendel said.

The journalist asked, "How many copies of your recipe book did you make?"

"A hundred," Terpsichore said. She realized as she said it that now that she hadn't won the twenty-five dollars, that wouldn't be enough. She'd need to sell another forty copies to have enough to buy the piano, and another twenty to pay back the school for supplies.

As if reading her mind, the reporter said, "I think you'd better make another hundred. After one of these pictures of you and Laura appears in tonight's paper, and I write about how you need that money for a surprise for your mother so she'll want to stay in Alaska, I suspect you'll get a lot of business tomorrow."

The boards beneath their feet on the loading dock beside the railroad station began to vibrate, and a shrill whistle broke into Terpsichore's calculations of how much paper she'd need to print a hundred more copies of her recipe book.

Before Gloria and Mendel could leave to find their families, Terpsichore pulled them aside. "Did you hear what the reporter said about the newspaper article helping us sell lots more recipe books? We need more copies by tomorrow, and with Grandmother coming I won't be able to get away!"

"If I can get the key from one of the teachers, I can run more copies in the school office," Mendel said.

"And I can put the pages in order and staple them," Gloria said.

Terpsichore squeezed their hands. "I knew I could count on you!"

CHAPTER 48

Grandmother

With a shriek, brakes slowed the train to a stop just in front of the Johnsons. The engines hissed and enveloped them in steam.

As soon as the train came to a complete stop, the conductor pulled down the steps at the door of the passenger car and spread his arms to cordon off clear passage for those getting off. Terpsichore shuffled back a few steps.

Mother held up Matthew so he could see over the grown-ups' shoulders. "Grandma's coming," she said. "Wave to Grandma."

Matthew waved both hands at everyone getting off. Just when Terpsichore was beginning to think Grandmother had missed the train, a porter descended the steps lugging two monogrammed leather suitcases. He set those down with a thump. Then, both he and the conductor reached out a hand to assist the tall woman in an ermine coat down the two steps onto the platform.

Mother thrust Matthew into Pop's arms so she could wave with both hands. "Mother, Mother, we're here!"

The sun, at a low angle above the mountains, put a golden glow on Mother's face, but some of that glow also radiated from inside. She looked so happy! Terpsichore hadn't thought about how much her mother must have missed her own mother, thousands of miles away.

Mother led her mother back to the rest of the Johnsons and took back Matthew so she could reintroduce him to his grandmother. "Matthew is two now, and already knows all his letters."

Grandmother cooed approvingly and reached out to touch Matthew's hair. "He's perfect!" she said. Matthew shyly buried his head in Mother's shoulder.

"Oh dear," Grandmother said. "I see I should have come up sooner. A little boy should always know his own grandmother. And the twins, Calliope and Polyhymnia! What little beauties you've become!" Grandmother stooped to take one twin in each arm for a hug. Last, she turned to Terpsichore.

"Well," she said, "here is Terpsichore, our junior librarian."

"Your books helped us off to a good start, Grandmother," Terpsichore said. "Thanks!"

"Not only a junior librarian but a blue-ribbon pumpkin-grower," Pop added, and pointed to Terpsichore's pumpkin, still on the loading scale and sporting a blue ribbon rosette on its stem.

"It's very . . . big," Grandmother said as she took a closer look at the blue ribbon. "Congratulations!"

When Grandmother hugged her, Terpsichore felt the silkiness of her fur coat against her cheek. The fragrance of Grandmother's Joy perfume brought the memory of the other scents of Grandmother's house: beeswax polish, bouquets of flowers from her garden, and the bread her cook baked every day.

Pop took Grandmother's coat as they walked to the wagon. Beneath her coat she wore a bias-cut frock of silk crepe. Her only concession to being in Palmer instead of her mansion in Madison was her low-heeled oxfords instead of high-heeled shoes. "I thought you'd have three feet of snow by now," she said.

"Snow will come around late September or early October," Pop said. "And we had a couple of days last month that were nearly ninety degrees."

"Well," Grandmother said, still looking around as if she suspected snow was lurking somewhere. "This isn't what I expected."

As they approached the wagon, Cally and Polly ran ahead to greet Smoky. He whinnied a greeting and lowered his head so Cally could rub his forehead between the eyes and around the ears. Polly combed her fingers through his mane.

"Did you miss us?" they crooned.

Grandmother looked warily up at Smoky. "Do horses grow bigger in Alaska too?" she asked.

"He's a Percheron," Polly said.

"They're always big," Cally said. "And wonderful!"

Grandmother took a skittish step back. "My father had horses, but none like this."

"Don't worry, he's gentle," Polly said. To prove it, she pulled a carrot out of her pocket and held it on the flat of her hand so Smoky could take it gently with his lips.

Pop helped Grandmother up to the middle of the wagon seat. She checked the wood for splinters (there were none; Terpsichore knew her father had burnished it smooth as a mirror) before settling down and reclaiming her coat.

Grandmother relaxed as they approached the house. "At least you have a house now instead of a tent," she said.

Mother led her mother into the house and took her upstairs. Terpsichore had moved into the twins' bedroom with a pallet so Grandmother could have Terpsichore's room during her visit.

After Grandmother unpacked and came back downstairs, Terpsichore asked, "Would you like to see the farm?"

"Your grandmother is probably tired from her trip," Mother said.

"Nonsense," Grandmother said. "I'd love a tour from the girls."

Terpsichore and the twins took Grandmother back outside to show her the farm.

"This was the first building Pop built," Terpsichore said as they passed the chicken coop.

"Pop said we would have had to sleep in it ourselves if the house didn't get built before winter," Cally said.

Grandmother shook her head in dismay at the thought of living in a chicken coop.

"And here's the barn," Polly said.

"We got to sleep in the loft of the barn while the house was being built," Cally said.

Terpsichore remembered cuddling together with the twins, with the smell of hay and newly sawn wood. In Wisconsin, the twins had always seemed in their own world, with no need for anyone else. Alaska brought them all together.

Grandmother was less skittish around Clarabelle, the milk cow, than she had been around Smoky, who was now settled into his stall. "I remember getting up early to milk our Maisy," Grandmother said.

"You milked a cow?" Terpsichore couldn't imagine her grandmother in her silk dresses milking a cow. But of course she wasn't born a grown-up. She had been a girl once too. What had that girl been like?

"I grew up on a farm," she told them. "I wasn't always a matron of the Assistance League and Friends of the Opera." She looked appraisingly at the barn, closed her eyes, and inhaled. "I remember the smell of a clean barn, the warmth of Maisy's flank against my cheek as I milked her, half asleep. My mother always said milking gave me strong piano hands." She held out her hands, with their buffed fingernails and rings that glittered even in the dim evening light of the barn.

"That was a lifetime ago," Grandmother said. "But seeing what you've done here makes me remember my years growing up on the farm. I was happy then. Are you happy too, on this farm in Alaska?" She looked at each of the girls.

"We are! We are!" Terpsichore joined the twins in reply.

They all paused on the way back to the house so Grandmother could admire the plowed fields and the remains of the kitchen garden.

Once inside the house again, Grandmother said, "I didn't expect to be impressed, but I am. In a little over a year you've established a tidy little farm. You must miss your piano, though, Clio. It's a shame you and the girls don't have one here in Alaska. Every year counts when a young person shows such promise." She shook her head over the tragedy of wasted talent.

Then Grandmother sighed. "But I suppose there are worse things. I miss you all. It gets lonely sometimes in that big old house by myself. A house with just one person doesn't seem like a home."

CHAPTER 49

A Knock at the Door

When the knock finally came, Terpsichore ran to the door. She closed it behind her just as Gloria and Mendel gently set down the cardboard box they carried.

"Here you go," Gloria whispered.

"We ran out of paper, so it's only thirty more," Mendel said.

"Only thirty?" Terpsichore's temples pounded.

"I know that's not going to be enough," Mendel said. "But we tried, we really did."

"Miss Zelinsky even stayed at the school to help us with the mimeograph machine," Gloria said.

"If you don't make enough money with the recipe books, we'll help make up the difference," Mendel said. "Today in the craft hall, a tourist saw my *Erebia rossii* and *Pieris angelika* butterflies you can only find in the far north. He's offered to buy them."

"And I could sell my autographed movie star photos," Gloria said.

"But I can't ask you to give up your best butterflies and movie star collection," Terpsichore said. "You've already done so much. Thank you for trying." Tears pricked her eyes.

"I'd rather part with my collection than my best friend," Gloria said.

"And a couple of dead butterflies," Mendel added.

They draped their arms around each other and touched their heads in the middle. When they drew back, Terpsichore said, "I still don't . . ."

"We don't want you to go," Gloria said.

"You're the best," Terpsichore said. She opened the door and shoved the box into the room with one foot. She stood for a moment at the open door, watching Gloria and Mendel head home before she shut the door.

"Who was that?" Pop asked.

"Gloria and Mendel," Terpsichore said. She leaned over to shove the box a little farther into the room. "Pop," she said, "could you haul this box upstairs for me?" With only thirty copies, she could have carried the box herself, but she wanted to get Pop away from Mother so she could explain her project and how she might need his help at the fair.

Pop picked up the box and started up the stairs with it. Cally and Polly clomped upstairs too.

With Pop and the twins looking on, Terpsichore unfurled the crosshatched flaps of the box of thirty copies of her Alaska cookbook. Her nose wrinkled at the smell of mimeograph fluid. Her forehead wrinkled in concentration as she did the figures in her head. Five dollars from the pumpkin prize, fifty dollars from the one hundred recipe books she'd already printed, fifteen dollars from this batch . . . She was still five dollars short of enough to buy the piano, and she also had to pay the school back for the supplies she'd used. How could she make up the difference? And what if she didn't even sell all the recipe books?

Pop picked up the top copy of the recipe book and flipped through it. "Jellied moose nose? I'm not sure if I want to try that one," he said. "Terpsichore, do these recipe books have anything to do with your secret plan to make your mother vote to stay in Alaska?"

Cally and Polly bounced on their cots. "They do! Terpsichore's going to buy Miss Zelinsky's piano. With the bathroom you built *and* a piano she'll be happy here, won't she?"

Pop shook his head and dropped the book back in the box. "Hmm. I just don't know."

Cally and Polly stopped bouncing on the beds. Terpsichore drooped, then straightened. "But if I do earn enough money for the piano, can you pick it up from Miss Zelinsky? Once Mom sees the piano . . ."

"When I see how much your mother has missed her mother, and how much your grandmother looks forward to having us with her, I don't know if even a piano will make a difference," Pop said. "You can count on me to get the piano moved, though."

He hugged each of his Muses in turn. "Give it your all, Terpsichore. At least we'll know we tried."

CHAPTER 50

The Fair, Day Two

PALMER WAS AT ITS BEST THE NEXT MORNING. THE SKY was cerulean blue. The Chugach and Talkeetna Mountains, frosted with early snow, guarded the Matanuska Valley. As the gates opened for day two of the fair, many tourists clutched a copy of the *Anchorage Daily Times* with the picture of Terpsichore and her pumpkin, Laura, on the first page.

Laura rested proudly on her nest of straw, the star of the Palmer Fair. Cally and Polly stood on each side of the pumpkin, and Gloria peeped over the back, fluffing her hair and displaying her perfect teeth in a Hollywood smile. Mendel was there too, ready to take the money and keep a running total of all the money they'd collected.

Tourists surrounded the booth and everyone who had a camera wanted a picture of the biggest pumpkin they had ever seen. One of the tourists straddled his toddler's legs around Laura's stem and backed up far enough to get his little boy and all of the pumpkin in the picture. "How much for a picture?" he asked.

Charging for a picture? That was the answer! Terpsichore couldn't raise the price of the cookbook, since the *Anchorage Daily Times* article said she was selling them for fifty cents, but she could sell pictures. "Seventy-five cents for a picture *and* a copy of the cookbook," Terpsichore said. Her voice rose like she was asking him if that was a reasonable price.

The man eagerly dug in his pocket for change.

He picked up a copy of the cookbook and turned the pages. "Low-bush cranberry cobbler, pickled salmon—hey, here's that recipe for jellied moose nose. What a hoot! I'll take a recipe book for myself and the picture of my son on the pumpkin. But I'd also like two more recipe books and two photos of all you kids and the pumpkin, for folks back home."

"That's two dollars and twenty-five cents," Mendel said, grinning at Terpsichore.

Terpsichore grinned back. Twenty-five cents more just to let someone take a picture! Easiest money she'd ever made. Or maybe not really, as she thought of scraping off hundreds of squash bugs, lugging water, and everything else she'd done to grow the biggest pumpkin in the valley.

In the lull between trainloads of tourists, Terpsichore ran her fingers through all the nickels, dimes, quarters, and dollar bills in the coffee can. "So what are we up to, Mendel?"

He slid his glasses down his nose and rechecked his column of figures. "Forty-three dollars and twenty-five cents," he said.

Mendel and Terpsichore hunkered down over the box and counted the remaining recipe books. Out of the total one hundred and thirty copies, they still had nearly half of them.

Cally said, "We'll make sure you sell every last recipe book."

Polly said, "And sell lots of pictures."

Just before noon, the train made its second trip into the Palmer station, and the next batch of tourists streamed toward Terpsichore's booth. The twins jumped up from the straw where they'd been giggling and whispering. As the first tourists approached, they hummed their starting pitch, traded smiles, and began. It was their own version of the folk song "The Pumpkin Pies That Grandma Used to Bake."

> *"My sister was a wizard*
> *At baking pumpkin pies;*
> *The things you would find in them*
> *Were surely a surprise!*
>
> *Mom canned a ton of salmon*
> *To save us from a famine*
> *But jars vanished just like snowflakes on a lake.*
> *When Halloween came around,*
> *Guess where those jars were found?*
> *In the pumpkin pies that sister Tipper makes."*

As the crowd around the stand grew, the twins became more theatrical yet. They opened their eyes wide in surprise and spread their hands in mock amazement as they came to the lines announcing the location of the missing objects.

> *"We thought we'd lost our dogsled.*
> *The winter we would dread.*
> *We'd have to get to town on rusty skates.*
> *When Thanksgiving came around,*
> *Guess where that sled was found?*
> *In the pumpkin pies that sister Tipper makes."*

Gloria knew the tune and joined in with a hummed alto harmony and added some flourishes of her own. By the second repeat, the booth was surrounded by both tourists and locals watching the show. Gloria signaled the twins to stop singing for a minute and waved a copy of the recipe book. "Get your recipe book here, including the recipe for Tipper's famous pumpkin pies!"

"Come on, Trip—Tipper, it's your pumpkin, get up here!" Mendel said.

Terpsichore clambered up on a bale of hay and stood. "See the biggest pumpkin ever grown in the Matanuska Valley! Get your Alaska souvenir with genuine Palmer Pioneer recipes! Get your picture taken with the giant pumpkin!"

Cookbooks and photos were selling so fast Mendel could hardly keep up with the hands thrusting quarters and dollars at him. He shouted out updates every few sales.

A familiar voice cut through the hubbub of questions about

growing pumpkins, the recipe book, and taking pictures. "My word!" It was Grandmother, holding Matthew. She was followed by Mother, who had left the school bake sale booth to follow the crowd to Terpsichore's giant pumpkin. "What are you doing to attract such a crowd?"

"Mattie down!" Matthew wriggled out of Grandmother's arms. Mother lunged toward him, but he darted through a sea of legs to reach Terpsichore. "Tip," he said. "Pick you up!"

Mother caught up with Matthew and held onto the straps of his overalls with one hand as she held up her copy of the newspaper in the other hand for Terpsichore to see. "And what's this in the newspaper about raising money for something for me, so I'll want to stay in Alaska?"

"Just a minute," Terpsichore said. "How much money do we have now, Mendel?"

Mendel added the last few pictures and recipe book sales: "Sixty-eight dollars and twenty-five cents."

"Gloria, how many books do we have left?" Terpsichore asked.

Gloria shuffled through the remaining books in the box. "Just fourteen."

Gloria shouted out her spiel again. "Only fourteen copies left of the most authentic souvenir of your trip to Alaska! Be the one who buys the copy that puts this project over the top! Help the Johnsons stay in Alaska!"

"Are you the sister Tipper those girls were singing about?" one tourist asked.

"Cute nickname! Never heard it before," another said.

As she handed out another recipe book and posed for another picture, Terpsichore tried out her new nickname. "Tipper," she said to herself as she smiled for another camera. *Trip* sounded like a clumsy slip on a banana peel. *Tipper* was light and cheerful, just like she felt.

She stepped away from Laura to hug Cally and Polly. "Thanks for your help today, and thanks for the new nickname," she said.

"It fit the rhythm," Polly said.

"And it sort of fits you too," Cally added.

"I like it!" said Mom. "And it's a bit like the 'Tip' that Matthew already calls you."

Finally, the last recipe book was sold, but people were still lining up with quarters to have pictures taken with the pumpkin nearly as tall as the girl who grew it.

"We're over the top, Tipper!" Mendel shouted.

In the flurry of sales, Mother, Matthew, and Grandmother had been edged to the outskirts of the crowd. Cally ran back to hold her mother's hand, pumping it up and down in excitement. Polly held her grandmother's hand, although she resisted having her hand pumped.

Tipper called out instructions. "I'll stay with the pumpkin. Mendel, can you run to Miss Zelinsky at the school bake sale booth and give her the money? Gloria, will you go with the twins to Pop at the hobby and crafts tent and tell him it's time to round up that truck and a dolly?"

As the crowd drifted away, clutching cameras and recipe books, Grandmother strolled over to Terpsichore. "Now honey, can you please explain what all this hullabaloo is about?"

Before Terpsichore had a chance to answer, someone called out, "Is that you, Happy?"

CHAPTER 51

Home Sweet Home

TERPSICHORE ALMOST DIDN'T RECOGNIZE HIM AS HE approached her stall. His lower face was white where the beard used to be. He was wearing a suit instead of a flannel shirt and dungarees. She recognized his voice, though.

Grandmother fanned her face with a fair program and squinted toward him. "Do I know you?"

Mr. Crawford grinned all the way back to his molars. "Happy?" he said again.

"Why, my goodness! No one's called me that in over thirty years." She stopped fanning her face with the program and peeped over the top of it. "Nathaniel?" Her eyes were wide, and though her lower face was covered, anybody could tell she was smiling behind that program.

"Grandmother, this is Mr. Crawford," Terpsichore said. "He's our friend and he's one of the genuine old-timers in the valley. He's been here since just after the Nome gold rush. Mr. Crawford, this is my grandmother, Mrs. VanHagen."

Without his beard, his blush showed up, rosy as radishes. Grandmother matched his blush, cheek for cheek.

"I believe," Grandmother said, "we have been introduced, although it was long ago."

"So we were. And now, here you are in Alaska!" Mr. Crawford said, with another smile. "What do you think of Palmer? This town's growing just like one of Terpsichore's pumpkins and your family is helping it happen. Terpsichore and her friends got a library started, and Pastor Bingle told me he hoped your daughter would volunteer to be the music director of the new church."

"Really? But how can she be a music director if she doesn't have a piano?" Grandmother said.

Their conversation was interrupted as Pop tooted the horn of Mr. Crawford's pickup and inched toward the rest of his family. The twins started bouncing again.

Terpsichore couldn't help bouncing too. "What do you mean, no piano?" She pointed to the piano in the back of the pickup. "Here is your piano, Mom!"

As Pop jumped down from the truck, Mother transferred Matthew's hand into Grandmother's and raced up to hug Pop.

Pop reached for her hands. "Terpsichore's the one to thank, not me," he said. "She bought it herself with her pumpkin prize and recipe book sales."

Mother ran one hand through her hair. "Terpsichore? But you don't even like to play the piano."

"But I know you miss it and I want you to vote to stay.

We all do." Terpsichore's voice faded out as she watched her mother's face for a clue on whether the piano was enough to change her mind.

"You still haven't voted," Pop said. "But come up here first."

Pop reached down to pull Mother up to the back of the pickup with the piano. She sat on the bench and ran through some arpeggios. She grinned to have the feel of piano keys under her fingers.

A crowd gathered. Among them was Scoop Swanson, the reporter from the day before. "Was this the surprise for your mother you were raising money for?"

"Yes!" Terpsichore shouted over the murmuring of the gathering crowd.

"Hey," Scoop Swanson shouted back, "the picture of you and your pumpkin was picked up by the Associated Press and is appearing today in newspapers across the country. Even President Roosevelt will probably see it!"

Terpsichore almost forgot to breathe. Even President Roosevelt would see her pumpkin? And President Roosevelt would see Terpsichore's grin, and eyes sparkling with faith, optimism, and cheer, just like she'd imagined he might when she listened to his fireside chat. That was amazing!

But she couldn't bask in fame. After one wave to thank the reporter, she riveted her attention back on her mother.

Mr. Crawford lifted Matthew to the back of the pickup and then hoisted Grandmother up to the pickup too, despite her protests.

Terpsichore and the twins were right behind them, along with Mendel and Gloria. Scoop Swanson took picture after picture.

Mother said, "I guess I'd be a spoilsport to say I want to leave now . . . after all Terpsichore's—Tipper's—work for the piano." She turned on the piano bench to hug Terpsichore.

"Then how about it, Mrs. Johnson, are you going to stay?" That was the reporter.

Still holding one of Terpsichore's hands, Mother said, "Yes. My answer is yes."

"Hooray!" shouted Cally and Polly.

"It worked!" shouted Mendel and Gloria.

Pop hugged Mother. Mother hugged Terpsichore again. Terpsichore hugged Cally and Polly, and Gloria and Mendel bent down to hug Matthew. Pop hugged Mr. Crawford. Mother hugged Grandmother. "If you were in Alaska," Mother said, "I'd have everything I need here. If you're lonesome in Madison, why don't you stay too?"

Grandmother looked at Mr. Crawford with a slight nod and surprised everyone by saying, "I'll think about it. Perhaps I'll give Alaska a try."

"Alaska grows on you, Grandmother, see if it doesn't," Terpsichore said.

Mother laughed. "I hated to have people tell me that. I thought I would never get over missing Wisconsin. But it's true. Alaska does grow on you."

"Do you miss your old home?" Terpsichore asked Mendel and Gloria.

"I did at first," Mendel said.

"Only until I made new friends," Gloria said.

"Me too," Terpsichore said.

Somebody in the crowd shouted, "Hey, are you going to play that piano, or what?"

Mother's hands hovered over the keys while she thought about what to play, then she decisively struck a three-chord introduction and began to sing. "'Mid pleasures and palaces though we may roam . . .'"

As people in the crowd recognized the song, their voices gradually joined in for the next line: "'Be it ever so humble, there's no place like home . . .'"

The hundreds of voices singing together gave Terpsichore delicious shivers. Some sang on-key, others sharp or flat, but the imperfections evened each other out to something perfect.

As Mother began to play the second verse, Grandmother nudged Mother to make room for her on the left-hand side of the piano bench. She played slow, rich, grounding chords to Mother's melody that made the spinet sound almost as good as the piano Mother had sold back in Little Bear Lake.

When they stopped playing, Grandmother turned on the bench to take Mother's hand into her own. "It's been a long time since we've played a duet," she said.

"Too long," Mother said. "I hope you'll also decide to stay."

Pop was standing behind the piano bench, one hand on Mother's shoulder. "Me too," he said. "I know Clio's missed you."

Low rays of sun made Laura gleam like solid gold.

"That's some pumpkin," Gloria said.

"The size of all these giant vegetables is attributable to the longer hours of sunlight of Alaska's summer days," Mendel said.

"Yes," Terpsichore said, "but it also takes hard work and luck." She looked fondly at Laura, still surrounded by people amazed at her size. "No wonder folks dream big here. Who'd ever have imagined that a pumpkin seed from Wisconsin would lead to a champion like Laura and a piano that would convince Mother to stay?"

Cally and Polly slipped their arms through Terpsichore's and sang, "Just our sister Tipper."

"Yep, she sure has the pioneer spirit I love," said Mr. Crawford. He jumped down from the back of the truck. "Let's get that piano home!"

Author Notes

My son inspired this book by purchasing a house from the 1930s next to a potato field in Palmer, Alaska. As I followed my curiosity about the early settlement in Palmer, I was astonished to discover accounts of a New Deal program that took two hundred and two families off relief and shipped them up to Alaska to become self-sufficient farmers.

Some of those families left behind tar-paper shacks, and some left solid homes with electricity and indoor plumbing. No matter what life had been like for them before, in Palmer they were equal, all starting out in identical tents with shared outhouses.

You'd think that with mud and mosquitoes, and living in tents in the snow, people would have unhappy memories of the early days of Palmer, but most of those interviewed remembered their childhoods in Palmer as a happy time. After all, instead of living on isolated farms, for the most part, they had dozens of children their own age nearby in the colony to play with.

Although I made up Terpsichore and her friends, other people, including Dr. Albrecht, Pastor Bingle, and Don Irwin, were real people who were credited with the survival of the colony. Major incidents, such as the measles outbreak, children dying and the telegram to Eleanor Roosevelt, management problems that left many families still in tents as the first snow fell, and Will Rogers's visit and plane crash, are all based on real events.

A notable omission in accounts I read of the Palmer Colony was reference to the people who were in Alaska for thousands of years before the colonists: the various Eskimo, Aleut, Athabaskan, and other Indian tribes. Since I married into a part-Native family, I was concerned about this omission, but finally decided not to create contacts with Native peoples if the colonists themselves did not mention them. However, I hope as many readers as possible will visit the Anchorage Museum to learn more about the *original* colonists of Alaska.

The colony started with two hundred and two families, but over fifty percent of the original colony members left within five years. Thirty years later, only ten percent of the original families remained.

The Matanuska Valley, an hour's drive from Anchorage, is now the fastest-growing area of Alaska. You'll find a Fred Meyer store where colonists once planted potatoes. But you'll still find remnants of the colony era: the water tower, the railroad station, and even Pastor Bingle's Church of a Thousand

Trees, where my son and his wife were married. The early colonists are honored every year in early June with a parade, a salmon recipe contest, and a tour of the Colony House Museum on old Tract 94.

The Talkeetna and Chugach mountains still preside over the Matanuska Valley, and the wind still blows. On street signs, businesses, and mailboxes you will still see the names of the stalwart colonists and their descendants who stayed.

Resources

HERE ARE THE RESOURCES I RELIED ON MOST IN WRITING *Sweet Home Alaska*. If you get a chance to see these books yourself, you'll find photographs that inspired several scenes.

Atwood, Evangeline. *We Shall Be Remembered*. Anchorage: Alaska Methodist University Press, 1966.

Hegener, Helen. *The Matanuska Colony Album; Photographs of the 1935 Matanuska Colony Project in Palmer, Alaska*. Anchorage: Northern Lights Media, 2014.

Hill, Paul and Joan Juster, Mark Lipman, and Jim Fox. *Alaska Far Away; The New Deal Pioneers of the Matanuska Colony*. (DVD) Paul Hill and Joan Juster, Producers, 2008.

Lehn, Lynette A., and Lorraine M. Kirker. *Matanuska Colony 75th Anniversary Scrapbook*. Anchorage: Pyramid Printing Company, 2010.

Matanuska-Susitna Borough. *Kink Matanuska Susitna; A Visual History of the Valleys*. Sutton, Alaska: Brentwood Press, 1985.

Terpsichore's Favorite and Not-So-Favorite Recipes:

Terpsichore's Pumpkin Oatmeal Cookies

2 cups flour

¾ teaspoon baking soda

1 ¼ teaspoons salt

½ teaspoon nutmeg

1 ½ teaspoons cinnamon

1 teaspoon ground ginger

1 cup butter or shortening

1 ¼ cups sugar

1 egg plus 1 egg yolk

2 ⅓ cups rolled oats

1 cup canned pumpkin

¾ cup walnuts or pecans
  (optional)

½ cup raisins (optional)

Directions

Heat oven to 375 degrees.

Sift together flour, salt, soda, and spices.

Cream shortening until fluffy and gradually add sugar,
    creaming until light.

Add egg and egg yolk.

Beat well, add pumpkin, oats, and flour.

Add nuts and raisins if you are using them.

Mix and drop by heaping teaspoonfuls 1 ¼ inches apart
    onto greased baking sheet.

Bake for fifteen minutes, but start checking at ten minutes
    in case your oven runs hot.

Jellied Moose Nose

Put a large kettle of water on to boil.

Hack off the upper jawbone of the moose just below the eyes and boil it for forty-five minutes.

Dip the jawbone in cold water and pluck the hairs from the nose. Wash the nose thoroughly.

Boil the nose again in fresh water with chopped onion, garlic, and pickling spices until tender. Cool overnight in the water it was boiled in.

The next morning, remove the meat from the broth and remove the bones and cartilage.

Thinly slice the meat, pack it in a glass dish with high sides, and cover with the broth. Season with salt, pepper, or vinegar to taste.

Refrigerate. As the mixture cools, it will jell so it can be sliced.

"When It's Springtime in Alaska" (song)

"WHEN IT'S SPRINGTIME IN ALASKA" IS A PARODY OF "When It's Springtime in the Rockies," a song Mary Hale Woolsey published in 1929 and Gene Autry made famous with his recording. The tune was probably based on old folk melodies. The new words were made up by colonists as they rode the train from their homes in Wisconsin, Minnesota, and Michigan toward the Matanuska Valley.

When It's Springtime in Alaska

When it's springtime in Alaska
And it's ninety-nine below,
Where the Eskimos go barefoot
Through the white and drifted snow,
When polar bears get sunburned
At midnight or by day,
When it's springtime in Alaska—
In Alaska far away.

Where the berries grow like pumpkins
And a cabbage fills a truck,
Where milk and cream are flowing,
For a market we're not stuck,
Where the sun is always shining
And the seals sing all the day,
When it's springtime in Alaska—
In Alaska far away.
Some people think we're foolish
And are sure we will regret;
I'm afraid they are mistaken,
For I see no sign as yet.
We want to make a new start
Somewhere without delay,
So, here we are Alaska,
AND WE HAVE COME TO STAY!

Acknowledgments

I THANK ALL THE AUTHORS OF CHILDREN'S BOOKS WHO inspired me as a child to turn a flowered couch into a covered wagon, a ship, or a house in the big woods. I still like to play make-believe, but now I call it research for the historical fiction I write today.

My agent, Steven Chudney, found me the perfect team to work with: Nancy Paulsen and her imprint at Penguin Young Readers. Nancy gently coaxed me into revisions and additions that gave the book its heart. Her assistant, Sara LaFleur, eased me into modern online editing. Robert Farren, meticulous copy editor, and Kathleen Keating, equally meticulous proof-reader, saved me from anachronisms, time warps, and assorted boo-boos. Erika Steiskal painted the captivating jacket art. My thanks also to everyone else at Penguin who helped get this book out into the world, and to librarians and booksellers who will put this book into the hands of readers.

I started research with books, and thank the staff of libraries in Palmer, Alaska; Everett, Washington; and the University of Alaska. Outside the library, I appreciate the help of longtime friends who live in the valley, Bill and Caroline Prosser, their sons Loren and Alan and their families, and Bill Prosser's mother, Sophie, who invited me to their fish camp to see how salmon are caught and canned.

Weekly emails with my writing friends helped me finish this book with sanity intact: Amy Fellner Dominy, Alissa Grosso, Kiki Hamilton, Penny Holland, Julia Karr, Deb Lund, Christina Mandelski, Gae Polisner, Bettina Restrepo, Caroline Starr Rose, Angie Smibert, and Ruby Tanaka.

I couldn't write without the support of my family:

My sisters, Helen and Randi, still my best friends, who never doubted I could write this book;

My son, Rolf, who started it all with his Palmer house, and his wife, Lilly, who reminded me to include Palmer's winds;

My daughter, Emily (also a children's librarian and one of my best boosters), and her husband, Hampton;

My grandsons, Gosta (junior editor in training), Arthur (who reminds me to laugh), and Iggy (the jellied moose nose recipe is for you);

My cat, Billi (named after Billiken, the symbol of the 1909 Alaska Yukon Pacific Exposition), who herds me like a sheepdog to the computer to write every day;

And through it all, my husband, Gosta, who converted the woodshed into my quiet writing hideaway and humors his writing wife.